SEER

The Seeker Series: Book Three

By Amy Reece

SEER

Limitless Publishing, LLC
Kailua, HI 96734
www.limitlesspublishing.com

Formatting: Limitless Publishing

ISBN-13: 978-1-68058-209-3
ISBN-10: 1-68058-209-7

DEDICATION

For the girls who feel like they can't go home yet.
And for the boys who love them enough to wait.

CHAPTER ONE

"O wonder!
How many goodly creatures are there here!
How beauteous mankind is! O brave new world
That has such people in't!"
—Shakespeare, *The Tempest*, 5.1

"Ladies and gentlemen, as we start our descent, please make sure your seat backs and tray tables are in their full, upright position. Make sure your seat belt is securely fastened and all carry-on luggage is stowed underneath the seat in front of you or in the overhead bins. Please turn off all electronic devices until we are safely parked at the gate. Thank you." The message was repeated in French.

I stared out the airplane window, hoping to see a recognizable landmark, like maybe the Eiffel Tower, but glimpsed only vague brown and green squares below. We were still too high for any sightseeing.

"Stop biting your nails," Rémy admonished,

taking my hand away from my mouth. "Why are you so nervous?"

"Oh, I don't know, Rémy. How about the fact that I just flew across the Pacific Ocean with a 22-year-old Seer who has been masquerading as a high school student? Or the fact that my mother and grandmother think I'm landing in Dublin right about now?" I had an unfortunate tendency to get cranky—okay, bitchy—when I got nervous.

"Oh, calm down," Rémy said, unfazed. You'll be able to call them as soon as we land. This is important, Ally. We must get you to my grandmother before it is too late. Your Seer Council never would have let you come voluntarily. It was necessary to do this."

He referred to the fact that he and I had boarded a plane to Paris when everyone thought I was flying alone to Dublin and then on to Galway. I was going to be in so much trouble when I got back to Albuquerque, but Rémy was right; I needed to meet his grandmother, the Oracle, and the Irish Seer Council never would have granted their permission. They had a pretty good reason: they thought the Gaulish Seers had kidnapped the Oracle more than fifty years before. In reality, she had eloped with her boyfriend, a Gaulish Seer, and had lived happily and voluntarily in France ever since.

"I know, I know. I'm sorry. I'm just scared. And I miss Jack so much. I wish I told him about this; I'm not going to be able to contact him for so long!" My boyfriend was in Missouri for Army basic training for the next ten weeks and would be unable to contact family or friends for at least two weeks.

"What's he going to think when he finds out I sneaked away to France with you?"

"That you finally saw the light and dumped him for me?"

"Oh, my God! That's exactly what he's going to think!" I buried my face in my hands as I wailed.

"Ally, Ally, shhh." Rémy put his arm around me and pulled me close. We were seated in first class, so we had some small semblance of privacy. "You're working yourself up over nothing. We'll send messages to everyone just as soon as we land, I promise. As for Jack, well, I wish he would be insanely jealous, but I think not. He really loves you, chérie. He must trust you too. It will all work out, so stop worrying."

I nodded and tried to believe him. He was right and it was too late to change my mind, anyway, as we were about to land in Paris.

"Now, when we land, we'll go directly to our hotel so you can get some rest before we drive to Rouen tomorrow. You'll feel more yourself when you have some good food and some sleep. You'll see," he assured me.

It took an inordinate amount of time to deplane, gather our luggage, and navigate our way through the hideous lines—or queues, as Rémy called them—at customs. I was exhausted and craving nothing more than a soft bed as we headed toward the pick-up area. I expected to join yet another queue for a taxi and was surprised when a chauffeur holding a sign that said 'M. Giles' approached and took my bags from me. We followed him to a gleaming, black limousine and I slid into the back seat as he held the door.

Rémy laughed delightedly at my shocked expression. "What? Did you think the Conseil would let the next Oracle travel in a common, dirty taxi cab?"

"The what?" I asked, confused.

"The Conseil des Voyants is our version of your Seer Council. They have arranged for you to be well cared-for on your visit."

"So, this is all for me, huh? If I wasn't here, you would be taking a common, dirty taxi cab to your hotel?" I asked pointedly.

He shrugged. "No. If you weren't here, I would rent a car and drive home to Rouen tonight."

"Rémy, why don't we do that? I don't need a limousine and a fancy hotel tonight. I assume it will be a fancy hotel?" I asked, eyebrows raised.

"Yes," he admitted. "It is a very nice hotel. And you do need it. Tomorrow will be stressful for you, so tonight you will rest and enjoy a fine Parisian meal. No arguments."

The limo deposited us in front of Le Méridien Etoile on **Boulevard Gouvion Saint-Cyr** and Rémy checked us in, speaking in rapid French. We were shown to a two-bedroom suite, the likes of which I had never seen before. The decor was ultra-modern and sleek, with a living room in between two bedrooms.

"Wow, Rémy. This is beautiful!" I wandered around touching the metal lampshades, smoothing my hands over the butter-soft, white leather couch as he tipped the bellhop.

"It's all right." He shrugged in his signature

Gallic manner. "You can have this bedroom." He motioned for the bellhop to deposit my bags in the larger of the two bedrooms. "Why don't you get settled in, perhaps change clothes, and then we'll go to dinner downstairs, yes? I'm not letting you sleep until later tonight. It's the only way to deal with jet lag."

I really craved a nap, but knew he was right from my experience during my trip to Ireland. So, I instead took a shower and changed into a fresh outfit, by this time starting to feel hungry. Then I called my grandmother and Fionnuala, head of the Irish Seer Council. I was correct: I was in deep trouble with both women. My grandmother promised various kinds of punishment, including grounding until my 21st birthday, but she agreed not to tell my mother until she returned from her honeymoon. Fionnuala was nearly speechless with anger. She said she would have to speak to the rest of the council before getting back to me. Then she hung up. I didn't have any way to get in touch with Jack, so I called his Aunt Trina and told her where I was, although not the true reason why I was in France. Jack's family knew nothing about my psychic powers or Seers. He would be able to call home a few weeks into his training, but there was no way he would be allowed to make an international call. I don't know why it was important to me to let her know where I was; maybe because it was the closest I could get to Jack at the moment.

We ate in the hotel restaurant, Ma Chère & Tendre, a trés expensive steakhouse with an incomprehensible menu, but Rémy ordered for me in rapid-fire French and I ended up with a vegetable side dish plate that was exquisite. He ordered a Charolaise filet, rare, for himself. I had to avert my tender, vegetarian eyes while he cut into the bloody, oozing mess.

"Mmm," he moaned, chewing. "It is so good to be back in France where they know how to prepare food correctly. No offense, chérie, but American food leaves much to be desired."

"I don't recall you complaining while you were chowing down on cheeseburgers," I replied.

"Well, yes, that is one thing you Americans do very well," he admitted. "But I never acquired a taste for New Mexican food. I don't understand your state's love affair with red and green chile. It is on everything." He shuddered and stabbed another piece of hemorrhaging beef.

"Yes, as God intended. Chile should be on everything. But I will admit that this is delicious. Thanks for dinner, Rémy."

"Of course. I must take good care of you while you are in my country. Are you sure you don't want some wine?" He held up the bottle he had ordered and was enjoying with his dinner.

"No thanks." I shook my head. "Just out of curiosity, what is the drinking age here?"

"Well," he paused to take a sip of the ruby red liquid, "there is no explicit consumption age, but it is illegal to sell alcohol to anyone under the age of 18. Wine is important in France. We are not so prudish and judgmental as you Americans."

"Oh, get off your French connoisseur high horse!

Okay, I'll try some." I held out my glass, stopping him from pouring more than a small amount. I took a sip and made a face at the sour taste. "Eww. Gross. How can you drink this stuff?"

His expression was horrified. "*Mais non!* You just committed a crime, the way you slurped and gulped down this beautiful cabernet."

"A wine crime? Really?" I asked in the most sarcastic way possible.

"Yes, definitely. Here, I will show you. First, you must appreciate the aroma. Smell it. Now take a small sip and hold it in your mouth, on your tongue." I did as he said. "Now concentrate on the taste and feel of the wine. Can you detect the cherry?"

As I concentrated, I could, indeed, taste the subtle cherry flavor.

"Good," said Rémy. "Now swallow and take another sip. This time see if you can detect the blackberry." I was able to taste it. "Now, one more time. See if you can taste the violet." I tried, but didn't even know what a violet might taste like. "So, you see there is much to learn about wine, no?"

"I guess. I still don't like the taste. Sorry. But I can see that there is a lot to it. So, you missed wine while you were pretending to be 17 in the U.S.?"

"Oui. I am used to drinking wine with lunch and dinner. I was raised this way, you understand?"

After dinner, he insisted we spend an hour or so listening to music in the Jazz Club Etoile, next to the restaurant, where he introduced me to more wonders of French wine. When he finally decided we could retire to our rooms, it was nearing midnight. I washed up quickly before sinking gratefully into my bed.

***

The next morning, Rémy and I walked a few blocks to a small sidewalk cafe where he ordered *le petit déjeuner* for two. This consisted of a croissant, café au lait, and freshly squeezed orange juice. I watched as he tore off a piece of croissant and dunked it in his coffee, noticing that other diners were doing the same. This was apparently *de rigueur* for a French breakfast, so I did the same, rolling my eyes in gastronomic ecstasy at the flavor explosion taking place in my mouth. We didn't have croissants like this in the U.S.! It was so fresh and buttery that I could have cried.

"It's good, no?" Rémy smiled. His accent was much thicker since we had arrived in France.

I nodded because I was too busy stuffing more croissant in my mouth to speak. After breakfast, we walked back to the hotel, where the limousine was waiting to transport us the one hundred thirty kilometers to Rémy's hometown, Rouen.

I was contemplative on the drive and grateful that Rémy seemed inclined to leave me to my thoughts. As I watched the gorgeous French countryside speed by, I reflected on the events of the last semester that had brought me here. I had returned to Albuquerque from Ireland without the answers that I sought; in fact, I was more confused than ever since the Irish Seer Council told me that I may be the next Oracle, a sort of leader of all the

Seers in the world.

It had been a stressful semester in other ways, as well, what with the strange nightmares about a kidnapping that turned out to be psychic messages from beyond the grave from a girl named Ashley Hayes, who had been murdered in 1984.

The other stressful event was my break-up with Jack. It was still hard to think about the month we had spent apart because of his inability to deal with conflicting emotions over his father's re-emergence in his life. We eventually patched things up, and he was now trying to develop a relationship with his dad, Marcos.

Lost in thought, I was surprised when the limo slowed down and turned into the driveway of a palatial estate; I had apparently daydreamed away the entire trip.

"Come, Ally," said Rémy as he held out his hand to assist me from the limo. "It is time for you to meet the Conseil and my grandmother. They are very impatient to make your acquaintance."

I swallowed my nerves and took his hand. He led me into a grand marble-tiled foyer where we were met by a stern-looking man in a black suit.

"Bonjour, Monsiuer Rémy," he said in a deep voice. *"Ça fait longtemps que nous ne vous avons pas vu."*

"Ah, bonjour, André! Merci. Voici notre invitée spéciale, Ally. J'espère que vous vous occuperez de tous ses besoins." He turned to me. "Ally, this is our majordome, uh, butler, André. If you need anything at all during your stay, you have only to ask him."

"You have a butler?" I squeaked. "This is your house, Rémy?" The place was a freaking palace! Suddenly, his spendthrift ways made perfect sense. He was literally rich.

"Oui, although technically it belongs to my grandparents. I grew up here, but I now have an apartment near the university. The Conseil hold their meetings here. Come. They are waiting for us." He led me up a winding staircase and into a large living room where a group of about seven men and women were sitting on couches and in easy chairs, conversing in rapid French and drinking coffee. Although the house itself appeared to be several hundred years old, the room was furnished in a modern, comfortable manner with leather couches, glass tables, and modern art.

"Rémy!" A young woman rose from one of the couches and ran to Rémy, launching herself into his arms. *"Tu es enfin rentré!"*

He laughed and kissed her on both cheeks. *"Oui, me voilà…ca fait plaisir de te voir, ma petite."* He turned to me. "Ally, I would like you to meet my cousin, Geneviève. This is Ally Moran." When he said my name, all the conversation in the room stopped and everyone turned to stare at me. He put his hand on the small of my back and guided me to one of the couches where an elderly couple sat. "Ally, I would like to introduce you to my grandparents, Mary Katherine and Phillipe Giles. Grand-mère, Grand-père, this is Alethiea Moran."

They both rose, and the woman leaned forward to kiss both my cheeks, grasping me solidly by the upper arms. I could feel the psychic energy flow between us. "Please, call me Kate. Ally, it is wonderful to meet you. It is good that my grandson has brought you here." She turned to greet Rémy, folding him into a tearful embrace and murmuring to him in French. Her accent was an interesting mix of French and Irish lilt.

"Ally, it is good to meet you." Rémy's grandfather kissed both of my cheeks. "Come, while my wife assures herself of our grandson's health and well-being, I will introduce you to the rest of the Conseil." The others had risen and now stood in a semi-circle. "This is Francoise," Phillipe gestured to a tall, stern-looking woman with improbably black hair. "She has the dubious pleasure of leading this rambunctious group."

"Oh, Phillipe! You are such a tease. Welcome, Ally. We are pleased that you have come. This is Hélène, Corinne, and Arnaud." She gestured to two other women, both middle-aged, and a 30-something man. "And this," she led me to a man who stood somewhat apart from the rest of the group, "is Luc." He was tall; I had to crank my neck back to see his face, which was lean with pronounced cheekbones. His eyes were a cool gray, perusing me from head to foot; I had the horrible feeling he found me lacking somehow.

"Mademoiselle Moran," he said as he lifted my hand. "Wonderful to meet you." I knew he thought it was anything but wonderful as waves of ugly thoughts inundated my mind. Although I picked up nothing specific, I felt greed, ambition, and a desperate need for power. His eyes squinted as he stared into mine too long and too deep. I withdrew my hand from his and barely resisted wiping it on my jeans. I couldn't wait to ask Rémy about him. Who was he and why was I getting such negative feelings from him?

***

André announced lunch and Geneviève put her arm through mine, pulling me away from Luc. "Come, Ally. I am claiming you for lunch. I haven't had anyone my own age to talk to in too long." I was grateful to be away from Luc's intense stare.

"Don't believe her, Ally," Rémy said, appearing at my other side. "She just posted a girl's night out on her Facebook page."

"We were at a club, so there was no chance to talk. Why are you cyber-stalking me, anyway? Is your social life so pathetic that you have to live vicariously through mine?" Geneviève flashed him an arch look.

"He's probably just jealous because he's spent the past six months babysitting teenagers in Albuquerque," I offered with a laugh. "Go easy on him. American teens are brutal."

"*Mais, non*. I loved my American friends and will miss them now that I am back in France," he replied gallantly.

"Especially Veronica, huh?" I said, hoping Geneviève would zero in and want details. She didn't disappoint me.

"Veronica? My cousin found a girlfriend in America? Tell me everything," she demanded as we took our seats. Rémy rolled his eyes and took his place at the opposite side of the table.

I filled her in on how I had tried for weeks to ferret out the information about who Rémy was crushing on, while a bevy of waiters began placing bowls of soup before each diner. I looked down into my bowl and was dismayed to see some sort of seafood bisque. I glanced across the table at Rémy, but he was too busy digging into his soup to notice my issue. He had apparently not called ahead to notify his family that I was a vegetarian. A room full of psychics and not one of them could figure out that I didn't eat meat? Seriously? Oh, well. It's not like I've never faced this dilemma before. It's just that I could usually count on raiding my own refrigerator later in the evening. On the bright side, I probably wouldn't be gaining a bunch of weight while I was here. I didn't want to make Rémy's family feel bad about not knowing I was a vegetarian, so I picked up my spoon and stirred my soup, hoping to disguise the fact that I wasn't actually eating it. Once Geneviève had exhausted the topic of Veronica, she began quizzing me about my own love life, which gave me an excuse to talk rather than eat. When the main course arrived, I picked around the chicken and ate the potatoes and vegetables. I practically wolfed down my fruit tart, relieved that the French love their desserts.

"Ally," Kate addressed me from the head of the table. "Would you care to walk with me in the garden after lunch?" Although I had no intention of refusing her, I got the message it was more of a command than a request.

"Of course. I'd be happy to," I said as she rose

and motioned for me to follow her into the garden, a wonderland of flowers and greenery with a winding path covered in bits of stone.

"This garden is my pride and joy." She leaned her head back, enjoying the sun on her face. "Well, one of them. Rémy is the other. You got to know him over the past few months, no?"

I quickly glanced at her, noting the too-innocent look on her face. I rolled my eyes and said, "Yes. We became good *friends* while he was in the U.S." I made sure to emphasize the 'friends' part. "He helped me through a rough time this last semester."

"Why don't you tell me about it while we walk off that delicious lunch that you ate so little of? I will make sure the kitchen knows of your dietary preferences before dinner." She winked at me with the last statement.

"Thanks. I appreciate it." While we strolled through the gorgeous gardens, I told her about how Rémy had helped me deal with my breakup with Jack. I wondered if she was bored hearing about my teen drama, yet I felt it was important to mention that I currently had a boyfriend and that Rémy and I would never be anything more than friends. I knew she and the rest of the Conseil had chosen to interpret the prophecy in a way that meant Rémy and I should be together.

"So, you are in love with this Jack?" I nodded. "There is no chance for you and my grandson to…" She left the question dangling.

"No. None at all. Sorry." I replied firmly.

"Oh, don't apologize, my dear. I am the last person on earth to tell someone whom they should love or what they should do with their life. I left my family to be with the man I love, you know?" I nodded, but said nothing. "I don't understand what the prophecy referred to any more than you, Ally. I saw a vision of you and where to find you, and then I had the prophecy. You and my grandson are connected, important in some way, but we don't know how. You may be the next Oracle, or you may not. That is why Rémy brought you here, so we can find out. Now, I know you can't stay too long on this visit, but I hope we can begin to build a relationship. I do realize we will have to share you with the Irish Council, but I must impress on you the importance of spending time here with us. I understand you just graduated from high school. How would you feel about attending the university here in Rouen? I could arrange it easily."

I was sure she could. I began to realize this group could arrange a great many things. "Thanks, but no, Kate. I don't mind splitting summer vacation and possibly Christmas breaks between here and Galway, but my life is in Albuquerque. I don't want to leave my grandmother. And I need to be there when my new little brother or sister arrives. Plus, I absolutely insist on being home by the time Jack gets back from basic training."

"Ah, he has joined the military? That is very noble. What branch did he join?"

Before I could answer, Rémy appeared around the corner. "Here you are. I have brought you a peace offering so you don't hold it against me that I forgot to tell Grand-mère that you are a vegetarian." He handed me something wrapped in a cloth napkin. I opened it to find a sandwich made with a delicious-looking piece of baguette. I lifted the top piece and saw lettuce, tomato, and something creamy. I raised my eyebrows questioningly at him.

"It's cheese. Proper French cheese—none of that disgusting orange 'cheese product' you Americans are so fond of. Now eat. You must be starving. We can't have you fainting in the garden from weakness."

I took a bite and wasn't surprised to find it delicious. I'm a huge cheese fan and the French certainly have a way with it. "Thanks, Rémy," I said with my mouth full.

"Ally was just telling me that her young man has joined the military. I think that is very noble." Kate put her arm through Rémy's and pulled him along with us deeper into the garden.

"Oh, yes. Jack is all that is noble and good," Rémy said, dripping sarcasm. "He is so good that we mere mortals must bask in his virtuosity. Oww." He rubbed the arm I punched.

"Now, children. You mustn't fight. Don't make me send you to your rooms," Kate teased. "We must make good use of Ally's limited time here to try and figure out what you two have to do with the prophecy. It would be so much easier and make more sense if you were destined to fall in love with each other," she sighed.

I swallowed another bite of sandwich. "I really don't think prophecies should go around telling people who to fall in love with. That's not right. I didn't choose to fall in love with Jack; my heart chose him and I had to go along with it." They both stopped in the path and stared at me. "What?" I asked.

"That was very beautiful, Ally. And very profound. I can see I would be wise not to underestimate you, my dear. Now," she said as she led us briskly down the path, "why have you two been brought together, if not to unite the clans through a marriage alliance?"

The mere thought of marriage to Rémy made me cringe. I mean, he was gorgeous, but we would kill each other in about an hour. "You don't think we can bring the clans together any other way than marriage? That's really limiting, you know? Not to mention medieval."

Rémy snickered and Kate gave him a dirty look. "Ally is correct. And far, far in the future, when I begin to look for a wife, I will require someone a good bit more biddable than Ally," he said.

"Yes," I sneered. "You'll need someone who adores you nearly as much as you adore yourself."

"Remind me why I went to the trouble of bringing you a sandwich?"

"Children," Kate warned.

"Sorry," we both murmured.

"Now, we must use what little time we have for Ally's visit to try and figure out what in the world is going on with you two. We will have to run various tests…"

Her voice faded away in my mind as Rémy sent me his thoughts. *Please be patient with her, Ally. She has been very concerned ever since she received the prophecy. I worry for her. Please, just go along with all this?*

Of course, Rémy. She's wonderful. I would never want to upset her. I do realize we need to figure this out. But I don't have to marry you to do that.

Kate stopped and stared between the two of us. "Amazing. Simply amazing. I have never seen such communication possible between two Seers. This is quite remarkable."

"Grand-mère, could you hear us?" Rémy asked.

"No, nothing specific. I'm not that powerful. I could only feel the energy flowing between you. You are both much more powerful than I realized. This will take much thought. You must excuse me. I need to be alone. Rémy, you will see that Ally finds her way back to the house?" At Rémy's bemused nod, she scurried away down the path.

He sighed and led me to sit on a nearby bench in the shade. "Well, that was apparently a mistake. I'm sorry, chérie. I didn't think." He dropped his head into his hands and sighed again.

"Yeah, I didn't especially like the gleam in her eyes, either. She's not going to let the couple thing go, is she?"

He shook his head. "No, probably not."

***

Over the course of the next week, Kate managed to throw Rémy and me together more often than not, ostensibly so she could observe the connection we had, but I knew it was merely an excuse to force us to spend time together. Rémy and I were both frustrated with her casual treatment of our personal wishes in the matter, but he feared upsetting his grandmother so he went along with it, on the surface at least. The rest of the Conseil skirted around us for the most part, letting Kate have her way. The bright spot in the whole situation was the surprising friendship developing between Geneviève and myself; we hit it off and enjoyed spending my limited free time together. The evenings frequently found the two of us, joined by Rémy and Arnaud, enjoying the nightlife Rouen had to offer.

On Thursday evening of my second week in France, we sat in a club waiting for the guys to return with drinks. "So, what's between you and Arnaud? I'm sensing some romance there." I leaned toward her to be heard over the music.

"I wish! I have been in love with him forever, but he thinks he's too old for me," she said with a sigh.

"How old is he?" I had figured 30-something when we were first introduced.

"He is 28 and I'm 19. Do you think that is too old?" She looked adorably unsure as she pushed her golden-brown hair behind her ears.

It was a big age gap, but who was I to judge? "My grandfather was ten years older than my grandmother and they had a great marriage from what I've always heard. How does Arnaud feel? Do you have any idea if he reciprocates?"

"I don't know! Sometimes I think he does, but he never acts on it. Never. I've tried flirting. I've tried making him jealous. What should I do?" Geneviève grasped my hand desperately.

I placed my other hand on top of hers and

squeezed lightly. She was beautiful and one of the sweetest girls I had ever met, so I wanted her to get the guy she was in love with. "First of all, calm down, okay? Don't freak out. My boyfriend is older than me and I had to pretty much stalk him until I wore him down. Although in my case, it was Jack's legal troubles more than the two-year age difference. Maybe you just need to be persistent."

"Maybe. Thanks." She smiled. "Tell me more about Jack. What is this legal trouble? It sounds intriguing."

I told her about Jack's troubled youth, his time spent in jail and juvenile detention, and his years on probation. "I finally bullied my way into going to his final probation hearing and he kissed me afterward."

"That's so romantic!" She sighed. "He sounds dark and dangerous."

"Not at all," I said, laughing. "He's the sweetest guy ever. I miss him so much." I sighed and looked away.

"I hope to meet him someday. You must love him very much. You should see your face when you talk about him, Ally. It's really sweet. It certainly doesn't look like that when you talk about my cousin. I think my grandmother is destined to be disappointed, no?"

"Definitely! Thanks for understanding, Geneviève. Listen, I will help you with Arnaud if you help me with your grandmother. Deal?"

"Deal." The guys returned at that moment with drinks for everyone.

"Why don't you two go dance?" I suggested.

"Rémy and I will guard the table." He smirked at me, obviously seeing through my suggestion.

"Good luck with that." He gestured toward his cousin and Arnaud, who were just taking to the dance floor. "He thinks he's too old for her."

"What do you think?"

He shrugged his signature shrug. "I don't think an age difference should keep anyone apart. If two people love each other, nothing should keep them apart."

"Wow, Rémy, you are such a romantic! Who would have thought? Why don't we try to get them together?"

"Because I am not a matchmaker, chérie. Arnaud is a grown man and can manage his own love life. He still thinks of my cousin as a child and I don't see that changing anytime soon. Now, let us not waste this opportunity to dance." He stood up and held his hand out to me expectantly. I stared at him for a moment and then sighed and accepted his offer. We danced several fast songs and then he pulled me close when a slow song came on.

"Shh," he said when I balked. "Just go with it. It's what everyone wants. Why don't we give it a chance?"

I shook my head, but allowed him to slide his arm around me. I held myself rigidly away from him for a few moments, but then put my head against his chest, tired of it all suddenly. What if it was our destiny? What if the prophecy did mean we were supposed to be together? I was so tired of fighting and Jack seemed so far away. And Rémy smelled better than anyone had a right to. He must have sensed my acquiescence, because he raised his head from where it rested atop mine, lifted my chin with his finger and lowered his lips to mine. "Rémy, no. I don't—" I whispered.

"Everyone expects it, Ally. Just try, please," he whispered back and closed the distance between us. His kiss was soft and slow, allowing me to get used to him.

I was so torn. Part of me felt that he was right: everyone in the Seer world interpreted the prophecy to mean that Rémy and I should be together. But I loved Jack. We were meant to be together, weren't we? I was so confused. I just finished telling Geneviève how much I loved Jack and that there was no attraction to Rémy. What was wrong with me? I couldn't sort my thoughts out. So I allowed him to kiss me. Thoroughly. And then I kissed him back. It was nothing like kissing Jack, but I knew enough to recognize that Rémy was quite an accomplished kisser. His lips were soft, yet firm and I allowed him to open my mouth and slide his tongue against mine. I answered in kind, analyzing his taste and texture, hoping my technique was not as sloppy as I feared. Then I realized that I was actually analyzing his kiss rather than enjoying it or being swept away with desire. When Jack kissed me, I never had a chance to analyze anything; I could only hold on and go with the flow. Kissing Rémy was nothing like kissing Jack. At least I knew. I pulled away and frowned at him.

"Well," he sighed, leaning his forehead against mine, "we did try. No offense, chérie, but kissing you is like kissing my sister."

"Yeah, same here. I mean, you're a good kisser, but it just doesn't do anything for me. God, Rémy! I feel so guilty! What am I going to tell Jack? I cheated on him! What kind of person does that?"

"Why on earth would you tell him? You didn't cheat on Jack, although I wouldn't blame you if you did. Shh," he said as he wiped away the tears that started to slide down my cheeks. "You are making too much of this. I kissed you. So what? We just needed to see if the Conseil was right about us. Now we know. We are not meant to be together as a couple. The prophecy means something else. There is no need for Jack to know anything. It was just a kiss."

"Why do I feel so guilty?" I leaned my head against his chest and sniffled.

He pulled me close and chuckled. "Perhaps because you are only seventeen years old and you've been thrown into some situations that a much older person wouldn't handle as well? You deserve to react like a teenager to some things in your life."

I laughed slightly. "Thanks, old man. Way to compliment me and call me a child all in one statement."

"Ally, listen to me. You are very beautiful. Who can blame me for wanting to kiss you? Jack certainly wouldn't, although he would probably punch my face. Now that we know, we can stand firm against my grandmother and the rest of the Conseil as we try to figure out what the prophecy truly means. You are very special to me, but not in a romantic way. I swear I will protect you."

"So, you are assuming that you are the 'protector, the strength of many' that the prophecy refers to?" I asked.

"Well, yes. I guess I do. You don't?" he asked.

"God, Rémy. I don't know what to think." All I knew was how horrible and guilty I felt for having doubted my relationship with Jack and kissed Rémy. I must be a terrible person, that's all. Why was I having second thoughts about my love for Jack? That wasn't supposed to happen, was it?

CHAPTER TWO

"Go bring the rabble,
O'er whom I give thee power, here to this place:
Incite them to quick motion; for I must
Bestow upon the eyes of this young couple
Some vanity of mine art: it is my promise,
And they expect it from me."
—Shakespeare, *The Tempest*, 4.1

I cried myself to sleep later that night, obsessing over what Jack would do when he found out I kissed Rémy. He had been livid when Rémy had kissed me once before but had quickly calmed down when I reassured him that it was not a romantic kiss—simply Rémy's way of telling me he was a Seer. But this was different. It was a romantic kiss, even though it had convinced us both that romance was not part of our future, and I had willingly and knowingly participated. I tossed and turned for hours, creating dozens of scenarios in my head about how the conversation with Jack would go, alternating between happy and awful endings.

Rémy didn't think it was worth telling Jack—it was nothing, after all. Oh, to have such a casual view of what, in my mind, amounted to dirty, rotten cheating! Of course I would confess to Jack. I couldn't keep something like this from him. I desperately hoped he could find a way to forgive me.

The next morning Rémy and I confronted Kate with our discovery of the night before: we were not meant to be a couple. We were both dismayed when she dismissed this revelation as nothing.

"But Grand-mère," Rémy sputtered. "We tried, as you wished. There was nothing, no feeling at all when we kissed. It was as if I were kissing Geneviève."

"Kate, please," I began. "I am not in love with your grandson, but I am in love with my boyfriend back home. You said you understood, that you of all people should not tell me who to fall in love with, remember?"

She stood up and began to pace in front of the couch where Rémy and I were seated. "I do remember, Ally. I'm not trying to pressure either of you, but I am also old enough to know love can grow. I don't want you to so easily dismiss what the prophecy may mean. I have never seen two people have such a strong psychic connection and I have a hard time believing you are not destined to be together. I think we had better wait and see. Now, let's continue your training." She proceeded to push us especially hard during our session. She had found out about my physical powers, both the electric shock I had given Rémy during our first kiss and the violent blue energy pulse during the showdown with David Moore at the end of last school year, and attempted to provoke a similar reaction. Today I was angry enough that she might be successful! Thus far I hadn't been able to recreate anything, but I hadn't been angry like I was both previous times. Today, I was excessively pissed off and needed to vent. I wasn't angry at Rémy, and I couldn't begin to direct any anger at a little old lady, so after taking all I could handle of Kate's nagging 'just concentrate, Ally!', I muffled a scream of frustration and directed all my pent up feelings at a small vase resting on a side table in the room where we trained. We were all shocked when it exploded, showering the three of us in sharp ceramic fragments. I felt horrible when I saw a small drop of blood on Kate's cheek from a shard of the vase.

"*Merde!* Ally, what did you do?" Rémy exclaimed as he rushed to his grandmother's side, examining the small cut.

"Oh my God, I'm so sorry, Kate! I didn't mean to hurt you!"

"It's nothing, Ally. Rémy, don't fuss! I'm fine. It's just a scratch." She took the tissue from his hand and pushed him away impatiently, going to look at the remains of the vase. "This is extraordinary! I have never seen such power! Has this ever happened before?"

I shook my head. "No, never like this. I've never destroyed anything before. The last time it was just a pulse of energy that knocked Jack and a crazy, sadistic murderer down. Sorry about the vase. I hope it wasn't antique or anything."

"Of course not. It was nothing. Something I picked up in a market. It was my fault for doing this in the middle of my living room, anyway. We'll find a more suitable place for training from now on. That's enough for today. I need to talk with the rest of the Conseil. Rémy, why don't you drive Ally into town for some lunch and shopping? I'm sure you both would appreciate some time away."

We didn't speak at all as we got into his car and drove into Rouen. I leaned my head against the headrest and closed my eyes. Finally, I rolled my head toward Rémy and opened my eyes. "It was an antique, wasn't it?"

"18th century Meissen. Worth several thousand euros." I saw a half-smile as he stared straight ahead at the road.

"Oh, my God. I'm a disaster. What is happening to me?" I wailed.

He reached over and clasped my hand. "Don't worry, chérie. We will figure it out. It will just take time."

"How much time?" I sighed. "Rémy, I want to go home."

"Ally, it's only been a few weeks. Please, give it another week at least."

I pulled my hand away to wipe my tears of frustration. "What about your grandmother? She keeps trying to throw us together. She won't take no for an answer and I'm tired of compromising my relationship with Jack. I'm done, Rémy."

"I know. Listen, we don't have to do anything we don't want to do. She can try all she wants, but you and I know what is in our hearts, no? We will concentrate only on our training, nothing else. Please, stay another week."

"One week. That's all. Then I'm going home." I sniffed, trying to sound firm.

"So, you will not go on to Ireland then?" he asked, turning to look at me briefly.

"I don't think I'm invited anymore. Fionnuala was livid when I talked to her. I think I'll just go home."

"I'm sure she's calmed down by now. You should definitely call her before you decide. But it is ultimately your decision. I will support you in whatever you decide. I do hope you'll give us another week, however."

It was my turn to give him a half-smile as I reached for his hand again. "Thanks, Rémy. Your support means a lot, you know? I feel kind of like it's you and me against the world right now."

He took me to lunch at Le Mouton Noir, a small crêperie where I had one of the most delicious meals I have ever had: a savory crepe with Pont-l'Évêque cheese and herbs, a sweet crepe with honey and nuts, and a glass of le cidre de Normandie, a slightly alcoholic apple cider that was apparently a regional specialty. The bill for lunch was accompanied by two small glasses of cider liqueur. I would need an AA program by the time I left France. After lunch, we walked along the Rue du Gros-Horloge, stopping in at whatever shop looked interesting, all the while working our way toward the giant clock that watched over the street. We exited a small boutique when a vision, my first in months, slammed into my mind.

Jack, running through the rain. Mud covered his combat boots and water streamed down his face, into his eyes, making it difficult to see where he ran. He followed another soldier closely, trying to make it through the obstacle course, but it rained so hard he couldn't see what was ahead. He didn't see the low-hanging branch in time to duck. He ran into it at full speed and went down, unconscious, blood streaming from a head wound.

I gasped and reached blindly for Rémy, my breath coming in gasps. He led me to a nearby bench and sat down with me, rubbing my hands between his.

"It's all right, Ally. Show me what you saw."

I shook my head, but he saw the vision that I couldn't erase from my mind. I wrenched my hands from his and fumbled through my pockets, searching for my phone, trying to control my shaking hands enough to dial Trina's number. It took an agonizing amount of time for the international call to connect. "Trina? Is Jack okay? I don't know; I have a really bad feeling that he's hurt. Yeah, please call the base and find out, okay? I know it sounds crazy, but please just do it for me. Thanks. Yeah, I'll wait for your call." I hung up and sat staring at my phone, willing it to ring and for Trina to tell me he was all right. Rémy didn't say anything, but rubbed my back soothingly while we waited. I spent the longest fifteen minutes of my life waiting for my phone to ring. "Trina?" I practically yelled when it finally did. "He's okay? Oh, thank God! What happened?" She proceeded to tell me that Jack had been hurt that morning during a routine training exercise, hitting his head and splitting it open on a tree branch. He had been taken to the infirmary where he had been stitched up and checked for a concussion.

"He's okay, mija," Trina assured me. "But how on earth did you know? You and Jack must have some sort of crazy mind connection. I don't know what to think about this." I could picture her crossing herself.

"I don't know, either, Trina." I hated lying to her, but had no intention of telling her how I really knew. "I just got this really bad feeling about him. But you're sure he's okay?"

"Yes. They actually let me talk to him for about two minutes. He said that he's just embarrassed and the rest of the guys are teasing him ruthlessly. He said to tell you that he loves you and misses you. I didn't have time to tell him you were in France, sweetheart. I'm sorry."

"That's okay, Trina. Thanks for calling and finding out. Sorry I freaked out. I'll talk to you when I get back to Albuquerque, okay?" I hung up and looked at Rémy. "He's fine. Just a few stitches. Sorry for the drama scene."

He laughed a bit and pulled me up from the bench. "It is not a problem. I'm glad Jack was not seriously injured." At my doubtful look, he continued, "You wound me, chérie. Just because I don't particularly like him doesn't mean I wish him harm. Now, let us find a place to get you some refreshment. I think sugar helps you after a vision, no?" He led me a little further down the street to a small sweet shop called Chocolaterie Auzou, where he introduced me to the wonder of French macarons. Oh. My. God. I fell in love with the brightly colored cream-filled cookies, unable to decide whether I liked pistachio or coconut better. Or maybe chocolate. Yum. We walked down the street, eating our treat, laughing at how we each ate the cookies: Rémy ate his in what he said was the 'grown-up manner,' biting through the cookie, while I pulled the cookies apart to get to the cream filling, like I ate Oreos. I stuck my tongue out at him and enjoyed the cookies my way. My phone buzzed with a text notification and I struggled to juggle my cookies and reach for my phone. Rémy took my packet of cookies so I could check my message.

Jack: I'm fine. I swear. Stop worrying.

I gasped and texted back quickly, wiping away a sudden tear.

I had a vision. Are you sure you're okay?

Jack: Fine. Gotta go. Luv u.

I stared at my phone, willing him to text something else, although I knew he couldn't. I gave a small sob and lowered my forehead to my phone. Rémy led me to a bench and sat me down, rubbing my back softly as I cried. "He's fine. I don't know why I'm crying." I sat up and wiped my eyes, determined not to fall apart.

"It's a natural reaction, chérie. You are relieved now that you have heard from him." He remained silent for a few moments. "I'm sorry about last night, Ally. I'm sorry I kissed you."

"Oh, Rémy," I sighed.

"I mean it. I'm sorry. I see now the depth of feeling you have for Jack. He doesn't begin to deserve you, but you love him very much. I am done trying to come between the two of you."

I stood and pulled him up with me. "Come on. Let's get a drink and then head back to your mansion." He smiled and led me farther down the street to a bar called Delirium, where he had a beer and I had another glass of cidre.

We chatted amiably on the way back to the estate and were still talking as we entered the house, where Geneviève met us with a dour, "We have guests."

***

Rémy and I, with some trepidation, followed Geneviève into the living room where Francoise argued with none other than Fionnuala.

"We didn't kidnap her! The child came here of her own free will!" I certainly didn't appreciate Francoise referring to me as a child.

"She knew nothing about you until you sent a spy to seduce her into coming here!" Fionnuala didn't give an inch.

"Seduce?" I cried.

"Spy?" Rémy yelled at the same time.

"There you are, Ally dear." Fionnuala rushed over to hug me and otherwise fuss. She had apparently moved past the fury with which she had greeted my earlier phone call. "Are you all right?"

I hugged her briefly, but then pushed away impatiently. "Of course I'm all right. I did come here of my own free will. Rémy is not a spy and there was absolutely no seduction involved! Jeez, Fionnuala! That's just inappropriate!"

"Well said, Ally." Kate floated into the room, followed by the rest of the Conseil. She came to a halt in front of the Irish Seer. "Are you going to stand in *my* house and accuse *my* grandson of spying on and seducing the new Oracle?" The two elderly women stared at each other for a moment. Fionnuala's body language, from her pinched mouth to the arms crossed tightly in front of her, made me wonder when the yelling would start. Kate was not much better, with hands on hips and her chest heaving with indignation. Her next statement caught me completely by surprise. "It's been a long time, sister."

Wait, what?

The two women stared at each other for a full moment longer before Kate moved forward to throw her arms around Fionnuala, who remained stiff and unyielding for a few seconds before melting into her sister's arms. I turned to Rémy, my mouth hanging open like a fish. "Wha—?"

Geneviève appeared between the two of us, squealing, "Oh my goodness! Can you believe it?"

I shook my head, disbelieving. "Rémy, did you

have any idea?"

He said nothing, shaking his head as I had, apparently speechless.

The two women finally disengaged and turned to us as Kate spoke. "Fionnuala, I want you to meet my grandson. Rémy, come and greet your Aunt Fionnuala."

I stood in the background, watching as Rémy met his long-lost aunt and Fionnuala and Phillipe got reacquainted. I tuned back in when Kate turned to peer behind Fionnuala, asking, "Are you going to introduce your friend?" I had been so focused on the events unfolding in the center of the room I hadn't noticed the other guest. We all turned to look now; the young woman standing off to the side appeared embarrassed at the sudden attention.

"Of course." Fionnuala reached out to pull the girl forward. "This is my young protégé, Mina Addair. She is showing signs of great power, much like Ally, and we are working with her. I thought it would be a good idea to bring her with me."

I experienced a sudden feeling of something like jealousy: Mina was beautiful, with long, black hair and piercing blue eyes. And she was powerful, too? Even as I chastised myself for my unreasonable, instant dislike of this new girl, I felt relief that maybe there was another contender for the Oracle title. I watched her flush becomingly as Rémy lifted her hand and kissed the back, murmuring, "Enchanté."

I must have vocalized my disgust, because Geneviève leaned in, whispering, "What? She is lovely, don't you think?"

"If you like that obvious sort of beauty," I said and sniffed.

"Well, Rémy apparently does. You're not jealous, are you?"

I gave her a look that hopefully said I found her remark ridiculous. She just laughed. I rolled my eyes and stepped forward to interrupt the mutual admiration society between Rémy and this new girl, Mina. I reached my hands simultaneously to pull Rémy's hand away from Mina's, touching both of them at the same time. What happened next took the snarky comment I planned to make right out of my mouth. My hands felt instantly glued to their arms as the room faded away and a loud buzzing engulfed me. The word 'Jessamine' appeared in my mind, as it had months ago when Rémy first kissed me, and I'm not sure if I said it aloud or if I only thought it. I heard glass shattering as if it were from a great distance, accompanied by screams. That brought me out of the trance, or whatever it was, to see the room was much darker than it had been and the curtains were blowing in at the windows.

"What happened?" I asked as I dropped Rémy and Mina's hands. They both shrugged, looking around in confusion.

"Kate!" Phillipe cried as his wife collapsed on the sofa. Fionnuala and Francoise rushed to Kate's side as I looked around the room at the others. Arnaud attended to Geneviève, brushing pieces of what looked like glass out of her hair. I noticed others doing the same.

"Aw, crap! What did I explode this time?" I sighed.

"I'm not sure it was you this time," Rémy said as he and Mina looked around the room. "Or that it was *only* you, Ally. I think all three of us may have had a hand in this." He turned to address his cousin. "Geneviève, what happened?"

"I'm all right, Arnaud. Thank you," she assured him. For someone who felt he was too old for her, Arnaud certainly rushed to her side when things got dangerous. *Very interesting.* Geneviève approached the three of us, still brushing bits of glass from her hair. "When Ally touched you and Mina, the lights flickered and then burst. Then the windows exploded and there was a sort of glow around you three. That's when Grand-mère started speaking a new prophecy, right before she fainted."

"I'm fine!" Kate interrupted, sitting up on the sofa. "I did not faint. I felt a little weak. That's all."

Rémy walked over to the sofa and knelt in front of his grandmother, taking her hand between his. "Grand-mère, can you tell us the prophecy?"

She cupped her hand against his face and leaned forward to kiss his forehead. "Oh, my dear boy. Ally, Mina, come here, please. You all need to hear this." We both followed Rémy's lead and knelt on the floor in front of Kate. The rest of the Conseil gathered close, although they had already heard the prophecy while Rémy, Mina, and I were in our trance, or whatever it was. Kate held on to Rémy's hands as she spoke:

"The binding is before you. The time of the Seers is at hand. Before you stands the Oracle, the Shield, and the Heart of the Oracle. Behold the power of the three."

We were all silent for a moment before Geneviève broke in. "What is 'Jessamine'? Rémy and Ally said it at the same time."

Mina spoke for the first time. "It's my name."

***

While the Conseil began to debate all the possible meanings and ramifications of the new prophecy, Rémy pulled Mina and me aside to a corner where we could talk quietly. It was nearly impossible amidst the increasing volume and rancor of the older Seers in the room.

"Tell us, Mina, please. We have been hearing the word 'Jessamine' in our heads for months now. You say it is your name?" Rémy began.

"Jessamine Elizabeth Addair is my full name. I go by Mina. What do you mean you've been hearing my name for months? I didn't know you two existed until today; Fionnuala and the rest of the Council told me nothing." In addition to being extremely pretty, she had an enchanting lilt to her voice. Ughh!

"Well, when Rémy and I found out we were both Seers—" I began.

"How did you find out? Did you know when you met? How long have you known each other? I don't know any other Seers, except the Council," Mina broke in, grabbing my hands. She seemed so alone and confused, but I hardened my heart, determined to dislike her. I know—I'm a horrible person.

"We've only known each for about six months. Rémy went to the United States to find me because of a vision his grandmother had, but we didn't know about each other being a Seer until he, w-well, um, actually, w-when we—" I stuttered.

"I kissed her and we were instantly inside each other's mind, both of us hearing the word 'Jessamine,'" Rémy finished. I rolled my eyes at his brusqueness.

"Oh. Ohhhh," Mina said, looking between the two of us and dropping my hands. "I'm sorry. I didn't realize you were together."

"We're not," I said firmly. "It was a mistake. Rémy is like a brother to me. An annoying, much older brother." It was his turn to roll his eyes at me. "But I didn't read anything from you, Mina, when we touched. Did you, Rémy?"

He stared at her, an intense look on his face. "I did. I felt you in my mind, as well. Did you feel me?" he asked her.

She nodded, smiling slightly at him. "I did. I couldn't tell anything really specific, just a general presence. But Ally, what I felt from you was just, well, power. It was quite shocking."

Her comment made me feel more of that unreasonable dislike toward her and I turned away. "What does this mean, Rémy? What does this 'binding' mean? What is 'the power of the three'?"

"I don't know, chérie, I don't know. Perhaps we—"

Luc's shouting interrupted him. "You can't be serious! She can't leave! None of them can! We must keep them close to find out what this prophecy means!"

The three of us stared at each other, wide-eyed,

before returning to the rest of the group.

"Did you not hear what the Oracle prophesied?" Luc continued. "*The time of the Seers is at hand.* This is what we've been waiting for. This is our call to action. Do you not see that these young people are developing more powers than our kind have seen for a thousand years? This must be a sign! A sign that we are meant to rise up and claim our true place in this world!" The entire room listened to his rant as if under a spell. "Ally, Rémy, and this Mina are clearly the key to a new day for Seers. We must keep them here in Rouen, to test them, to find out what they can do together. That demonstration of power they just gave may be just the beginning. Think of the possibilities!"

"I can't stay here!" I objected, breaking away from the charisma of his voice. "I have to go home! My mom and my grandma need me there. I need to be back when my boyfriend gets home from boot camp." I looked frantically around at the Conseil members to see if anyone might be sympathetic to my plight.

"Your silly teenage romance is unimportant." Luc waved his hand dismissively. "We are talking about changing the power structure of nations! You are the next Oracle and should be above such petty romantic entanglements!"

"You have no right to say anything about my love life!" I sputtered.

"What can a child possibly know about love?"

"Luc, that's enough!" Kate's voice shook as she rose from the couch. "We don't know for sure that Ally is the next Oracle. We don't know anything for sure yet. What you are saying is crazy! Seers have always kept to themselves, stayed behind the scenes. Changing the power structure of nations? What are you talking about?"

"Oracle, can you not see the future? Your short-sightedness will be our downfall," he sneered.

This clearly made her angry. "No, Luc. Your blind ambition may be, however." They stared at each other, eyes narrowed, until Luc turned abruptly on his heel and left the room. Kate stared after him.

"I want to go home," I whispered.

She turned back to me, clasping my hand in hers. "Of course you do, my dear."

"So, you won't keep me here?"

"Of course not! You are free to leave whenever you like. However, I think Rémy should go with you. I believe the prophecy means that you are the Oracle and he is the Shield. I think it is important that the two of you remain close, for your protection."

"What about Mina? Is she the Heart of the Oracle? What could that mean? Should she stay close, as well?" Rémy asked.

Kate shook her head. "I don't know. That is the confusing part of the prophecy. I don't understand it at all. Perhaps it would be better for the three of you to remain close to each other."

"So, we're all going back to Albuquerque? Does Mina have any say in this? What about her parents? Is she in school? What about her friends? What if she has a boyfriend? My God, what if she's married or something?" I started to blather as I panicked.

Mina stepped forward and put her hand on my

shoulder. "It's all right, Ally. You have family and friends back home that you need to return to. I actually don't. I can go wherever I need to go. After what happened earlier, I think it might be a good idea for us to stay together."

She had been nothing but nice, and I realized that my unreasonable dislike of her had to go. How old was I, anyway? I was acting like a bratty child. And since it looked like we were going to be together for a while, it would be a whole lot easier to be friends.

***

We spent two more weeks in France, dividing our time between training with Kate and exploring the countryside around Normandy. We spent much of our time practicing reading each other's thoughts. Rémy was unstoppable, clearly the most talented of the three of us, but Mina came in a close second, able to read anyone with only a few seconds of intense concentration. It took me much longer, and when either Rémy or Mina really tried to keep me out, they were mostly successful. It really made me feel like a complete loser compared to the other two, let me tell you. I was supposed to be the next Oracle, and here these other two were exhibiting more mental powers than me! Neither of them had anything like my ability to break things, however, which made me feel nominally better. Kate worked with me to concentrate and focus my power without me having to be completely pissed off. She was still baffled by my ability since there was no evidence that any Seer had ever had anything like it.

Luc skulked around the estate, staring at me and making me feel extremely uncomfortable. He had apologized to me the day after his outburst, but I could tell Kate had forced him to do it. He seemed to come and go from the estate frequently and Rémy told me he lived in Rouen, as did many of the other Seers. I kept hoping he would go back to his home and leave us alone, but he always returned.

One afternoon, as I paced in the back garden, trying to work off the frustration of a particularly difficult training session, I stumbled upon Luc and a man I had never seen before, deep in conversation. Although I understood nothing of the French they spoke, I got the unmistakable feeling it was secretive, a feeling reinforced by the fact that they stopped as soon as they noticed me. The strange man melted away into the garden as Luc came forward to talk to me.

"All alone, Mademoiselle Moran? Your guard dog dares to leave you alone for even a second?" He obviously attempted to tease, but I didn't like the undertones. This guy seriously gave me the creeps.

"You know, I don't really think I need a guard dog. If someone tried to hurt me, I could always explode something," I answered and walked away. I didn't have time for his crap. I returned to the living room where we had been working earlier to find Rémy and Mina sitting together on the couch, laughing quietly, and Kate missing.

"There you are," Rémy said. "Feeling better?" He was surprisingly understanding about my frustrations, often advising his grandmother not to push me too hard.

"Yeah, I guess." I blew out a breath. "Where's Kate?" I asked, looking around.

"She went upstairs to take a nap," Mina answered.

"Is she okay?" I asked Rémy, worried about Kate's health; she was an old lady, after all.

"She's fine, chérie. She's just feeling her age, although she would never admit to it. Why don't we take advantage of this extra time and go to Les Andelys for the rest of the day? It's only 40 or so kilometers from here. We could take a picnic."

"Really? I would love to get out of here for a while." I was desperate for a break from all the stress. I looked at Mina hopefully.

"I would love to go," she said quietly.

"Then it is settled. I'll get the kitchen staff to pack a lunch while you two go do whatever it is that takes girls so long to get ready." Rémy said the last part as he exited the room.

We had a wonderful afternoon climbing to the top of a steep hill and exploring the ruins of the Chateau Gaillard, a castle built in the twelfth century by Richard the Lionheart, then eating a delicious lunch while resting in the shade. After we ate, we headed down the hill toward the picturesque town of Les Andelys where Rémy let Mina and me shop to our heart's content along the Promenade des Pres and admire the half-timbered houses on the Rue de Remparts. I took lots of photos of everything, but for some reason I especially fell in love with the Church of St. Saviour, with its flying buttresses and tall spire. Maybe I loved it because it was a cool, calm respite in the midst of a stressful period in my life. I could have stayed all day. I wandered around looking at the dozens of beautiful statues staged throughout the sanctuary until Rémy and Mina dragged me away, claiming they were dying of thirst. We had cake and cidre (Rémy had a beer) at the Fort de Thé, a lovely teashop we spotted in town.

"Mina, you mentioned you don't have family or friends to return to in Ireland. What did you mean?" I was curious about this quiet addition to our group and she had been frustratingly tight-lipped about any personal details. "Is it a deep, dark secret or something?"

She smiled softly. "No, of course not. It's simply not very interesting. My parents died three years ago, as I was finishing secondary school. I didn't have any relatives to rely on so I had to quit school and get a job. I found work in a small dress shop in Galway, which is where Fionnuala found me. When I accidentally touched her hand she sensed my power and, well, here I am, I guess." She shrugged and picked up her glass of cidre, but found it empty and set it back on the table awkwardly. Rémy motioned the waiter to bring another round.

"So, are you really okay about coming with us to the U.S.? What about your friends? You don't have anyone special back home?" I found it hard to believe that someone so beautiful didn't have a guy in her life.

She shrugged again. "I work a lot. I don't have much time for friends. What little free time I have I like to spend in my apartment with my cat." She bit her lip as she said the last part and I got a horrible feeling.

"Mina, what happened to your cat?"

"I gave her away," she whispered miserably. "I didn't know when or even if I would be going back."

"God, Mina, that's awful!" I clasped her hand and squeezed. I would never give Wicky away for stupid Seer crap! A girl's bond with her cat should be sacred! Rémy rolled his eyes as he read my thoughts, but when the waiter delivered the new round of drinks he put the beer in front of Mina, taking the cidre for himself, obviously feeling she needed something stronger. "What are you going to do in the U.S.? I mean, are you going to work? Or do you want to go to school? Where are you going to live?"

"I don't know." She shook her head. "Fionnuala said not to worry, that we would work it all out, but I can't help it. I guess I will need to find a job, but—"

"But what? What do you really want to do?" I pressed.

She shrugged yet again, as if her desires were not important. "I excelled at computers in school. At the dress shop, I created a website—a simple one, for sure—but I liked it. I had thought maybe I would try to get some computer training. I managed to get my Leaving Cert last year so I thought maybe—"

At my confused look Rémy spoke up. "A Leaving Certificate is similar to a high school diploma or a G.E.D. Mina, I'm sure we can make that happen if that's what you would like. There should be *something* beneficial in all this for you."

He forced her to meet his eyes and they stared at each other for a long moment. I started to feel like a third wheel when they finally looked away and Rémy signaled for the check.

We ended our perfect afternoon with a dusk walk along the Seine before heading back to Rouen.

CHAPTER THREE

"All three of them are desperate.
Their great guilt,
Like poison given to work a great time after,
Now 'gins to bite their spirits. I do beseech you
That are of suppler joints, follow them swiftly,
And hinder them from what this ecstasy
May now provoke them to. "
—Shakespeare, *The Tempest*, 3.3

Fionnuala broke the news over dinner: it was expected—no demanded—that we spend several weeks in Ireland with the Seer Council before returning to the U.S. I can't say I was terribly surprised, so I just sighed and made it clear that I would be home before the beginning of August, when Jack was due back from basic training. Nothing in this world would keep me from being at the airport to welcome him home. Absolutely. Nothing.

Rémy also remained stoic about our upcoming trip. "It is to be expected, chérie. Your Seer Council wants equal time with the chosen ones."

I saw Mina smile into her water glass, but I took exception to everything he said. "It is not my Seer Council! We are not the chosen ones! And why is it that you never call Mina 'chérie'?"

"I'm sorry. I didn't know it bothered you so much." He held his hands up in surrender. "In the future, I will be sure to not call you anything nice. Perhaps you would prefer if I called you—"

"Rémy! Ally! Stop your infernal bickering!" Kate banged her hands on the table, rattling the china. "You are giving me a headache." She pinched the bridge of her nose.

"Sorry, Grand-mère," Rémy said contritely.

"Sorry, Kate," I echoed.

"Now, Ally, I'm afraid Rémy is correct: the Seer Council does view you three as the chosen ones. So do we, for that matter. The prophecy is clear about that, at least. The three of you have been chosen to usher in this new age of Seers. We are all trying to figure out what this will mean. I'm sorry. I know it is not what you want to hear."

"I never wanted any of this! Why would the prophecy choose me to be the Oracle? I'm going to be the worst Oracle ever!" I whined.

Rémy got up, came over to my chair and pulled me up into his arms. "Shh, chérie." We both laughed at his unconscious use of the endearment I despised. "You are going to be a great Oracle. I'm going to make sure of it." We might fight like cats and dogs, but he was always there for me. I hugged him back and felt slightly better.

We left two days later. We flew from Paris to

Shannon, Ireland, approximately 85 kilometers from Galway. We rented a car and Fionnuala kept up a running monologue the entire way, telling us we would be staying with her a short distance from Galway. Long car rides always made me sleepy, so although I tried to stay awake so as not to seem rude, I eventually gave up and fell asleep on Rémy's shoulder. I didn't wake up until we were pulling into the circular driveway of a lovely gray stone house surrounded by a wild-looking garden, huge trees, and rocky fields. It wasn't nearly as large as Rémy's palatial estate, but it had an untamed charm that appealed to me. "This is your house, Fionnuala? It's gorgeous!" I enthused.

"Oh, thank you, Ally. My husband and I bought it after the birth of our first son. I hope you young people will enjoy your stay here. I've always loved living here."

I tried to wrap my mind around the fact that there was a Mr. Fionnuala, much less little Fionnualas and didn't reply. Rémy snickered as he read this last thought, but said, "Thank you. I'm sure we will be very happy for our short visit."

"I don't understand why you are in such a hurry to get back to the United States. I really think we deserve the same amount of time you gave to the French Council. It's only fair," she said huffily.

"Fionnuala—" I warned. "We have talked about this. Two weeks is plenty of time. Stop bugging us to stay longer!"

"Fine, fine," she mumbled. I noticed Mina smiling to herself during the exchange. She didn't say much, but she noticed everything.

We unloaded our luggage and followed Fionnuala into her house. She showed Rémy to a bedroom at the top of the stairs and then took Mina and me to the bedroom across the hall, which we would share. It was different than the luxury I had experienced in Rouen, but I actually felt more comfortable; it was much more like my real life. Fionnuala told us to unpack and make ourselves at home until dinner, so I heaved my giant suitcase on my bed and flopped next to it, not wanting to face the chore of unpacking yet. Mina, of course, had already opened hers and begun unloading piles of clothing. Ugh! Why did she have to be so industrious and perfect?

"Mina! Stop working. Let's explore!" I begged. "We've been cooped up in a plane and a car all day! Come on!"

She smiled slightly. "Give me ten minutes. I want to unpack first."

I threw myself back on the bed, blowing a breath out. "Whatever."

Rémy poked his head in the door. "Come on, you two. Let's get some fresh air while we have a look around the grounds."

I hopped up eagerly. "I'm ready, but Mina is being a busy little worker bee. Make her stop, Rémy."

He chuckled at my childishness. "I can't make her do anything, chérie. Why don't we let her join us when she is ready? Maybe she needs a few moments to herself without your constant chattering."

"Hey!" I punched him lightly on his arm. "Don't

be mean. All right, let's go. Mina, see you at dinner, okay?" She simply nodded. I waited until we were outside to ask, "Is it just me, or is she the most reserved person you've ever met? She barely talks!"

"And you never stop, so you should be great friends."

"Nice, Rémy. Thanks a lot."

He laughed. "I'm kidding. Mostly. But I agree: she is very reserved. It may be difficult to get to know her well, but we must try, nevertheless. She is bound to us somehow. I don't understand it any more than you."

"She's really pretty—" I let it hang out there, waiting for him to respond.

He rolled his eyes. "We are not having that conversation. I've told you before I don't need your help finding dates. Besides," he put his arm around my neck and pulled me to him, mussing my hair in a horrible big-brother way, "if you're the Oracle and I'm the Shield, then that would make her the Heart of the Oracle. You think she's pretty, so—"

"So, I'm supposed to dump Jack in favor of Mina? Wow, if only I were a lesbian. Sorry, but the prophecy is whacked in that regard. And you may not want to have the conversation, but you can't deny the chemistry between you and Mina." I ducked out from under his arm and tried to straighten my hair.

"You are imagining things, chérie. I'm a man." He shrugged. "I look the same way at any beautiful girl."

"Aha! So you admit she's beautiful!" I exclaimed triumphantly.

"I never thought to deny it. Mina is very beautiful. So are you, for that matter. Why did you dislike her when we first met her?"

Crap. It was really inconvenient to have him in my mind whenever he wanted. I still wasn't very good at keeping him out. "Oh, I don't know. She shows up all of sudden and I'm supposed to instantly like her?"

"You were jealous, maybe? You have no reason to be jealous of her looks, but perhaps you are jealous of her power?"

"God, it's hard to be mad at you when you insult and compliment me in the same sentence." He smirked as I continued. "What is her power, anyway? Fionnuala says she's as powerful as me, but I haven't seen anything at all. Have you?"

He shook his head and stared out over the rugged landscape surrounding the house. "No. I sensed great power in her when we touched for the first time, but I still don't have any idea what it is. Hopefully we can find out while we are here in Ireland."

I looked around to make sure we were alone. "Do you trust her? Should we trust her?"

He shrugged again. "I don't know. Time will tell."

"I hope we can. I feel bad about not liking her in the beginning. She seems so sad sometimes. I guess I would be too, if I'd been through everything she has."

"You're too nice sometimes, Ally. You really can't handle not liking someone, can you?" He put his arm back around my neck and pulled me close.

"No! I was perfectly happy not liking Veronica," I objected.

"No you weren't. You forget I'm in your head, chérie. Let's go back to the house. It's getting late and I'm starving. Irish food! God help us all."

"Cheer up. We'll be back in the U.S. soon and you can have all the cheeseburgers you want. Hey, I haven't had a chance to ask if you're okay with babysitting me again. What are you going to do for school? I feel selfish about insisting we go back to the U.S., but—"

"Don't worry about me. You are the Oracle and therefore must be taken care of. It's my job and I'm happy to do it. Besides, I finished my undergraduate degree a few weeks ago and Grand-mère is working on getting me into your University of New Mexico for an MBA program. She is rather good at pulling strings, so I should be well occupied this fall."

"Rémy, you graduated from college? Why didn't you tell me? That's great! Why didn't we go to your graduation ceremony? Why didn't we have a party at least?"

"Don't fuss, Ally. It is not the big deal you are making it," he said dismissively.

"Your accomplishments are a big deal. They are to me, at least. I'm proud of you, Rémy."

"Thank you, Ally. You are sweet." He seemed determined to downplay his achievements.

"Hey." I stopped and turned to face him, looking up into his handsome face. "Don't let all this Oracle crap totally mess up your future. You are important, too, Rémy. It can't be all about me. Please," I begged. "You and Mina can't put your lives on hold so I can carry on like normal. We have to figure something out! We can't let the older Seers just push us around!" I started to get worked up.

"Okay, calm down, chérie." He pulled me into his arms, rubbing my back with his warm hands. "We will figure this out, I promise. Don't worry about Mina and me right now. For myself, I am happy to return to the U.S. where I have the opportunity to study in an American university. I will make sure Mina has the chance to study computers if that is what she wants. We will be fine. Besides, I liked my friends in Albuquerque. I was happy there. So, don't worry so much."

"Okay, I'll try," I promised. "It just doesn't seem fair."

"Life rarely is."

"So, are you going to date Veronica when we get back? You two seemed pretty cozy at Tara's party."

He smiled and let me go, continuing our walk toward the house. "Always so interested in my love life, chérie. We can't all be like you and Jack, you know, finding the love of our lives so young. Veronica and I were never serious. Besides, she is going to university in California. Hadn't you heard?"

"What? God, I'm always the last to hear anything!"

"Yes. She wants to get a fresh start where people don't know her history. I can't say I blame her," he mused.

"Yeah, me neither. I just wish I had known, I guess. Well, good for her. Okay, so you are fine with living in Albuquerque again. I just hope Mina likes it."

***

Dinner was an enjoyable affair. Fionnuala's husband, who had prepared the meal, devoted himself to drawing out each of his dinner guests, seeming to take Mina's lack of involvement as a personal challenge. By the time dessert was served, she was laughing quietly and teasing back. It was nice to see there was a personality there if one cared to dig deep enough to access it.

"Jon, you've done it again. This was a wonderful meal. Thank you, darling," said Fionnuala. He had prepared some sort of smoked salmon dish that the others seemed to enjoy and had thoughtfully presented me with a roasted vegetable tart. Dessert was a decadent lemon mousse that I would probably dream about. We all added our thanks for the delicious meal. "Jon was a chef for many years before retiring. He now writes a foodie blog and has several cookbooks published."

Jon smiled modestly and said, "I've been very lucky. I was in the right place at the right time when New Irish cuisine appeared on the scene. Not what you expected, eh, Monsieur Giles?"

Rémy had the grace to appear somewhat abashed. "No, not at all. I fear I am something of a food snob. I hope it is my worst failing."

"It's definitely not. I can think of several others that are much worse," I piped in. The others chuckled.

"Anyway, my faults aside, it was a delicious meal. And I wholeheartedly approve of this Irish

56

stout," he said as he raised his glass of dark beer in a toast. "To our hosts, Fionnuala and Jon. My thanks for your splendid hospitality." We all raised our glasses. I had opted for water instead of beer, not out of prudishness, but because I found beer disgusting. The only beer I had ever had tasted like cat pee. Well, what I imagine cat pee would taste like.

"The rest of the Seer Council will arrive tomorrow," Fionnuala said. "We will have a busy two weeks, so I suggest you all get rested up tonight."

"Will they be staying here?" I asked. I had only seen three bedrooms upstairs and couldn't imagine the other six council members sharing one room.

Fionnuala smiled. "Yes, dear. You are staying in the original part of the house. After dinner I'll show you the new wing, if you like." It turned out that Fionnuala and Jon had built a large addition to their house that wasn't visible from the front. It more than doubled the square footage and included four additional guest rooms, two bathrooms, and a large recreational room, where we would apparently be working. Yay. It made me tired just thinking about all the training they had in store for us. My dreams of a relaxing summer disappeared.

The ladies arrived bright and early the next morning; the sound of their chattering and laughing pulled me from sleep way too soon. I peered at the bed across from me and saw Mina was already up, bed made—of course—and gone from the room. By the time I showered, got ready, and made my way to the kitchen, elderly women were perched all over the room. The whole crew was here: Fionnuala, Caoimhe, Iona, Aine, Eithne, Bridget, and Maire. The noise level was incredible and I wished I could retreat back to my bedroom. I found an empty seat next to Rémy and gratefully sipped the hot, black coffee that Jon brought me.

"How about an omelet, Ally? I can have one whipped up in a few minutes."

"I don't want you to go to any trouble," I began.

"No trouble at all," he brushed off my concerns. "It's what I do. I enjoy cooking." He bustled away to prepare my breakfast.

"Where's Mina?" I asked after another sip of coffee.

"It was too chaotic here for her. She went out for a walk," Rémy said over the top of the newspaper he read. "Did you sleep well, chérie?"

"I guess." I shrugged. "I'm dreading this training, though." I shuddered as I looked around the room at the noisy members of the Seer Council.

He folded his paper and nodded in agreement. "This is going to be a long two weeks."

Once I finished my breakfast and Mina had returned from her walk, we all retreated to the large recreational room in the new wing of the house; all except Jon, who didn't belong to the council and left to shop for what he needed to prepare the rest of the day's meals. They started things off by having Bridget take turns touching each one of us separately in order to get a baseline reading. I got to go first.

"Oh, Ally," she sighed after a moment. "I was right. Your powers have developed so much in just a few short months. Your abilities far out-strip anything I have ever encountered. My goodness. I don't know what to think about this destructive power you seem to have. I just don't know." Well, that made me feel *so* much better.

She turned next to Mina. "How are you, dear? We missed you while you were gone." Bridget smiled at Mina and stroked her cheek before taking her hand. "Oh, my dear. Your ability to read others is incredibly strong. There's more there, too, that is just out of reach." Before moving away, she leaned forward and whispered something in Mina's ear. Mina appeared relieved and whispered 'thanks.'

I wasn't sure I approved of these secrets and was about to say something when Bridget approached Rémy. She seemed unsure and asked, "May I?" before taking his hand. I remembered all the Seers in their experience were women and this whole business of male Seers must rock their world a little bit. She grasped his hand and closed her eyes. After a few seconds she shifted uncomfortably and added her other hand. After another few seconds she lifted her hands away and frowned into his eyes. "You're blocking me," she accused. "No one has ever been able to block me before."

"Rémy," I began.

"It's all right, Ally. I will play nice. I just wanted to make it clear I am here voluntarily. For the moment. And it would be better for all involved if we cooperate with each other." He looked around at each council member, forcing them to meet his intense gaze. "Our two clans have a history of distrust, made much more serious by your generation. If there is to be a renewal and rebuilding of relationship, it will start with the three of us: Ally, Mina, and myself. You would all do well not to forget that." It was moments like this when I was reminded he was not simply the happy-go-lucky teen he enjoyed portraying; he was a full-grown man who could handle himself in the adult world. I felt very young and naïve in that moment. He smiled a smile that didn't quite reach his eyes and gave his hand back to Bridget. "Shall we try again?"

She looked around at her fellow council members before taking his hand somewhat shakily. She held on for a few seconds before letting go and whispering, "Amazing." She turned to look at the rest of us. "He is indescribably powerful. I just, I don't know…"

I was shocked. I knew Rémy was good at reading my thoughts and keeping me from reading his, but I had no idea of the depths of his power. He certainly downplayed his abilities. I wondered what else he kept from me.

Next, the council wanted to see my destructive abilities. I had worked with Kate enough so I only needed to think of something that annoyed me to make it work. Plenty of things annoyed me, including being here in Ireland instead of home in the U.S., so I gladly gave a demonstration. Fionnuala picked a cheap knickknack she claimed she didn't mind losing and set it on a low table. It took me about two seconds to focus my annoyance and turn it into powdery shards. I had also gotten better at making smaller, more controlled explosions so nobody got hurt. The council ladies were quite impressed by my abilities, which gratified me somewhat. They all then wanted to hear the story of how I made contact with Ashley Hayes's spirit and solved her murder. Rémy piped in with details every so often, especially his view of the final chapter outside David Moore's house. He told them how the blue pulse had exploded from me, knocking down both Jack and Moore right as he fired his shotgun.

"Ally, dear, I cannot approve of your involvement in this kind of criminal activity!" Caoimhe exclaimed.

I laughed slightly and gave my favorite council member a hug. "Believe me, I have no desire whatsoever to get involved in any more criminal situations. I just want a calm, peaceful year."

"Good luck with that," muttered Rémy. "You are a trouble magnet, chérie."

I glared at him as Fionnuala announced that it was time to break for lunch.

***

After lunch, several of the older women claimed they needed an hour or so of rest time before we resumed our training. I was about to say that I would enjoy some time to write Jack a letter—snail-mail letters were all he was allowed at this stage of his training—but suddenly heard Rémy's voice in my head telling me to say I wanted to explore the gardens. I gave him a curious look and noticed Mina doing the same. He raised his eyebrows expectantly at both of us, so I duly claimed my desire to take a walk after lunch, which Mina echoed. Rémy then declared his desire to join us.

"So, why did you want to get us away from everyone?" I asked when we were a good distance from the house.

"Before we get any deeper into this training, I think we need to come to a few agreements I do not wish the council to be privy to," he replied.

"Such as?" asked Mina.

"Nobody except my grandmother knows the extent of our mental communication abilities, and she will keep it to herself," he said to me. "And nobody knows how well Mina and I can communicate."

"Including me! What am I missing?" I stopped and faced them both. "Spill!"

"Calm down, chérie. Mina and I seem to have a direct conduit to each other's thoughts. That's all. It is even stronger than the bond you and I share."

"Oh, that's all, huh? When were you going to tell me? I thought we were supposed to trust each other! You guys have been keeping secrets from me! Ugh! Do you have any idea how that makes me feel?" I fumed.

"Apparently it makes you angry," he said with a smirk.

"Yes, it does! Don't be such an ass, Rémy!" I turned toward him and let loose with a small pulse of energy that knocked him to the ground, sprawled ignominiously in the dirt.

"Rémy!" Mina rushed to his side to help him up.

He took her hand and stood back up, brushing leaves and dirt from his backside. "I'm all right,

Mina. Thank you." He smiled at her gently before turning to me with a scowl. "Merde, Ally! I will try not to make you mad again! That was incredible, by the way."

"Ally, we weren't trying to keep anything from you," Mina broke in. "It's just—"

"It's just that Mina is not ready to talk about any of this, yet," Rémy interrupted. "She has not been close to any one for years, and suddenly she has two people invading her thoughts whether or not she wishes it. I'm sure it must be disturbing."

"It's not like any of us asked for this!" I was still mad, but I could see where they were coming from. I paced for a few seconds before hanging my head in defeat. "Yeah, I get it. Sorry, Rémy. I didn't mean to hurt you."

"You didn't, chérie. Don't worry about it. Still friends?" He looked at me hopefully.

"Of course," I said, impatiently waving aside his concern. "So, you two are able to read each other even better than Rémy and I? Are you constantly in each other's head? That must be kind of miserable."

Mina shook her head. "No. Rémy is incredibly gifted at blocking people from reading his thoughts."

"That's an understatement," I muttered.

"You are not too bad at it yourself, Mina. It is only when you are not paying attention that I am able to get in," observed Rémy.

"I would really appreciate if you would refrain from doing that," Mina whispered and turned away from Rémy and I.

I looked at him with raised eyebrows. *Jeez,*

sensitive much? I asked silently.

He shook his head slightly and approached Mina, putting his hand on her shoulder. "I'm sorry. I will be more careful in the future, I promise." She nodded and turned back around.

"Why are you both able to block people out better than me? I would really like to be able to keep Rémy out of my head," I groused, my crankiness showing yet again.

"Stop whining," Rémy said, laughing. "Neither Mina nor I can explode anything or knock people down with our thoughts. Don't be greedy. Do you think I enjoy being inside your head when you're thinking about Jack? I assure you I don't." I made a move toward him, but Mina stepped between us with a warning look. "Can we get back to the reason I brought us out here?" he asked and Mina and I nodded. "I think it would be best if the council remains in the dark about our mental communication abilities. I have a feeling that it could be our 'ace in the hole,' if you will."

Mina and I looked at each other for a long moment before turning back to Rémy and nodding.

"I'm not completely convinced that either group—this Irish council or the French conseil— has our best interests at heart," Mina said. It shocked me to hear her express this distrust. "I'm not sure their agenda allows for the feelings or desires of three young adults."

I appreciated her referring to me as a young adult rather than a teenager. "I agree with Mina. There are several agendas going on around here and none of them are ours. I think we should consider what's best for us. We're the ones who have to live with the prophecy, after all. We're the ones who have to figure out the stupid who's who riddle. This is such bullshit!"

Rémy and Mina stared at me with wide eyes for a moment before bursting into simultaneous laughter. I narrowed my eyes at them evilly, but couldn't hold out and joined them, laughing until I snorted, which made the other two laugh harder. It was therapeutic for all of us, easing some of the strain we had been feeling. We returned from our walk ready to train, but prepared to keep some of our mental gifts to ourselves.

The council wanted to see what would happen when the three of us touched, as we had in Rouen when the windows exploded. Because of said explosion, I insisted we conduct the experiment outside. We stood in a small circle under the shade of a grove of trees, joined hands, and…nothing happened. Absolutely nothing. I opened my eyes—which I had closed in expectation of flying splinters of wood—and stared at Rémy and Mina.

—*What is going on, Rémy?*

—*We expected it. We all have our barriers in place.*

—*So, should we let them down, or what?*

—*Perhaps just a small amount, enough to give them a bit of a show. That should satisfy them.*

—*Are you in, Mina?*

—*I suppose.*

I wondered why she was so reluctant to let us in, even for the briefest time. What was she trying to hide?

—All right, on three. Rémy thought. *One…two…three.*

We all let down our mental barriers, a little bit at the same time. I felt a mild version of the energy that had glued my hands to the other two the last time, but was still aware of what was happening around us. I felt the energy radiate out from us and shear a large branch from the nearest tree. It fell a few feet away from the members of the Seer Council, causing an outburst of squeals. We released our hands, but I could have sworn Rémy held Mina's hand a second longer than was absolutely necessary.

"That was amazing!" Caoimhe exclaimed. "Is this what happened last time?" she asked Fionnuala.

"Yes, but it was even more violent. I'm certainly glad you insisted on coming outside, Ally. I have no desire to have my windows replaced," Fionnuala said.

"But what does it mean?" Bridget asked. "What is the purpose?"

Nobody had an answer for her.

***

The rest of our visit was fairly uneventful; we trained, explored, ate, slept, and trained some more. We managed to keep our direct lines to each other's minds a secret from the Seer Council and thus felt like we had accomplished something, no matter how small. I tried to get to know Mina and felt like our friendship had progressed to the slightly-better-than-acquaintances stage. We weren't besties or anything yet, and I still wondered what secrets she kept from us. Or me. I got the distinct feeling Rémy knew what she kept from me, but when I asked him, all I got was "Leave it alone, chérie. Everyone deserves their privacy."

"But how can we trust her? She just appeared out of nowhere!"

"So did I, if you remember. You trust me, don't you?" he pointed out.

"Well, yes, but—"

"Just give her time, Ally. I have a feeling she really needs a friend right now."

Aw, crap. Way to make me feel guilty. Thanks a lot, Rémy! "Fine, fine," I muttered. "I'll work on it. No need to pour on more recriminations."

He laughed and hugged me to his side. "Your vocabulary never ceases to amaze me. Do you read the dictionary for fun?"

"No, but I do read a classic every now and then. You should try it, you know. Broaden your horizons beyond the *Wall Street Journal*, read something with an actual plot."

"No thank you. I have no need to read about make believe worlds. That's what movies are for."

"God, Rémy!" I rolled my eyes. "You are such a Neanderthal! I thought the French were supposed to be cultured and into art and literature."

"I don't know where you get your misinformation, chérie. You cannot simply categorize people by their country of origin. If so, I could say that all Americans like football and chicken wings. As far as I know, you like neither."

"All right, smart ass! Let's go see if Mina wants

to drive into Galway for the evening. I desperately need to get away from the senior citizen reunion for a while."

"I'm going to remind you of that comment in about sixty years. But I agree: it would be good to get away for a while," he said.

***

Although the council tried to get us to stay for a few more weeks, I put my foot down. Two weeks to the day after we had arrived, Fionnuala drove Rémy, Mina, and me to the airport in Dublin. I hugged her and promised to take good care of Mina and then we made our way through security and on to our gate. I was soon relaxing in my first-class seat—Rémy never flew coach—sipping orange juice and planning the epic nap I would take on the overseas flight. In a little over seven hours we would land in New York and it was my fondest dream to sleep through at least six of those. The dream died when Rémy plopped next to me and insisted on discussing our plans for getting Mina set up in Albuquerque and making sure she felt comfortable.

"I have made a few inquiries about web design training programs and feel certain I can get her accepted into a good one. My apartment complex is sure to have an opening soon and she can stay in my guest room until then."

"Well, that does sound cozy, but I've already asked her to stay with me at Gram's house. If she and Tara get along we might consider getting a three bedroom apartment to share." Was I imagining the disappointment on his face?

"Oh. Well, yes, that is probably a better idea," he sputtered a bit, but then regrouped. "I'll help you all find an apartment, perhaps in my complex."

"Right!" I said, laughing. "As if we could afford that! No, we will find a cheap place by the university. What?" I asked at his confused look.

"It's nothing. I just thought you and Jack might—"

"You thought Jack and I were going to move in together? You don't know him very well. He is not the type to shack up with a girl. Anyway, he's moving in with Mat as soon as he gets back from boot camp."

"I didn't know living with a girl required a type. So, you'll have two roommates and Jack will have one. Won't that make…things…awkward?"

"Wow, Rémy. Are you really asking me about my sex life?" Or lack thereof, but that was nobody's business but my own.

"Just idle curiosity, chérie."

"I'm sure we'll manage." I sniffed and pointedly looked out the window. I swear I could feel him smirking behind my back.

"Hey." He pulled my shoulder back gently. "I'm sorry. It's none of my business."

I turned back around, but stared straight ahead. "You're right. It's not."

He put his hand over mine. "Ally, chérie. It's okay. There's no shame in it. It is actually very sweet. It's not something you should rush into. Jack better not be pushing you," he warned.

"Ha!" I laughed. "Not at all. He's the one holding back." I couldn't meet his eyes.

"Ally." He rolled his eyes. "Don't even think it! Of course he wants you. He's a man. He will always want you. He apparently has a great amount of respect for you, not to mention restraint." He chuckled a bit.

"I know. It's just that—"

"What? Go ahead—ask," he offered.

I was silent for a long moment. "So, it's okay? I mean, that we don't—"

"Of course it's okay, chérie. You are very young. It will be all the more special for not rushing it. If you and Jack are meant to be together, it will happen when the time is right."

"But he's already—" I couldn't say it.

"Of course he has. But he is in love with you and you're special. You are worth waiting for. Don't ever let anyone tell you differently."

I gave him a half-hearted smile. "Thanks, Rémy. So, have you—?"

He rolled his eyes again and laughed. "I'm 22, chérie. Yes, of course I have. But there has never been anyone special, anyone worth waiting for."

"Okay. Let's change the subject. Or better yet, let me get on with my nap."

He did, moving back to sit by Mina for the remainder of the flight, leaving me to catch up on some missed sleep. Both he and Mina slept on the connecting flight from New York to Albuquerque, which gave me a chance to read and write a letter to Jack. I started to get antsy about an hour from landing, eager to see Grams, Mom, and Brian, all of whom had said they would be at the airport to meet me.

We finally landed, gathered our belongings, and made our way off the plane, through the deserted airport, past the secure area, and there was my family. I reached Grams first, throwing myself in her arms.

"I missed you so much!" I pulled back. "How long am I grounded?" I knew I wouldn't be completely off the hook for sneaking away to Paris without telling anyone.

"At least a year. Or maybe a week," she said through her tears. "I missed you too. The house was too quiet. Wicky has gotten fat."

"My turn, Mother." My mom nearly yanked me out of my grandmother's arms. It was difficult to hug her with her hugely pregnant tummy. "Oh, Ally!" I could feel her tears on my neck; mine were flowing freely, as well. "Don't ever do that to us again! We were worried sick!"

"I know. I'm really sorry. Rémy and I thought it was best. I'll explain more later," I said quietly. "Mom! You are huge!" I rubbed my hand on her swollen belly. "Hello, baby! It's your big sister, Ally."

"Thanks a lot! I feel enormous and fat."

"You are gorgeous, Mom. You're supposed to be huge. You're about to have a baby. How are you feeling? Are you getting enough rest?" I held her at arm's length and looked carefully at her face. She looked tired and her face was swollen with late-term pregnancy, but she glowed with happiness.

"She's not resting as much as she should. She's

nesting, apparently. It's good to see you, Ally." Brian, my new stepfather, gave me a quick hug.

"I'm not nesting!" my mother exclaimed. "It's too early for that since I'm not due until early September. I won't start nesting until late August. I'm just trying to get Brian's former bachelor pad in order."

"It's good to see you too, Brian. How was the honeymoon?" I asked as I stepped away.

"Great, very relaxing. You definitely need to go to Hawaii sometime. How was France and Ireland?"

"What little I saw of each was fine. It wasn't really a sightseeing tour. You all remember Rémy? And this is Mina. She's from Galway and she'll be staying with Grams and me for a while." I pulled both of them forward to greet my family. I had already talked to Grams about Mina staying with us; I didn't think it would be a good idea to spring a houseguest on her unexpectedly. She had converted my mom's bedroom into a guest room over the last few weeks so Mina would have her own room for as long as she stayed with us. I wondered how long that would be.

CHAPTER FOUR

"in my false brother
Awakened an evil nature, and my trust,
Like a good parent, did beget of him
A falsehood in its contrary as great
As my trust was, which had indeed no limit,
A confidence sans bound..."
—Shakespeare, *The Tempest*, 1.2

We all met at Grams' house for what I thought was an impromptu welcome home dinner. I was disabused of the impromptu aspect of this notion when we walked in and I smelled ambrosia of the gods, i.e. enchiladas. I had been away from New Mexican food for over six weeks and seriously needed a chile fix. Since neither my mother nor grandmother had ever made enchiladas, it could only mean one thing: Trina was here, a fact substantiated when Megan ran out of the kitchen and threw herself in my arms, squealing, "Ally!"

"Hey, squirt! Oh my gosh, I missed you!" I hugged her tightly as Trina came out of the kitchen, wiping her hands on a dishtowel. I let go of Megan to hug Jack's aunt.

"I'm glad you're back, mija." She enfolded me in her warm arms and I inhaled the scent of her perfume mixed with cooking smells; it comforted me, almost like I was hugging Jack. Yeah, weird, I know. I hadn't seen him in so long I was getting loopy.

"Trina, you didn't have to cook for me. But I'm really glad you did. I haven't had a decent meal in weeks! They do not know how to cook over there!"

"I provided you with the finest French cuisine, chérie! I do, however, agree with you about the food in Ireland," Rémy teased.

"Hey!" Mina interjected.

"I don't mean to be ungrateful," I said, "but I have missed New Mexican food. Mina, you will see why when you taste Trina's enchiladas. Rémy, of course, doesn't appreciate chile. I hope your tastes are more sophisticated."

We were just settling down to eat when Tara and Mat came in. I abandoned my plate of green chile cheese enchiladas for the moment as I hugged my best friend, rocking back and forth.

"You are not allowed to leave for this long anymore!" she said, sniffing. "I nearly went crazy with only Mat for company!"

I met Mat's eyes over her shoulder and rolled my eyes. Tara could be a bit melodramatic.

"Okay, babe. Let Ally get back to her food before it gets cold. Let's get you a plate. I bet you haven't eaten all day." He pulled her away and steered her toward a seat. It was sweet to see him taking care of her. It had taken them a long time to start dating, but they were so good together.

Later, we relaxed in the living room with coffee and Trina's special natillas, a delicious custard made with flour, eggs, milk, and cinnamon. Mina seemed to enjoy the meal, gamely trying some of everything, while Rémy merely tasted enough to not be completely rude. He had never acclimated to New Mexican food.

"Ally, I'm so sorry I wasn't at the airport," Tara said. "My boss wouldn't let me off early, stingy bas—"

"Tara!" I gestured toward Megan.

"Oops! Sorry, Megan. Don't copy my horrible language, okay?" Tara apologized.

"That's okay," Megan said. "Jack says way worse words than that." We all tried not to laugh.

"How's the new job going?" I asked Tara. She had begun waiting tables at a local Italian restaurant a few weeks ago and said she could get me a job, as well. I needed to get some cash if we had any prayer of renting an apartment.

"It's all right, but I now hate lasagna. And spaghetti. And pretty much every other Italian food on the planet."

"Yeah, but I love the leftovers she brings home. I hardly ever have to cook." Mat laughed. He had moved out of Trina and Manny's house several months ago; Jack would be moving in with him soon after he returned from boot camp.

It surprised and pleased me to see Mina and Tara hit it off; I could never be sure what my somewhat volatile best friend would decide from minute to minute, but she and Mina as friends would make everything so much easier. They sat on the couch, getting to know one another, while I helped Grams with the dishes. We absolutely refused to let Trina help since she had slaved all afternoon and it was painful to watch my mom waddle around the kitchen, so we sent her out after a few minutes and ordered her to put her feet up.

Grams washed and I dried, and, as expected, the interrogation started along with the suds. "So, are you going to tell me why you and that French boy in there found it necessary to sneak off to France? I didn't know we kept secrets from each other," she said carefully.

"Grams, I'm sorry, but we did think it was necessary. I needed to meet Rémy's grandmother, and once the Seer Council got hold of me they were unlikely to let me go. The two councils don't get along. Rémy, Mina, and I have some seriously hard work ahead of us to get them to cooperate."

"So, you think it is your job to do that?"

"I do," I said firmly. "Kate's latest prophecy makes me think that's the least of what the three of us have to do. I just have no idea how we're supposed to actually do any of it." I gave her a rundown of the rest of our stay while we finished the dishes.

She dried her hands and pulled me close. "You're growing up so fast, Ally. I'm not happy that you disappeared without a word, but I guess I do understand. But please, please don't do that again. I'll try to understand, but I need you to tell me where you're going. Please, Ally? I was so scared when I didn't know where you were."

"Yeah, Grams. I promise. I'm so sorry."

"All right. Enough of this sappy stuff. You're not grounded. I guess you're getting too old for that, anyway. So, you and Tara are really going to move into an apartment together?"

"That's what we're planning," I agreed, watching to see how she reacted. "And Mina too, maybe. She and Tara seem to be getting along, so it might be a possibility."

She sighed and started wiping down the counters. "This all happened so fast. I'm not ready for you to be grown and on your own, I guess. It's going to be awfully quiet around here without you. First your mother and now you. I don't know what I'm supposed to do with myself."

I tried hard not to let myself laugh out loud at the thought of my grandmother sitting around, pining for my mom and me. The chances of her even noticing we weren't around were fairly slim because of her ever-increasing popularity at the senior center. She rarely spent a weeknight home, much less a Friday or Saturday. "Oh, Grams." I hugged her from behind. "I'll come over lots. I'll need to do laundry and raid the pantry, you know."

My own bed and pillow had never felt so amazing and I slept like the dead, but woke up at 7:00 a.m., unable to get back to sleep. The smell of coffee lured me to the kitchen, where I found my mom waiting for me.

"What are you doing here?" I asked, surprised to see her this early. "Are you already fed up with Brian?" When she didn't even chuckle, I knew something was up. "Aww, crap. What is it? Who died?"

"Oh, sweetheart. It's not that bad. But I do need to talk to you alone for a few minutes." She seemed nervous and unable to meet my eyes.

"O—kay," I drew out the syllables. "Shoot."

"Ally, honey, I need to, umm, I want to—shit." She stood up and began pacing.

I could count on one hand the number of times I had heard my mother use foul language. I wouldn't even need all my fingers. This was not good. I remained silent, waiting for her to finally tell me what was on her mind.

She took a huge breath and turned around to face me. "Okay. Ally, I need to tell you some things about your father."

"Excuse me?" Why on earth would she need to tell me about my father? "He didn't want anything to do with me. He deserted you, so why do I need to know about him?"

She pulled a chair up next to mine and clasped my hands between hers. "Sweetheart, that's not exactly what happened."

"Wait, what? What exactly did happen? Why are you just telling me now?"

"Shh, sweetie. Please, just listen, okay? This is really hard for me. I've been telling the lie for so long I think I started to believe it."

What. The. Hell?

***

"Mom, what are you talking about? My father

was someone you hooked up with at a frat party your freshman year of college. That's what you've always told me."

"I know. I'm so sorry. It was easier," she whispered.

"Easier for who?" My voice escalated to a near yell.

She winced and placed a hand on her burgeoning belly. "Please, Ally. Please calm down. I'll tell you if you'll calm down."

I immediately felt guilty and reached forward to cover her hand. "I'm sorry, Mom. I don't want to upset you. Okay. I'm listening. I promise to be calm. You just surprised me. That's all."

"I know. I never expected this. Ally, I have not been truthful about your father. It wasn't a drunken hookup at a frat party. It was my college boyfriend. My first boyfriend. We got way too serious way too soon and you were the result. I found out I was pregnant and I got scared and left. I never told him. He never knew about the pregnancy. He never knew he had a daughter."

"And you are telling me this now because—?" I wondered where on earth this was going.

She sighed. "Because he saw the media coverage of the Ashley Hayes trial. He recognized me. And he recognized you. Apparently you resemble his grandmother to a startling degree. He wants to meet you, Ally."

Now I stood up to pace. "Let me get this straight. You have been lying to me about my father all these years. You never told your boyfriend that he got you pregnant. What about Grams? Did she know?"

Mom shook her head, tears streaming down her face. "Oh, Mom! Why? Why didn't you tell anyone? Why the crazy frat boy story?"

"I don't know! I was scared and I just had to get away! I ran home and I never told Josh about the baby. I didn't want to ruin his life. He had a great future ahead of him and I didn't want to trap him with a baby."

Her unreasonable fear of telling Brian about this current baby suddenly made a whole lot more sense. I wanted to be mad at her, and I was—at least I think I was—but I also felt sorry for her. Grams had told me how much my grandfather's untimely death had messed Mom up, but apparently she had no idea how much. "So, he wants to meet me? What's he like? His name is Josh? I don't know if I'm ready to meet him. I think I need a few weeks to think about it."

"His name is Josh Harrison, and yes, he wants to meet you. He's a nice guy, Ally. He always was. I just wasn't ready for him at that point in my life. And you don't have a few weeks to think about it because he'll be here in an hour."

"What? No! I should have a say in this! I can't believe you expect me to meet him like this! In an hour?"

"I know, sweetie. I'm so sorry, but please do this. He's been here in Albuquerque for three weeks, waiting for you to get back. He's desperate to meet you. Please."

"Shit!" The curse burst out and, for once, my mother let it slide. "I can't believe this! He's coming here?" She nodded miserably. "Fine." I rolled my eyes. "I'll meet him." I looked at my mother, slumped in her seat, and again felt sorry for her. I knelt in front of her and took her hands. "Mom. Why did you keep this secret for so long? You could have told us. What about him? He never knew he had a daughter all these years. He must be pretty mad at you."

"Beyond furious. He's consulted a lawyer about his paternity rights."

"What? I'm almost 18. He's going to, what, sue you for custody or something? That seems ridiculous!"

"I know, but he has every right to be angry. I should have told him. I'm so ashamed of myself, Ally. You have every right to be angry too." She started crying in earnest.

I pulled her up and into my arms. "Shh, Mom. It'll be okay." She sobbed harder. "We'll figure this out, don't worry. Yeah, I'm mad. And completely shocked. But we'll figure it out, okay? I'll meet him and we'll see where it goes from there. After he meets me he'll probably be glad he didn't have to raise me." She laughed through her tears and pulled away. I gave her a wry smile and handed her several tissues. "All right. Pull yourself together and get out of here. I need to get a shower so I don't meet my long-lost father looking like a street kid."

"You don't want me to stay?"

I shook my head. "Not really. I think I should meet him alone. I mean, you're not worried about my safety or anything, are you?"

"No, of course not!" she scoffed. "Josh is perfectly safe. He was always sweet and gentle. I can't imagine he's changed that much. But I will keep my phone with me in case you need me for emotional support or whatever. I'll stay close, okay?"

"Yeah, okay. Thanks, Mom. Don't worry. I'll be fine." I ushered her out and then raced upstairs to get cleaned up, only to run smack into Mina and Rémy in the hallway.

"Ally, are you okay?" Rémy grabbed my arms and stared intently into my face.

"Yes, I'm fine. Why are you here? How did you get in? What's going on?"

"Mina let me in. We were both worried when your thoughts started going crazy and you wouldn't answer us. What's going on?" he repeated, shaking me slightly.

I brushed his hands away. "Calm down! I'm fine. My mom just told me that my father is on his way over here to meet me. I need to get cleaned up, so if you'll excuse me…"

"I thought you didn't know who your father was?"

"Yeah, well apparently my mother has been keeping secrets. I really don't have time to go into it now. I'll fill you guys in later, okay? Mina, can you get him out of here, please? Rémy, take Mina out for breakfast. My…dad," I choked on the word, "will be here soon."

"Come on, Rémy. Ally will be fine. We'll stay nearby in case she needs us." She tugged him away, continuing to soothe him as he sputtered his objections.

I pictured all the people that would be nearby in

case I needed them and had to laugh wryly at the mental picture of them bursting through the door to rescue me from my own father.

***

He was punctual, ringing the doorbell exactly one hour after my mother announced he would. I wiped my sweaty hands on my skirt and pulled open the door to see a man in his late thirties with brown hair and hazel eyes. He wore a blue chambray shirt, open at the throat, and casual khakis; he was good-looking, which didn't surprise me since my mom was beautiful. I stared at his face, trying to find any sort of resemblance. He stared back, probably trying to find the same thing.

"Ally. Wow. Um, hi." He sounded nervous; he shuffled his feet and didn't seem to know what to do with his hands.

"Hi, uh…" I had no idea how to address him, so I just let my statement die an awkward death. "Come in." I led him to the living room and invited him to sit on the couch while I took a seat in the chair across from him. Neither of us said anything for several minutes, and then both tried to speak at the same time. This at least broke the ice. "No, you go ahead," I said, laughing uncomfortably.

"I was just going to say I'm really glad you agreed to see me. I know you just got home last night and I really appreciate it."

While I wasn't aware I'd had much choice in the matter, I kept that snarky comment to myself. "Mom said you've been in Albuquerque for a few

83

weeks already?"

"Yeah. When I found out you were in Europe, I decided to stick around until you got back. I wasn't going to take a chance on missing you," he said quietly. Sheesh. That was a nice thing to say. It was hard to not like him when he said stuff like that.

"So, where do you live?"

"In Dallas. I'm in commercial real estate. I've been doing some business here in New Mexico for the last few weeks."

"Are you married? Do you have, um, other kids?" It was kind of an awkward question, but I wondered how he was able to hang around here waiting for me.

"No." He shook his head. "I was married once, a long time ago, but no kids. No other kids, I mean. Sorry. I'm not used to, um, you know."

"Suddenly finding out that you're a dad?"

He looked up. "Yeah. It doesn't come up every day." We both chuckled. "Listen, Ally, I don't want this to be weird."

"Well, that ship already sailed." This time we both laughed out loud. "So, um, crap. I don't even know what I should call you."

"How about Josh?"

I smiled. "Sure, okay. So, Josh, what do you say we go get some pancakes or something? I'm starving and I bet this conversation would be so much better on a full stomach."

"God, that would be great," he said, slumping in relief. "I was so nervous about meeting you that I couldn't even keep coffee down this morning."

***

I guess I shouldn't have been surprised to see Mina and Rémy sitting in a booth at the IHOP as Josh and I walked in.

—Are you all right, chérie? Rémy asked silently.

—Fine. I'm doing okay. We're just getting acquainted. I guess.

—We're here if you need us, Ally. This from Mina.

—Thanks, Mina. It's okay. I just need to get to know him.

"Ally?" Josh waited for my answer to some unknown question.

"Sorry. What?"

"Booth or table?"

"Um, booth." The hostess seated us in a booth near Rémy and Mina, but I shut both of them out of my head so I could concentrate on my father. We were both silent as we studied the menu. After a few minutes, I glanced up to see him staring at me.

"Sorry," he looked down quickly. "You just—"

"What?"

"You look so much like my grandmother."

"Excuse me? I look like a grandmother?"

"No," he said, laughing. "Like *my* grandmother. Like pictures I've seen of her when she was young. She was beautiful and had the same red hair. I can't believe I have such a beautiful daughter."

"Thanks. That's really nice." His staring made me uncomfortable; he seemed to understand and stopped when I looked everywhere but at him. "So that's where I got this hair, huh? I've always wondered."

The waitress came to take our orders, putting a momentary halt to our conversation. Once she left, he picked it up again. "So, your mom said that you already graduated from high school, a year early? You must be pretty smart. And you're going to start at the university this fall? Any idea what you want to study?"

"Um, I think I want to study English and education, maybe a double major. I'd like to teach high school English. I think."

"Well, that sounds great. What else do you do? What are your interests? What about friends? How about boyfriends?"

"Whoa, slow down," I said. "That's a lot of questions."

"Sorry, sorry. I just feel like I missed so much of your life already. I want to catch up, but I guess pummeling you with questions isn't the way to go about that, huh?"

"No, I understand. I have a lot of questions for you too. How about we take turns? So, my interests. Well, um…" I paused to think. I couldn't exactly tell him about my interests in the Seer world, so that limited my options. "I was a cheerleader this last year, mostly because I used to be a gymnast and I'm small. I was a flyer—you know, the one they throw around?"

"Yeah. Wow, that's great. Are you going to continue in college?"

"Oh, no. I'm not that good. Besides, I didn't really care for the social crowd that went along with cheerleading."

"Oh. What kind of social crowds do you like?" He looked puzzled.

"I think it's my turn to ask a question, actually."

He gave me a surprised, yet admiring nod. "Go ahead."

"Okay. Well, what are your interests? Besides real estate, I mean."

"Hmm. I like golf and biking. Not very exciting, huh?" He shrugged.

"Oh, I don't know. I've never tried golf. Biking sounds fun, though. Mountain biking or racing?"

"A little bit of both. Do you ride?"

I shook my head. "No. I mean I do know how to ride a bike, of course. Mom and Grams taught me but I haven't ridden since middle school." The waitress brought our meals and we spent a few minutes concentrating on our food. "Speaking of my mom, you're really mad at her, huh?"

He finished chewing and looked thoughtful. "Yeah, I am. I'm trying to understand everything she went through at the time, and I do. What I don't understand are the years since then. Ally, you're almost an adult. I missed your entire childhood. She stole that from me. I'm having a very difficult time forgiving that."

"I know, Josh. I'm not sure how I feel about it all yet, either. I mean, I haven't exactly had time to process any of it. But please, please don't sue my mom."

"What are you talking about?"

"Mom said you had consulted an attorney about your paternity rights. I know she should have told you, but I don't want her to have to face a lawsuit right now," I pleaded with him.

"Ally, I consulted an attorney about my paternity responsibilities, not my rights. I hope you want to spend time with me and that we can have some sort of relationship, but I realize that 17 and a half is a bit late to try and get parental rights or custody. I've never paid a cent of child support. That's what I asked about. I'm not going to sue your mother."

"Oh, thank God. I was worried. Yeah, of course I want to get to know you. And don't worry about child support. We've done fine through the years. I don't need any money." I was so relieved he wasn't going to take my mom to court for anything.

"Well, we'll see about that, okay? I take this responsibility seriously. I'm not going to be a deadbeat dad." We both chuckled at his attempted humor. I could probably like this guy. "So, is it my turn for a question? Tell me about your friends, especially any boyfriends that I'll need to run a background check on."

"Ha ha. My stepdad the cop has already done that, I'm sure. I don't have a ton of friends; I'm not really a social butterfly or anything. My best friend is Tara. We're planning to get an apartment together this summer. My friend Mina might move in with us if we can find a three-bedroom we can afford in a semi-decent area of town."

"What about boyfriends? You seem to be purposely avoiding that subject."

"You are really coming off as fatherly and over-protective, you know?"

He smiled. "Good. That's what I was going for. Okay, let's hear it. You do have a boyfriend, don't you? It's too much to hope for that you don't."

"Yes, I have a boyfriend. Calm down. He's really nice and I think you'll like him." I couldn't help but be flattered by his concern.

"And? How old is he?"

"He's 19."

Josh choked on his coffee. "Isn't that a bit old?"

"No, it's not. It's perfect, actually. You need to wait to meet him before passing any judgment, okay?" I knew I sounded defensive and cranky, but I was not about to put up with my brand-new dad butting his nose into my dating life.

"Sorry. It just took me by surprise. I'll withhold judgment until I meet him. When do I get to meet him? What's his name?"

"His name is Jack and you can meet him in about a month when he gets back from basic training. He joined the army right after we graduated."

"Army, huh? Well, I guess that's okay. Is he going to college?"

"Yes, of course. He's brilliant and is going to study mechanical engineering. My turn. What about you? Any girlfriends?"

"Not recently. So, I can't meet your boyfriend right away, but how about any of your other friends?" he asked, slyly changing the subject.

I stared at him for a moment, trying to decide if it was worth it to pursue my previous line of questioning. "Well," I sighed, giving up, "you can meet two of them now."

"Ally, chérie!" Rémy and Mina approached our table. "It has been ages!" Right. At least forty-five minutes.

I rolled my eyes and introduced them. "Rémy, Mina, this is my father, Josh Harrison. Josh, these are my friends, Rémy Giles and Mina Addair. Mina is staying with us for a few weeks." Rémy was his most charming as he chatted with my father for several minutes before ushering Mina away.

"So, they're not from around here, huh?" Josh asked.

I laughed. "No, they're not. Rémy is from France and Mina is from Ireland. I was overseas with them for the last few weeks. They're really good friends."

"Can I ask how old he is? I get the feeling he's not in high school."

"He's 22. Mina is 19."

"He's not your boyfriend, though, right? Please say no."

"Definitely not. Don't worry." I had a moment of guilt as I remembered kissing Rémy. I fervently wished that had never happened.

"Well, good. He seems way too sophisticated to be dating my 17 year old daughter." He picked up the check the waitress had left and pulled out his wallet to leave a tip. "I'd better get you back to your grandmother's house. I've got some work I need to do. Um, can I see you again? Maybe I could take you out to dinner tomorrow night?"

"Yeah. I'd like that, Josh." As we walked to his rental car I felt the hairs on the back of my neck raise as if I were being watched. I looked around the parking lot, trying to see who it could be, but saw no one. Creepy.

****

"Hol-y shit, Ally!" Tara flopped back on my bed as I filled her in on my bombshell du jour. "You have the most exciting things happen to you! My life is so boring!" She stared at my ceiling for a moment before sitting up and pulling me down beside her. "Are you okay? I mean, how are you doing with this?" That's why she's my best friend.

"I don't know, Tara. I'm kind of in shock, to tell the truth."

"What's your dad like? Is he nice? What do you call him?"

"Well, he seems nice enough, I guess. I call him Josh. 'Dad' would just be too weird. God, Tara! How could my mom do this to me? And to him? I'm so pissed at her right now I can barely think straight!" I reached up to wipe away the tears I couldn't keep from overflowing.

"Oh, sweetie! I know, I know. You have every right to be mad at her. It's perfectly normal," she soothed me, rubbing my back and handing me a tissue off my nightstand.

"But I don't want to be mad at her! She's pregnant and needs my support right now. How can I be mad at her? What kind of horrible person does that make me?"

"Okay, okay," she soothed. "Just cry it out. You'll feel better, I promise." She let me cry for a while before she went to the bathroom, got me a warm, wet washcloth for my face, and told me it was time to move on. Another reason she's my best friend. "Enough of this. Wipe your face and tell me about your trip," she ordered. "I cannot believe you took off with Rémy and didn't tell anyone! You could have told me, at least! I wouldn't have ratted you out!"

"I know and I'm sorry, Tara! I didn't even tell Jack. He still doesn't know. Rémy thought it would be better if we didn't tell anyone."

"What a jerk! I really hate him sometimes!"

I closed my eyes and lowered my head to my hands. "Oh, God, Tara!" I groaned. "I need to tell you something."

"Oh, my God! You slept with Rémy!"

I threw a pillow at her. "Of course not! How could you even think that?"

'Sorry!" She had the grace to look guilty. "What did you do?"

"I kissed him," I whispered.

"You mean recently? Since the last time?"

"Thanks for reminding me!" Why was she my best friend? "He kissed *me* last time, remember? He actually kissed me this time too. But I kissed him back."

"Was it, you know, a *real* kiss? And did you *really* kiss him back?"

"Yep. As real as it gets. I *really* kissed him back." I flopped on my bed and curled into a fetal position, hugging the stuffed cat Jack gave me a few months ago. "I'm so ashamed! I cheated on Jack! What am I going to do?"

She sat beside me and brushed my hair off my face. "Okay, tell me about it."

So I told her about the prophecy all the Conseil members seemed to want to interpret to mean I was the Oracle and Rémy and I were meant to be together. I told her how he insisted on slow dancing with me and holding me closer than I was comfortable with. I told her how he kissed me, saying that everyone expected it. And I told her how I kissed him back instead of pulling away. "I was so tired of everyone, especially Kate, trying to push us together. I thought maybe I was wrong and I should listen to everyone else," I said miserably.

"First of all, he kissed you. You didn't kiss him. That's an important distinction. How was it? Were they right? Are you two meant to be together?"

I shook my head. "No, we definitely aren't. I mean, he's a good kisser; there's no denying it."

"I know. You're right: the boy knows how to kiss," she said, reminding me that she and Rémy dated briefly when he first arrived in Albuquerque last winter.

"But I analyzed it the whole time: how he moved his lips, what he did with his tongue."

"Wow, you *really* kissed him, huh?" she interrupted.

I cringed and nodded. "I never analyze it when I'm kissing Jack. I can't even think straight when we're kissing. Kissing Rémy was like kissing my brother, if I had a brother. I don't know how I'm going to tell Jack."

"Why in the world would you need to tell Jack?" she asked incredulously.

"Because I cheated on him! I need to beg his forgiveness," I wailed.

"Ally, sweetie, you didn't cheat on him. You were confused and pressured into doing something you never would have chosen to do on your own. You have been under an enormous amount of stress lately with this whole Oracle nonsense and you were basically tricked into doing something you didn't want to do. That's not cheating. I guarantee you Rémy isn't losing any sleep over the kiss and you shouldn't, either. Just make sure it doesn't happen again."

"You really don't think I should tell Jack?"

"I really don't. I know you feel guilty, although I don't think you really have any reason to. Telling him would only make you feel marginally better. It will hurt him. I guarantee he won't understand. And it will probably be the nail in the coffin in his and Rémy's already tenuous relationship. He's already going to be pissed at Rémy for taking you to France, and since Rémy is an important part of your life, you need them to be able to get along somewhat."

"Are you sure? I feel like I'm lying to Jack if I don't tell him." Rémy had given me the same advice, but I wasn't sure. I felt naïve, gauche, and so far out of my depth it wasn't even funny.

"Hey, I'm no relationship expert. I just know that you love him. I think you should focus on the future, not the past. You've got what, four more weeks before he gets back? Why don't you let it rest for a few weeks and see how you feel about it closer to when he gets home? If you still feel like you have to tell him, fine."

"Okay. Thanks, Tara. I'm just so mixed up about everything right now. I don't know what to do."

"Well, for starters, let's get out of here. You owe me some girl time. Let's hit the mall and whatever else we decide to do before I have to go to work. Do you want to see if Mina wants to tag along? By the way, am I the only one sensing some sparks between her and Rémy? Aren't you able to read his mind or something? Does he like her?"

"There's something going on, but they have both firmly shut me out of that part of their minds, which is highly annoying," I said as I went across the hall to invite Mina to accompany us to the mall.

Mina did want to go, and we had a great afternoon shopping and showing Mina what American retail was all about. Tara and I were both amused at Mina's reaction to the grocery store we stopped by on the way home. Apparently grocery stores in Ireland were not nearly as big as ours and she wandered the many aisles, wide-eyed. We were just picking up a couple frozen pizzas and some salad for dinner, but it took her a full fifteen minutes to decide what kind of pizza she wanted.

"How do you choose between so many different types of food? It must take you hours to shop!"

"Let's really mess with her mind and take her to the ice cream aisle," Tara suggested.

"That's evil," I said. "But now I want ice cream, so let's do it."

***

Later that night, as I wrote a letter to Jack, my mom came in and sat beside me on my bed. "How often do you write to him?" she asked, idly picking up the calendar I had set down beside me. I was using it to mark off the days until he came home.

"At least twice a week. I don't get that many in

return, though. He's not a great letter-writer."

"Yeah, well, he's a guy." Neither of us said anything for a few minutes; I kept writing and she flipped aimlessly through the calendar. "Can I ask about the meeting with Josh? Did it go all right?"

I sighed and stopped writing. "Yeah, it was okay. Awkward, but he seems like a nice guy."

"He is a nice guy. Ally, I'm so sorry. I know you must hate me right now." She stood up and paced around my room.

"I don't hate you, Mom. I don't know exactly how I feel, to be honest. I'm mad, I guess, and I still don't understand how you could do that, how you could keep it from us all these years."

She shook her head. "I know. I don't have any excuse, sweetie. I was afraid. I made some really bad choices and I'm so ashamed of myself." She came back and sat down again. "Are we going to be okay, Ally?"

"Yeah, we will. I just need a while to get used to this and to think about it. I need time, okay?" I reached to rub the back of her hand.

She nodded sadly. "Okay. I understand." She rose and left my room, silently closing the door behind her.

I sighed and fell back against my pillows. Crap. I hated that my mom and I weren't in harmony right now. I much preferred to get along with her and Grams, but I couldn't get past what she had done to my father and me. I reached over and picked up the letter I had been writing to Jack, attempting to explain the huge change in my life. After a few attempts, I scribbled out what I had written and crumpled the paper. This was too big to write in a letter; I didn't want him to be distracted from his last few weeks of training by worrying about me and my crazy life. When he got home I would have lots to tell him. He still had no idea that I had defected to France with Rémy instead of going straight to Ireland and now I had to tell him all about my father. Yikes. I reached over and grabbed the calendar my mother had been looking at and crossed off another day: three weeks and five days until Jack came home.

CHAPTER FIVE

"a contract of true love to celebrate;"
—Shakespeare, *The Tempest*, 4.1

I spent quite a bit of time with my father over the next few weeks. He split his time between Dallas and Albuquerque, racking up a huge amount of frequent flyer miles as we attempted to get to know each other. Josh was a nice guy, so it wasn't terribly difficult, but there was still a certain amount of awkwardness, which we were finding a challenge.

"Josh, can I ask you something?" We were sitting in a secluded booth at The Rancher's Club, a pricey restaurant inside the Hilton Hotel. Josh enjoyed taking me out for expensive dinners when he was in town, and I loved eating at the kind of places my mom and Grams never took me to and that were well beyond the range of Jack's salary.

"Of course, Ally. You can ask me anything."

"How did you figure all this out? Mom said you saw us on the news or something, but I wondered how you knew." I felt like we were getting to know each other well enough to begin to talk about some harder issues.

He set down his fork and took a sip of wine, as if to fortify himself. "Well, that's true. I was watching the national news one evening last spring and they were covering the funeral of Ashley Hayes, doing a story about how the cold case was finally solved. There was a shot of you and your mom standing together at the funeral and they were talking about how you had been taken hostage by the killer and almost died in the shootout or whatever it was."

I remembered what he was talking about; Mom and I had refused to talk to the media at the funeral, but couldn't keep them from filming us from a distance. We didn't want to have to go into details about how I got involved in the whole situation and turned down multiple offers to tell our story. I probably could have financed my college education on what I was offered by the various media outlets, but I had no desire to talk about my psychic abilities on national television. We had also agreed to keep that information from my father, as well. I could think of no reason for him to know about our little family gift.

"Anyway, I recognized Jen right away. She really hasn't changed that much. She's still beautiful." He sounded wistful as he stared into his deep red wine. "And then I noticed the girl standing beside her." He looked up at me, pinning me with his gaze. "I can't begin to tell you how I felt at that moment, Ally. It all came back to me: the last crazy months of freshman year when Jen and I couldn't keep our hands off each other—"

"Oh, God, Josh! I was trying to eat!" I pushed my plate away.

"Sorry, sweetheart, but it's true. Anyway, Jen disappeared in the middle of finals week without a word to anyone. I couldn't find her anywhere on campus and when I got to her dorm room, she was already gone, along with all her belongings."

"Why didn't you go after her? If you loved her, why didn't you chase after her?" I had churned this question over in my mind since I found out about him. I couldn't understand why he had let her go without a fight. Jack would never do that. Would he?

"I tried, Ally. I really did, but I only knew she was from Albuquerque. I didn't know her home phone number or address and I couldn't find it in any phone book. We didn't have cell phones back then and the Internet was in its infancy. I was just a stupid kid and I thought she had got tired of me and left. I always worried she was out of my league and that was her way of letting me down easy. I never thought about her being pregnant. God, I'm such an idiot! I missed your entire childhood! You're nearly an adult and I just found out about you. I'm so sorry, Ally."

"Grams said Mom was really messed up after Grandpa died. She told me she just wasn't ready for you." I said nothing for a moment. "Did you love her?" I needed to know the answer to this and I really hoped he wouldn't lie.

He was silent too, and then said, "I don't know, Ally. I thought I did, but we were both so young. We got serious so quickly and weren't as careful as we should have been. And I'm really embarrassed to be talking about this with my 17 year old daughter. Look, I don't have all the answers. All I know is I have a daughter I never knew about. I want to get to know you and be part of your life. That's it. Can we just concentrate on that? Please?"

I half-smiled at him. "Yeah, we can. Dad." I tried it out for the first time. And I liked it.

A startling change came over him and I saw him surreptitiously wipe away a tear.

***

Tara succeeded in getting me a job at the restaurant where she had been working all summer and the busy schedule helped the time without Jack pass more quickly. I started as a hostess, but hoped to be promoted to waiting tables soon. I studied the menu every day in order to pass the 60-question menu test, the first barrier to becoming a waitress. Now that we were both gainfully employed, Tara started dragging me around to look at a plethora of different apartment complexes. I asked why we couldn't simply rent one in the same complex as Mat. Jack would be moving in with him as soon as he returned from boot camp. Wouldn't it be handy to live in the same complex? I hadn't seen it yet, but it sounded great.

"I'm not saying no, but I would like to look around first. I do have my name down on a waiting list for a three-bedroom in their complex, but we need to have a backup plan." So we toured apartments. A lot of apartments: Tara was a woman on a mission. Mina joined us when she could; Rémy had managed to get her a job in an Irish pub since she was old enough to serve liquor in New Mexico, although not old enough to drink it. I don't want to know how he managed to get her a green card and a server's license so quickly. He also found an IT program for her to start in the fall so she could learn web design. He had wanted to underwrite all her living expenses, but she was fiercely, yet quietly independent and refused to let him. After much negotiation, she agreed to let him pay for her initial schooling costs, but stated she would be reimbursing him. Period. When he tried to argue, I sent him a friendly mental message: *for God's sake, stop talking*. I began to recognize that when Mina set her jaw and narrowed her eyes it was best to let her have her way. Mina and I humored Tara up to a point, gamely viewing model apartments all over Albuquerque, but I held firm on a place that allowed cats; Mr. Wickham would definitely join me on my sojourn toward independent living.

***

Josh called later that week to arrange a lunch date on Saturday. It surprised me since he usually took me to dinner, but I agreed readily enough. Our time together was no longer awkward and I was becoming more and more comfortable thinking of him as my dad. Which he was. Of course. Okay, so, maybe I had some more work to do.

"Sure, Josh. Dad." I cringed as I said it. "Yeah, that would be great. What time should I be ready?"

102

"It's okay, Ally. It's hard, I know. How about I pick you up around 11? I have something I want to show you before lunch."

He picked me up in his rented Acura and drove us to a neighborhood close to my old high school, pulling in the driveway of a well-kept red brick home with a green, manicured lawn and a huge tree shading the front of the house. I noticed a realtor's 'sold' sign in the yard.

"Are we visiting someone?" I asked.

"Remember when I told you I wanted to show you something?" Josh said. I nodded as he got out of the car, opened the door for me, and ushered me up the front walk. I was surprised when he used his own key to open the front door.

"Oh, my God, Dad! Did you buy this house? Are you moving here?"

"Yes and no. Yes, I bought this house. No, I am not moving here. Would you want me to?" he asked.

"Of course I would. It would be great if you lived closer. Why did you buy the house if you're not moving here?"

"I bought it for you, Ally. Surprise." He pushed open the front door and led me inside. I said nothing; I was incapable of speech as he led me on a tour of the house, which was empty of furniture. I said nothing as he showed me the living room with a beautiful brick fireplace and dark wood floors. The kitchen was gorgeous, obviously recently remodeled, and the three bedrooms were spacious. The backyard was adorable, with the same lush, manicured lawn and a covered deck that wrapped around the side of the house. "So, what do you think?" he finally asked.

"You…you bought me a house? Why? Josh—Dad—it's too much. You can't buy me a house! What in the world?" I was flabbergasted.

"All right, first of all, yes, I can buy you a house. I assure you I can afford it. I've made a lot of money in real estate and I want to spend some of it on my daughter. As to why: you need a place to live and this would be much better than living in an apartment. Renting an apartment is throwing money away. A house is an investment. It's capital. You can start building wealth at a young age. With three bedrooms, you can have your two friends pay you rent." He sounded so logical.

"But it's so expensive! This is a really nice house, Dad."

"It is nice. I'm not about to buy you some hovel, sweetheart. It belonged to an older couple who maintained it well. I've had a few things updated and improved, but that's all."

A few things? Yeah, like the entire kitchen, all three bathrooms, and the flooring throughout the whole house! "Wait. An older couple? Nobody died here, did they?" What a horrifying thought; I'm not sure I could live in a house where people died. With my luck, they would probably stick around and want to visit with me.

Josh laughed. "No, Ally. Nobody died here, at least not recently. Realtors have to disclose a distressed property, so it was not the scene of some gory murder, either. The couple that lived here was tired of taking care of the yard and moved to a smaller condo. I'm nearly positive this house is not haunted."

"Oh, good. But that does not negate the fact that you can't just buy me a house! Who does that?" I exclaimed.

"A father who was absent for the first seventeen years of his daughter's life and has never paid a cent of child support. Ally, did you know that the average cost of raising a child to age 18 is somewhere around $250,000? That fits in well with the cost of this house. I'd rather do that than hand you a lump sum." He looked ridiculously hopeful so, although I still had major reservations about the whole thing, I gave in.

"Okay. Well, wow. I don't even know what to say except thank you. This is beyond amazing, Dad. Thanks." I initiated our first-ever hug. "Tara is going to flip out when she sees this. I guess our apartment hunting is over."

"So, you think your friends will want to move in with you?"

"Definitely."

"Well, good. I hesitated because I didn't like the thought of you living alone. And I absolutely hated the thought of your boyfriend moving in here with you. Please tell me that's not an option." He looked at me, pleading.

"Don't worry. Jack would never go for that. He's really kind of an old-fashioned guy. If you know what I mean," I said with raised eyebrows.

"I don't. And I don't want to know or even think about it. As long as you're okay with the house, there's one more thing I want to show you. Come on." He led me to the door in the kitchen that opened into the garage. "Ta da!" He opened the door to reveal an exquisitely clean garage in which was parked a brand new SUV.

"Oh, my God," I whispered.

"It's a Toyota hybrid, so you'll save on gas. It's four-wheel drive so you'll be safe when it rains or snows."

"A house and a car? No way, Dad. I just can't."

"Of course you can. It makes me happy, Ally. Please. I've never been able to provide for you. Now I finally have the chance. I already told your mom and grandmother and they're fine with it, if a bit surprised."

"Yeah, no kidding. Me too. But Dad, I have a car. Jack gave it to me. I don't want to hurt his feelings," I argued.

"If this young man is as wonderful as you say he is, he'll recognize that this is a much safer vehicle than that Volkswagen, which doesn't even have air bags. I hate the thought of you driving around town in it. And this is air-conditioned. And it has heated seats."

My dad didn't play fair. I had been sweating it out driving around Albuquerque in the summer heat. July temperatures typically hover in the high nineties, so air-conditioning would be so nice. And the thought of toasty-warm butt cheeks on a cold winter's day had me sighing. I had one thing left to say, however. "Dad, you know I don't need any of this. I still want to spend time with you whether or not you buy me stuff like some sort of fairy godfather. I need to know that's not what this is about."

"No. Absolutely not. I need to be able to do this for you, Ally. I can well afford it and it makes me feel better, so let me, okay? This helps me feel like I'm making up in the smallest way for not being there while you grew up."

"It's not like you had any say in the matter, you know?" I pointed out.

"I know, I know. Do this for me, okay?"

"Okay." I had no more arguments. I would accept my dad's extreme largesse and be happy with it.

He must have recognized my total capitulation, because he added, "Great. Let's take another look around then we need to grab some lunch and go furniture shopping." Of course. I should not have expected him to give me a house that I had to furnish all on my own. Perish the thought. I simply nodded.

We had lunch and then spent the afternoon picking out a living room set, dining room and kitchen furniture, a more casual sofa set for the den, and a patio set for the deck. I drew the line at bedroom furniture, stating firmly that each of us girls had our own stuff that we would be using. I also nixed the barbecue he wanted to buy, claiming a vegetarian had no earthly need for a device designed for grilling meat. I'm almost sure he had it added to the grand total on the sly, however. Oh well, it would be fun to have the whole family over for barbecues, I guess. Jack would probably enjoy it, as well. At the end of the day, Josh turned the keys to my new house and new car over to me. I drove the car home, but would not move into the house until the furniture had been delivered in a few days. Josh also informed me that he had set up a bank account for me, into which he would be depositing a monthly stipend for living expenses.

"Your mother informed me that you're attending the university on scholarship. I would have, of course, paid for your college, so I'll just put the money in the bank for you to use. I know you have a job," he said when I started to argue. "And I think you should keep it. It's important to build a good job history while you're in college, but this way you don't have to burn yourself out working so many hours. You'll have time to study."

What could I say? He was unstoppable. I started the day as a normal teenager—well, on the surface, at least—and ended it as a homeowner. Josh was listed as the official owner, but would sign it over to me on my eighteenth birthday.

As I got in the driver's seat of my new SUV—I had insisted on driving so I could check it out— after our shopping trip, the hairs on the back of my neck stood at attention. I turned around, looking quickly around the parking lot.

"What's wrong, Ally? Who are you looking at?" my dad asked, looking around as well.

"Um, no one. It's okay. I felt like someone was watching me, but I don't see anyone."

"Well, that sounds disturbing. Are you sure?" He looked around, concerned.

"No. I'm not sure. I just got a weird feeling, that's all. It's probably nothing." I laughed self-consciously. "Let's get going."

***

To say Tara was excited by my good fortune was a gross understatement. She was ecstatic and we had a wonderful time decorating and setting up the new furniture over the next couple weeks. Mat helped us move the heavy stuff when she had to try arranging it six or seven different ways. It turned out that Mina loved to cook and took over the majority of the kitchen chores. I tried to learn, but it looked like cooking might be my Waterloo. The three of us were having a blast playing house during the last few weeks of summer. Grams visited frequently as she tried to get used to me not living with her. Poor Grams! She was experiencing an empty nest for the first time in many years. Mina and Tara were patient with her when she repeatedly showed up with a bag of groceries or a plant and stayed for several hours.

I adored my new SUV: I loved the sparkly blue color, the smooth leather seats, and especially the ice-cold air-conditioning. I still worried about what Jack would think when he got back, which was less than two weeks away. Would he be hurt by my callous dismissal of his gift into which he had poured his sweat? I probably would if the situation were reversed.

The week before he returned, Tara, Mina, and I were watching a movie on our 46-inch screen television—Josh had insisted—when my phone rang.

"Ally, it's Trina. Honey, I have a huge favor to ask."

"Of course, Trina. What do you need?" I would do anything in my power to help Jack's aunt.

"Well, Manny and I are going to see Jack graduate, you know, and Shelly planned to watch Megan, but she's been put on bed rest by her doctor until the baby's born. Paul and his family are out of town on vacation and I just don't know what to do. Manny and I already have non-refundable tickets. Is there any way Megan could stay with you and Tara? It's just for one night. I'm sure Mat will help out." Paul and Shelly were Trina's older children who had children of their own.

"Of course, Trina. I'd love to take care of Megan. She won't be any problem and I can bring her to the airport to meet you all when you get back. Do you need a ride to the airport so you don't have to leave your car?"

"Oh, no, sweetie. We'll just leave it there. It's only one night. I'll get Megan packed and drop her off Friday afternoon, okay? Thank you, Ally. I worried that I wouldn't be able to go. I want Jack to know how proud we are. It would break my heart not to be there for him. I'll bet you're anxious to see him, aren't you?" she asked.

"Oh, Trina, you have no idea. This has been an eternal summer! I can't believe he'll finally be home this weekend. Have you talked to him recently?" I knew he was only allowed short, infrequent calls home to parents. Trina and Manny were as close to parents as Jack had; I couldn't see him calling his father, Marcos, from boot camp. They were cordial to each other, but not much else. There had been too much damage to that relationship to hope for closeness at this point.

"Yes, he called last night to see if we were able to come after all. We only talked for about five minutes. They are so stingy with his time! He said to tell you he loves you, Ally."

"Thanks, Trina. I guess I'll see you Friday when you drop Megan off. You remember where the house is?" She and Megan had brought a housewarming gift when I first moved in—another plant. I would be able to start a greenhouse soon.

"Of course. I'll see you Friday." She hung up and I began to look forward to a fun night with Jack's 7 year old sister. Their twelve-year age difference made for a relationship more like father-daughter than siblings. I loved Megan and never minded spending time with her, which was good since Jack and I frequently included her in our time together.

***

Although I thought it would never arrive, Friday finally made an appearance. Just one more day until Jack came home! This had been our longest separation, making the two weeks at Christmas seem like a drop in the bucket; I sincerely hoped it was our last for quite a while. Tara and Mina joined in the spirit of the occasion and helped me get ready for Megan's overnight visit. We might have gone a bit overboard buying beauty products for the girl's spa night we had planned: we bought face masks, foot soaks, and the wildest nail polish colors we could find.

Trina and Manny dropped her off around 3 o'clock with admonitions to behave herself and not make extra work for any of us. Megan was about the sweetest little thing I had ever seen and one 7 year old was not likely to make much of a mess. Other little girls might be more trouble, but she had had a rough time of it early on that left its mark. As a result, Megan was inordinately quiet with infrequent, yet serious bouts of anxiety. Their father's reappearance in their lives last winter, while a positive thing overall, had caused stress for both of them. Megan had become even more withdrawn when she met her father and had just recently started to return to her normal self. I was determined she would have a good time tonight.

We spent the first few hours getting her set up in my room and then baking cookies to eat later that night. I let the first batch burn and took the second out of the oven too early. They had to be eaten with a spoon. We finally got an edible batch on the third try when I let Megan be in charge. The realization that a 7-year-old was a better cook than I was a hard pill to swallow.

"Ally, don't worry about it," Megan said as she used a spatula to remove the perfect cookies from the sheet. "I help Auntie Trina all the time. Maybe she could teach you to cook."

"Maybe," I sighed. "I'm beginning to think I'm a hopeless case."

Mat and Tara showed up with pizza from the restaurant where Tara and I worked. I had taken the whole weekend off so I could be with Megan tonight and Jack tomorrow night; I owed Tara big time for covering my shifts. Rémy appeared halfway through dinner and presented Megan with a beautiful bouquet of colorful flowers, which she accepted shyly, awed by his overblown charm.

"What a suck-up," muttered Mat. Tara elbowed him to be quiet.

"That was nice, Rémy," I said as he kissed both my cheeks. He had made himself quite scarce for the last few weeks and I had missed him. I noticed that Mina's fair cheeks blazed pink when he greeted her with his typical European kisses. There was definitely something going on with them, but neither seemed willing to admit it. We had an enjoyable dinner with both guys complimenting Megan on her cookies, which endeared them to me even more. Nevertheless, we booted them out soon after eating and began our girl's night spa treatments. An hour later, the four of us were watching *Frozen,* all sporting green face masks while painting each other's toenails alternating blue, yellow, green, pink, and orange. Megan fell asleep two movies later, during *Aladdin,* and I had to wake her enough to get her into my bed. She slept soundly, although I had trouble getting to sleep because I was so excited about seeing Jack the next day. Megan and Mina made waffles the next morning and we spent the day playing with Wicky and watching more movies until it was finally time to go to the airport. Megan was beside herself with excitement to see her big brother and had a hard time sitting still as I re-braided her hair. I got her advice on what outfit Jack would like best and, finally, we were on our way.

We stood anxiously just outside of security, watching as passengers made their way from the gate area.

"There!" Megan squealed as she caught a glimpse of her aunt, uncle, and brother. "Can I?" she asked, tugging on my hand.

"Of course, sweetie. Go get him." She dropped my hand and ran toward Jack, who set down his duffle bag and scooped his sister up into his arms. She hugged his neck as if she would never let go and I felt my throat tighten with emotion.

"Meg!" he breathed. "I missed you, squirt! You grew while I was gone, didn't you?"

She giggled and pulled back to look him in the face. She pulled his uniform cap off his head, reaching up to feel his short military haircut. I didn't care what length his hair was; I was so glad to see him I was about to come out of my skin. He laughed along with her and placed his cap on her head. Then he saw me. He said something to Megan I couldn't hear and set her down before advancing toward me. I met him halfway and walked straight into his arms.

"Jack," was all I could say.

"Ally," he breathed against my hair.

As he held me, everything clicked into place, as if my internal gears had been slightly off kilter and now found the proper position. I could breathe fully again and felt that empty place in my heart filled. He pulled back, put his big hands on either side of my face, and kissed me softly, yet intensely. The sound of wolf-whistles broke us apart.

"Later," he whispered against my mouth.

"Count on it," I whispered back. He smiled.

"So, this must be the girlfriend you were always writing to." The speaker was another young man in camouflage army fatigues. "You gonna introduce us, Jack? Or are you ashamed of us?" The other soldiers with him laughed.

Jack rolled his eyes. "Ally, these are my friends from boot camp. This is Jason," he gestured to a tall, blond-haired guy who shook my hand. "This is Ryan, and this," he motioned to the original speaker, "is Barry. Guys, this is my girlfriend, Ally. And this," he picked Megan up again, "is my little sister, Megan. I got to know these guys real well in boot camp." We chatted for a few more minutes, but I was eager to have Jack to myself and couldn't honestly care less about his new buddies right now. I sensed his impatience, as well. They finally left with their families and Jack grabbed my hand as we walked toward baggage claim.

"Ally, why don't we take Megan with us? You and Jack can meet us at the restaurant. I'm sure you two would like a few minutes to yourselves," Trina suggested. I could have kissed her right then and there.

"Thanks, Trina. We'll meet you at Padilla's, okay?" We had arranged to have dinner at one of Jack's favorite Mexican restaurants, certain he would need a chile fix after ten weeks of army food. He gave Megan another hug before setting her down and picking up his giant duffle bag with one hand, engulfing my hand in his other huge, warm one. We practically ran to the parking garage, where I ushered him to my SUV.

"What's this? Did your mom get a new car?" he asked.

"Later, Jack. I've got tons to tell you, but right now I just want to kiss you." I launched myself at him, backing him against the side of my car. He happily obliged, swiftly turning us so I was backed against the vehicle and kissed me senseless. We surfaced a few minutes later, both of us flustered, but cognizant of the fact that we were actually in public.

"God, Ally," he breathed, resting his forehead against mine, "I missed you so much. Ten weeks is too long."

"I completely agree. Let's never do that again." I reached up and ran my thumbs across his raspy five o-clock shadow. "You're so handsome, Jack. I think I forgot."

"Well, I'm glad you think so." He kissed me again quickly. "I didn't forget how incredibly beautiful you are. I dreamed about it every night."

I smiled. "You say the nicest things, Mr. Ruiz." We kissed again, less frantically, until I stiffened in his arms and looked around the parking garage.

"What's wrong, babe?" Jack asked.

I was seriously sick of this feeling that I was being watched and wished I could figure out what was going on. Was someone watching me or was I imagining it? Was my stress finally getting to me? "Nothing." I tried to smile. "I thought I saw…someone. Never mind."

He looked into my eyes, searching, for a long moment. I dropped my eyes; there was no fooling Jack. "Okay. You'll talk to me about it later?" I nodded. "We better get going or we'll miss dinner. I am dying for some chile. The food in Missouri was miserable."

"Poor Jack. Let's get you fed. I'll tell you all my crazy news on the way to the restaurant." I insisted he drive so I could concentrate on telling him the basic points of all the crazy changes this summer had brought. Although it was a fairly short ride to the restaurant, it was important to get him at least a little bit caught up because there were sure to be comments about my house, my car, and my dad during dinner. So, I told him about my dad appearing in my life and about the new house and car. I held back the information about sneaking off to France for the moment, deciding I would rather tell him about that in private when we had more time for him to vent his anger against Rémy. I spilled everything else in a rapid info-dump and fell back against my seat, letting out a huge sigh.

"So, your mom lied to everyone all these years?" he asked, incredulous. "I'm having trouble processing this. Jesus, Ally! How are you doing with it? Are you okay?" He reached over and clasped my hand.

I entwined my fingers with his, loving that he was finally here and I could touch him all I wanted. Well, maybe not *all* I wanted, but still. "I'm okay. Confused, but basically good. Josh is a great guy, and not just because he has showered me with exceptionally expensive gifts. I like him, Jack. I'm glad he's in my life."

"How are you doing with your mom?" As usual, he zeroed in on the heart of the matter.

I breathed out another sigh. "I'm not sure about that. On one hand, I'm super pissed at her. But then I feel guilty about being pissed because she's been through so much and she's about to have a baby. Did you know she's due in three weeks? I'm kind of confused about how I feel about her right now, actually."

"Hey." He rubbed his thumb along the back of my hand. "It's okay. You're allowed to be confused. You don't have to have everything figured out. I just hope you'll let me be there for you and help you through it. Please don't be an idiot like I was when my dad showed up and shut me out. I want to be there for you, Ally. I love you like crazy, you know."

"Yeah, I know. But it's good to hear. It's especially good to hear in person. I can't even begin to tell you how much I missed you, Jack. I'm so glad you're home." Home. That's what I felt when I was finally in his arms again: I was home.

***

It was so good to have him back. That first night we sat on my new couch in my new house until 3 a.m., talking and holding each other close. There was also a fair amount of kissing, but we were careful not to let it go too far; neither of us were ready to take our relationship to the next level, mostly because we knew we would be inseparable once we started sleeping together, and that would get awkward with our roommate situation. It might sound terribly old-fashioned, but it worked for us. I knew in my heart of hearts that Jack was the one for me, but it wasn't time for more yet. I can't really explain it, but there it is. I also knew that my dear, wonderful Jack would not be able to live with the guilt if he pushed me into a sexual relationship at what he considered too young an age. So I tried not to push him, either. It was difficult, especially when I hadn't seen him in ten weeks. I had realized months ago that Jack would not feel comfortable with us having sex until we were engaged, at the very least.

He was amazed at my new house and we loved the fact that we had more freedom to see each other. I helped him move into Mat's apartment soon after he returned from boot camp. Since Mat was dating my best friend, both the boys spent nearly all their free time at our house; Mat complained they were throwing away money on the rent since they just slept there and teasingly suggested he move into Tara's room. She rolled her eyes and told him to dream on.

Rémy also spent much of his free time at my place. Jack had let him have it over taking me to France without telling anyone, but once he got that out of his system they went back to their guarded friendship. Jack would probably never fully accept Rémy because he still felt somewhat jealous of the inexplicable closeness we shared. I had decided not to confess the kiss Rémy and I shared while in France. Tara was right: it would hurt Jack and he wouldn't understand it. I swallowed my guilt and learned to live with it. The advent of Mina in our lives mitigated the ridiculous rivalry somewhat;

there was something deep, yet unacknowledged between her and Rémy. He flirted outrageously with Tara and me, but treated Mina with a cool, somewhat distant attitude. I could not get through the mental barriers either of them had in place to see what their true feelings were, but I frequently caught both of them looking intently at the other when they thought no one was watching.

We all enjoyed the last precious weeks of summer, spending our evenings lazing about, barbecuing, watching endless movies, and simply enjoying our free time. Jack still worked several shifts each week at Manny's shop and I put in at least 30 hours per week at the restaurant, but we hoarded each free moment we could find. My work schedule would need to be cut back sharply once classes started.

We were cuddling on my couch one evening about two weeks before the start of fall classes, having returned that afternoon from our mandatory freshman orientation at the university.

"God, Jack! I feel like the world's biggest idiot! Math 120? What are you taking?" Part of orientation was a math placement test, which I bombed and therefore got placed into Math for Dummies. How embarrassing!

"Don't worry about it. Math isn't your thing, that's all. I bet you tested out of all the beginning English classes. Didn't you? I'm stuck in English 101, you know."

"Hmm. Trying to change the subject by appealing to my vanity. You must have aced that placement test. What did you get? Are you in

Calculus? You are, aren't you?" I turned in his arms to confront him. When he wouldn't meet my eyes I realized the worst. "Oh, my God! You're taking Calculus II, aren't you? Admit it!"

"Shh." He pulled me close and kissed me, probably to get me to shut up. "I'm an engineering major, querida. It would be better if I had tested into Calc III. I'm going to have to huff it to catch up as it is. I'm good at math. I completely suck at English. I can't spell my way out of a wet paper bag. I probably wouldn't have graduated if you hadn't edited all my papers this last semester."

I ran my hands through his short, black hair, stopping to feel the small scar at his hairline where he had clocked his head on a tree branch during boot camp. My vision of the event had freaked me out and caused me to make an international call to Trina. "You are very sweet, but I still have a sneaking suspicion you are way smarter than me."

He laughed. "No way, babe. How about we agree that we are just as smart as each other, but in different ways. We balance, you know?"

"Okay, I'll give you that."

"I can think of better ways to spend our time than arguing over who's smarter." He began kissing along my jaw and neck. He was right: this was much better. Who cared which one of us was smarter? I was smart enough to find this amazing guy who was currently rocking my world and whispering sexy Spanish phrases in my ear.

"Good Lord, you two!" Tara said as she came in the front door after her shift at the restaurant. "Give it a rest and spare my delicate eyes. Some things can't be unseen." She flopped in the armchair across from us.

"Oh, whatever!" I scoffed, unwinding myself from Jack's arms. "I've lost track of the times I've walked in on you and Mat sucking face. I've seen his hands in places I'm sure your mother wouldn't approve of."

"Meow! Pull your claws in, kitty. I'm just kidding. It's good to see you together, actually. Beats the heck out of watching Ally mope around the house all day. 'Oh, I can hardly wait 'til Jack gets home! I miss him soooo much!' Ughh!"

"Hey!" I threw a decorative pillow at her. "Be nice! You don't know—" I was interrupted by my phone buzzing. I pulled it out of my back pocket and saw Brian's name on the caller ID. "Brian? Is everything okay?"

"Ally, it's time. Your mother's been in labor for a few hours and I'm taking her to the hospital."

"What?" I sat up on the edge of the couch. "Why didn't you call?"

"She thought it was false labor—you know, those Braxton-Hicks contractions or whatever. But her water just broke, so it looks like this is the real thing. Can you meet us at the hospital?"

Jack had heard the conversation and was already standing up, tucking his shirt in, and looking for my keys. "Of course," I replied. "We'll meet you there in a few minutes." I leaned over to put my shoes on and then stood up and began looking for my car keys. "Where the hell are my keys?" I yelled as I began flipping up the couch cushions.

Jack grabbed my shoulders and turned me

around to face him. "Babe, I've got them. Calm down, okay? Breathe. Your mom is going to need you to be strong tonight." He leaned forward and kissed me gently to soften his semi-harsh words. "Now, get your bag and let's go."

Tara handed me my purse, hugged me, and said, "Call as soon as the baby's born. Jack, you better drive. Ally's shaking."

"I know. I'll get her there safely, don't worry. I'll keep you guys updated," he promised.

Once in the SUV, I leaned my head back against the passenger headrest and closed my eyes, trying to still my trembling, clammy hands. After a few minutes of driving, Jack reached over and covered my hands with his large, warm one.

"She's going to be fine, querida. Brian's there with her."

I gave him a wobbly smile. "I know. I just can't help worrying. She's too old to be having a baby."

"Ally, she's not even 40. She's perfectly healthy and has had an easy pregnancy. You're going to make yourself sick. Now calm down," he ordered.

I nodded. "I know, I know. I just…I've been so mean to her," I whispered. "I've been so mad at her for keeping my dad a secret. I shouldn't have been so mean."

He pulled into a spot in the hospital parking lot and came around to open my door. He reached in, unfastened my seatbelt, and pulled me into his arms. "You haven't been mean. You've maybe been a bit…cooler to her lately, but I'm sure she understands. What she did was seriously messed up. But it's time to move past it, for both of you. Now let's get up there and get you a baby brother. Or sister."

Mom had just been settled into her room, a family birthing room, as she had decided she wanted her family around her for the entire process. I was excited, yet scared spitless about witnessing the miracle of birth. The nurse was hooking her up to the various machines to monitor the contractions and the baby's heartbeat.

"Mom!" The nurse moved aside and I leaned over her bed to hug her. "I'm so sorry."

"Ally? What in the world?"

"I've been so awful to you since I found out about Dad. I'm so sorry!" I cried against her neck.

"Oh, sweetheart. Please don't worry about it. What I did was terrible and I'll never be able to make up for it. You haven't been mean. Ooh!" She sucked in a breath. "Brian!"

I backed away, terrified, as Brian rushed to her side. "Okay, Jen. Breathe through it. Squeeze my hand, hon. It's okay."

Jack came and put his arms around me from behind, holding me as we watched my mother have a contraction. Grams arrived as my mother began to relax. In her usual efficient manner she bustled around, questioning the nurse and demanding to talk to the doctor. The nurse spoke briefly to her before moving to examine my mother. As she moved to lift the sheet, Jack whispered, "That's my cue to go fetch coffee for everyone." He scooted out the door.

"Okay, Jen. It looks like you're at about five centimeters. Just keep breathing. You might want to walk around some. There's also a bathtub here if you want to use it. It can help get you through this active phase of labor. You've probably got a couple of hours to go before the last stage. Try to relax. Brian, you should massage her lower back if she wants, okay?" The nurse patted her hand and wrote on her chart before leaving.

Mom decided a bath would feel good, so I left them to it and texted Jack to tell him to wait for me in the cafeteria. We drank coffee and ate the pie he insisted on buying for me, saying that the sugar would be good for me.

"Querida, you weigh like 98 pounds sopping wet. You don't have a lot in reserve. I don't want you passing out right in the middle of the action tonight. I need to keep you strong for your mom."

I leaned across the table and kissed him, tasting the tart cherries from the pie we were sharing. "You are quite possibly the sweetest guy I've ever met. Thank you for taking care of me, Jack. I love you, you know?"

"I know. But it's good to hear. I love you too. It's my job to take care of you."

"You don't have to stay here. It may be a really long night," I offered, hoping he would stay anyway.

"I'm not going anywhere. I'll just make myself scarce when it gets messy, okay?"

I laughed. "Yeah, that's okay. And I weigh more than 98 pounds, for your information."

"Oh, a whole 99, huh?" he scoffed.

"Maybe." I tried to sound offended, but couldn't keep from laughing. "Come on. Let's get coffee for everyone and head back upstairs. Maybe Mom's done with her bath by now."

Mom was in her bed, resting between contractions when we arrived with the coffee. "Mmm, that smells so good."

"Sorry, hon, you only get ice chips," Brian apologized. "Do you want us to take the coffee out of the room?"

"No, of course not. I want you all here," she said sweetly, reaching for his hand.

Three hours later her sweetness was a thing of the past as she transitioned into the final stage of labor. She had eschewed heavy drugs, opting to have as natural birth as possible, and dealt with her pain by yelling at Brian and using some of the most colorful language I had ever heard my normally placid mother use. Jack relegated himself to the waiting room as her modesty flew out the window along with her social filters. Her contractions were nearly on top of each other before the doctor finally arrived and told her to start pushing. I hadn't known how I would react when the time came for the baby to come, and I had certainly freaked out earlier when Brian called, but as soon as my mom started pushing, I positioned myself behind the doctor, watching as the baby's head emerged from my mother's body. It wasn't gross or disgusting at all; it was the most amazing thing I'd ever seen. Grams and Brian were on either side of her, holding her up and encouraging her to push.

"All right, Jen. Stop pushing for a minute." The doctor suctioned the baby's mouth and nose and rotated the head a bit. "Okay, Jen. This is it. One more big push."

Mom made a sort of growling noise as she made her final push. The baby slithered out into the doctor's hands. The nurse wrapped it in a blanket as the doctor cut the umbilical cord. The baby started crying. "Ally, what is it?"

"It's a boy," I said with tears running down my face. "I have a brother! He's beautiful. Oh, my God, he's so beautiful!" Minutes later, my mom held her new son while Brian, with the biggest grin I've ever seen on a man, hovered over both of them.

The doctor was still messing around with my mother's nether regions and shortly said, "Okay, Jen. I need you to push again."

"What's happening? Is everything okay?" I asked, concerned.

"It's fine. I'm just delivering the placenta. Push again, Jen." Okay, this time—gross. I wish I hadn't looked. That kind of thing will scar you for life. I moved around to gaze upon the adorable new baby rather than the red sludge that was being extracted from my mother's body.

Grams and I stayed a little longer before we decided it was time to leave the new family alone for a while. Jack was asleep in the waiting room, sprawled in a chair, with his head resting against the wall. I sat next to him and leaned over to kiss his cheek.

"Oh, hey. Sorry. I fell asleep." He sat up, rubbing his hands over his face. "What happened? Is it over? What is it?"

"It's a boy! I have a little brother, Jack!"

"Aww, that's great, Ally. Come here." He pulled me in for a hug. "Congratulations. You're going to be such a great big sister. I'm really happy for you. How is your mom doing?"

"She's tired, but fine. She was cussing like a sailor, by the way. The whole childbirth thing seems rather unpleasant. I'm not sure I want to go through that. Is that a deal-breaker for you?" I was only half-kidding.

He chuckled and pulled me close again. "Nope. I don't even want to think about kids yet. Plus, I'm sure we'll get our fill of babysitting in the not-so-distant future."

I took him in to see the baby for a few minutes and got my first chance to hold my new baby brother. He had been bathed and his warm little head smelled amazing. Jack even took a turn holding him and I must say, I liked seeing him hold a baby. It gave me warm, squishy feelings that I firmly tucked away for future reference. Far future reference.

"Have you decided on his name?" Jack asked.

"Elijah James Keller," Brian replied. He held my mother's hand and gazed at her with such visible love in his eyes I felt like an intruder. I was happy my mom finally found someone; it was impossible to stay angry with her about keeping my dad a secret. It was time to get over it and move on. As I watched my boyfriend hold my new brother, I realized I was lucky to have such a great dad in my life, no matter how late I met him. Jack wasn't so lucky; although they weren't estranged any more, their relationship was strained at best.

Jack passed little Elijah to me and I kissed his fuzzy head before placing him in my mother's arms so she could nurse him. I bent down and kissed her cheek. "You did great, Mom. I love you." She smiled up at me and I knew we were okay.

CHAPTER SIX

*"My charms crack not, my spirits obey, and time
Goes upright with his carriage."*
—Shakespeare, *The Tempest* 3.3

1 Year Later

*I wandered through the giant maze of a parking
garage, frantic to find—what? I couldn't remember,
but I knew it was imperative that I find it. Life or
death. What was it? Would I know it when I found
it? As I rounded yet another aisle, pausing by a
bright green Mazda 2 to gather my thoughts, I
became aware of the distinct feeling of being
watched. I could feel it on the back of my neck, as I
had felt it so many times this past year. This time,
finally, I caught a glimpse of a shadowy figure
wearing a dark hoodie pulled up over his—her?—
head. That had never happened. I always felt like I
was being watched, but could never see anything or
anyone who might be watching me. Too bad this
was only a dream. It was strange that I realized it*

was a dream. On second thought, maybe it was more. I had a history of dreams being more than just imagination. The figure disappeared and I looked back down at the blue Ford Fiesta. Wait a minute...so, definitely a dream. I started searching again. I had to find...something. The drone of a helicopter hovering over the garage hummed louder. I couldn't concentrate on anything but the sound, growing ever louder and invading my mind.

I woke to the sound of a lawnmower just under my bedroom window. It sounded nothing like the helicopter my wild imagination had conjured in my dream. I blew out a sigh of frustration. That damned dream again! I'd been having it for a week now, ever since I returned from my summer abroad. The two Seer groups, the Council and the Conseil, had really ramped up their ridiculous rivalry and insisted on Mina, Rémy, and me spending an entire month with each group. The three of us were heartily sick of the situation and secretly swore to each other that these little summer visits were at an end. Mina and Rémy would both be finished with their schooling at the end of this coming year, Mina finishing her associate's degree in computer/web design and Rémy finishing his MBA. I would be starting my sophomore year at the university in a few days, having successfully completed my freshman year in May. We had enjoyed a relatively peaceful year: no crazy visions or dreams leading me to serial killers, rapists, or cold cases to be solved. It had been nice to be normal for a while. The only thing that occasionally disrupted my peace was that unmistakable feeling of being watched. I had stopped mentioning it to my friends for fear they would have me committed or something, and controlled my wild urge to whip my head around, looking for my unseen stalker. It worked with everyone except Rémy, who could read my thoughts, and Jack, who could read my heart.

At the thought of Jack's name, I smiled and threw back the covers. It was, of course, he who was mowing my lawn. He did this regularly, showing up on a Saturday morning before he headed off to work in his uncle's garage all day. He had keys to my house and garage, of course, and made use of them most often to do repairs and little chores unasked. I know—he's a keeper. I threw on a short robe over my sleep shorts and cami, brushed my teeth, and splashed water on my face before heading out to the kitchen to make coffee. Once it started brewing, I looped my long, red hair into a messy ponytail and headed outside to see Jack. A gorgeous smile transformed his already handsome face when he noticed me standing on the edge of the patio. He turned the mower off and jogged over to pull me in his arms for a morning hug and thorough kiss. I was glad I had stopped to brush my teeth as his warm tongue swept inside my mouth and I forgot how to breathe for a moment. I was as susceptible to this man's kisses as I had been when I was sixteen years old. At eighteen-and-a-half my stomach still flipped when he walked in the room. I reached my hands up around his neck, running them through the soft, black hair that was slightly longer than it had been when he had returned from boot camp. He had gone through a growth spurt in the last year and was now close to 6' 1''. He had filled out as well, much of it due to the hefty physical fitness requirements courtesy of the United States Army. It all added up to an incredibly hot boyfriend. I hadn't grown as much as a centimeter, still topping the growth chart at 5' 1". I liked to think I had gotten slightly curvier, but that may have been wishful thinking.

"Good morning," I breathed as we pulled apart.

"Mmm. It is now. I'm sorry I woke you up. I noticed your grass was long when I got back last night and thought I'd swing by and cut it on my way to work."

"No problem. I have to be at work in a little while, anyway. Besides, you saved me from a bad dream." I pulled his head down for another kiss.

"You want to tell me about it?" he asked after a minute.

"No." I shook my head. "It wasn't that bad. You don't have to mow my lawn, you know. I am perfectly capable of doing it myself. It's not part of the whole boyfriend deal. I'm happy with just your body." I was kidding, since we still hadn't slept together, but I enjoyed keeping him on his toes.

He laughed and pulled me in for a hug. "Someday, Ally, I am going to call you on all your bluffs."

"Promises, promises. Coffee will be ready in a few minutes. I'm going to get some pancakes started since you refused my more carnal offer." That earned me a swat on my rear end as I sauntered away.

"And I like mowing your lawn," he called after me. "I get to see you first thing in the morning!"

"I can think of easier ways of making that happen!" was my parting shot before I retreated into the kitchen. We were in an interesting place where we weren't quite ready to have a physical relationship, but were starting to see that it was inevitable and definitely on the horizon. I wasn't positive about what held us back, but it had something to do with the unsettled nature of my…calling, for lack of a better word. If I was the Oracle, I wouldn't have as much control over my life as I might wish and I was hesitant to embroil Jack too deeply. Yes, our love and commitment to each other was complete, but that still hung over our heads. That and Jack's incredible sense of honor; he said he would never be able to leave once we had taken that final step, and living together was not an option for either of us. It was going to have to be marriage or nothing. It was the nothing I was afraid of.

I poured the second batch of pancakes onto the griddle, filling the kitchen with a delicious, homey smell—after I sprayed air freshener to cover the smell of the first batch that I burned—as he came in from the yard. He reached into the cabinet above the coffee maker to get himself a mug and settled at the kitchen table to enjoy his coffee. I loved that he was so comfortable in my house and looked forward to the day when we would share it.

"Hey, Jack." Tara stumbled into the kitchen and headed straight for the coffee. "Thanks for mowing the lawn so early on a Saturday morning. I didn't need that extra hour of sleep." She ruffled his hair.

"No problem. Any time," he answered, smoothing down his hair. "Maybe if you didn't stay out all night with my cousin, this wouldn't seem so early."

She waved vaguely in his direction and headed back to her room with her coffee. She wasn't much of a morning person.

I loaded a plate with a stack of pancakes and set it down in front of him before hugging him from behind. "Thanks for mowing my lawn. I'm so glad you're back." He had returned the day before from his summer army training and we had only spent a few hours together the night before because I could tell he was exhausted. "I hate that we get so little time together in the summer."

"Me too. In fact, I'm pretty much done with it. Is there any way you can be home more next summer?" He pulled me around to sit on his lap and looked earnestly in my face.

I nodded and kissed him softly. "Yeah. Rémy, Mina, and I were talking about it. We've decided that next summer will be different. We're sick of this ridiculous rivalry between the two Seer groups. It's time we exert more control over our lives."

At the mention of Rémy's name, I noticed Jack's jaw tighten. Sigh. They were getting along fairly well, but it still bothered Jack that Rémy and I were able to communicate so intimately in each other's mind. It was time to try something I had been working on all summer. I took Jack's face between my hands, leaned my forehead against his, and pushed my thoughts into his mind. *I love you, Jack.*

You are the only one for me, you know. Try not to be jealous of Rémy. It's a brother-type thing. Nothing else.

He stared at me for a moment, unaware of what I was trying to do, then exclaimed, "Holy shit, Ally! Was that you? Did you do that on purpose?" I nodded slowly, unsure of whether he was happy or appalled. "Oh, my God! That's amazing! Is that what it's like with Rémy and Mina?"

"Sort of. It's easier with them, because they're Seers, I guess. But I've been practicing so I could do it with you." I had never been very successful at the mental communication with non-Seers. I still wasn't as talented as Rémy; it seemed to come as natural as breathing with him. "I don't want this tension anymore between you and Rémy. I love him like a brother. You are the love of my life, Jack." I leaned back in to kiss him.

"Ally, I can't tell you what this means to me. Thank you," he breathed as he kissed me back. "Okay, I'm done acting like such an ass to Rémy. I swear." Jack's pancakes got cold as we sealed his vow with more kisses.

"Oops, sorry," Mina apologized, backing out of the kitchen. Sometimes having roommates was not convenient.

"Mina, come back," I called as I hopped off Jack's lap.

"I didn't mean to interrupt," she said softly as she returned to the kitchen to make tea for herself; she had never acquired a liking for coffee in the morning.

"No worries. It's your home too," I assured her.

"You want some pancakes?"

"Yes, thanks. I also know that you two have missed each other this summer. You need time alone together." She always understood Tara's and my needs, making herself scarce when Mat or Jack was over. Often, we spent evenings with all six of us together, but she and Rémy had yet to declare themselves a couple, although it was obvious to the rest of us that they had feelings for each other. Tara and I had fixed her up on a couple blind dates, mostly to see if we could get a rise out of Rémy, but although he seemed tense and irritated, he never said anything about it. Neither did Mina. Another frustrating side effect of not knowing what in the hell the three of us were supposed to do or be.

"So, Jack, speaking of brothers…I'm going to be babysitting mine tonight. Would you care to join me?" I knew he adored my little brother, Elijah, and would jump at the chance to spend time with him. Jack loved kids and was so good with them.

"Definitely. I've missed that little guy this summer. I'll bet he's grown a bunch. I'll come by after work. Should I stop and get a pizza or something?"

"How about you bring Megan? We can take them to the park or something and have a picnic dinner."

"That sounds great. I'll check with my sister and see if she can fit us into her busy social calendar. I gotta go, babe. I'll see you tonight. Thanks for the breakfast," he said as he put his empty plate in the dishwasher and leaned in to kiss me goodbye.

"Anytime." I kissed him back briefly. "Thanks

for mowing my lawn." He left and I busied myself cleaning up the kitchen. "What?" I demanded of Mina, who watched me over the rim of her teacup.

She set her cup down carefully. "Nothing. I'm just wondering why you don't marry him already."

"Oh, I don't know, Mina!" I threw the dishtowel on the counter in frustration. "Maybe because I'm only 18. Maybe because he hasn't asked me. Maybe because I'm probably the fucking Oracle and I won't be free to marry the man I want!" Neither of us said anything as the guilt over snapping at gentle Mina set in. "God, I'm sorry, Mina. I shouldn't have yelled at you. I shouldn't have cussed at you, either. It's just so…" I didn't finish; there was really nothing to say. The strain of the summer apart had reared its ugly head again.

She got up and came over to hug me. "Don't worry about it, Ally," she said with her soft, Irish lilt. "I have heard that word before. I've even used it a time or two myself, when the provocation was great. Your provocation is great right now too. It's not fucking fair what we're all going through, is it?"

We both laughed and I hugged her back. She had become a great friend in the last year and I was so glad she was sharing the house with Tara and me. "No, it's not. I'm so tired of it all, Mina. I just want to live my life. We have got to figure out what we're supposed to do. I can't take this much longer."

"Me neither. Rémy feels the same way. We are so done with the Council and Conseil jerking us around like they've been doing for the past year."

"That sounds great, but do you and Rémy have

anything in mind? Any plans?"

"Not yet." She shook her head and returned to her seat. "But give us time."

***

I decided to call Megan myself to see if she wanted to help Jack and me babysit my little brother. She was thrilled at the idea and a short conversation with Trina secured permission for her to come over. Megan would stay the night, something we did fairly regularly since last summer when I had taken care of her while Trina and Manny went to Jack's graduation from boot camp. I had finally managed to convince my mother it was time for Elijah James to spend the night for the first time as well, and thought it would be nice for Megan to be there. She was never any problem, and would, in fact, be helpful. I arranged to pick her up on my way home from work. Elijah had weaned himself in the last few months and only needed a nighttime bottle of formula, so it was a great opportunity for Mom and Brian to have a short getaway. I knew they needed some couple time and I was happy to help out before school started next week. I texted Jack later that afternoon.

Me: I have kidnapped your sister. She's already here, so just bring your gorgeous self tonight.

Jack: OK. THX. See u 2nite. Luv u.

Mom and Brian dropped Elijah off in the early

evening. Mom fussed, worrying about leaving her baby, while Brian tried to get her out of the house before she changed her mind. It helped that Elijah was excited to see Megan, barely noticing when his parents left. I waved them out to their car, promising to keep my phone close so Mom could call frequently to check in.

"Whew," I said to Megan as I leaned against the closed door. "I never thought they'd leave. Now we can have some fun."

"Lee-Lee!" My little brother held his arms up, bouncing ecstatically on his diaper-clad bottom. I was charmed that this form of my name was one of his few words. He was not walking yet, but was pulling himself up on the furniture, so it wouldn't be long. I obliged his desire to be picked up, holding him close until he squirmed to be let back down to play with Megan. She was extremely patient with him, playing blocks and reading him endless picture books. She was eight and proud of her ability to read any of the books I kept at the house for him. Because he was a frequent visitor, I kept a high chair, toys, books, and a playpen here for him. I had a car seat for him in the backseat of my SUV and I had bought a portable crib just for this visit. My dad gave me a generous monthly stipend and I enjoyed spending some of it on my little brother.

Jack arrived soon after, hair wet from the shower he had taken after work. I met him at the door, throwing myself into his arms and reveling in his warm, clean scent as I kissed him thoroughly.

"Ugh! Mind the young children present!" Megan

stood up and took the baby's hands, helping him toddle on his chubby legs. "Come on, Elijah. We'll wait in the kitchen while they make out. Gross."

"Why did you want the brat here again?" Jack joked.

"I heard that," Megan called from the kitchen door.

"Hmm." I was distracted by his freshly shaven jaw that demanded my lips' attention. "Maybe because I know you missed her while you were gone. And because I love spending time with her. You should be glad she thinks kissing is gross. She won't always."

"God, I dread that day," he replied. "Can't she stay little and cute forever?"

"That's not the way it works. Okay, I could kiss you all night, but we better go take care of the children."

Elijah's little face lit up with delight when he saw Jack. He didn't try to say his name, but he held his arms out to him, wanting Jack to hold him. He was an affectionate baby, and I watched my tough, rugged boyfriend melt into a puddle right there in my kitchen.

"Hey, little buddy. Aww, you got so big this summer! Come here." He picked him up from the floor. "Oof! You got fat too. What have they been feeding you, huh?"

I smiled at the adorable picture they made and then bustled around the kitchen getting the items for our picnic packed. Megan helped, and when were done, Jack carried the heavy basket out to my car. I loaded Elijah into his car seat and while Megan buckled herself into the seat beside him I handed Jack the keys and he drove us to a nearby park that had a nice play area with baby swings for Elijah.

Twenty minutes later, we had a blanket spread under a shady tree and were diving into the dinner I had packed. I fed Elijah his baby food, but he was more interested in Megan's food. I managed to get a small amount of food into him before he demanded to be taken to the swings. It amazed me that such a small child could absolutely direct the actions of two adults and a young girl. Elijah was clearly the one in charge of our agenda this evening. He finally wore down an hour later and crashed for a nap on the blanket next to Jack and me. Megan headed off to the playground to play with some new friends, so Jack and I finally had a few quiet moments to ourselves.

"Tell me about your summer, querida. You didn't tell me very much last night," Jack ordered, combing his hands through my hair as I lay my head in his lap.

"Probably because I couldn't keep my hands to myself. I missed you, Jack. I'm tired of being apart."

"Me too, babe. Me too. Now spill."

"Yes, sir. Well, it was pretty much the same as last summer: we spent a month with Kate and the rest of the Conseil. We mostly trained with short breaks for Kate to question me endlessly about any visions I've had. I think she hopes I'll make a prophecy of some sort soon. It was pretty miserable," I sighed.

"What about that creepy guy, Lance? Larry? I

forget his name."

"Luc. Ugh. Yeah, he is creepy. It seems like every time I turned around, he was there watching me. Thankfully, I didn't have to talk to him much and he was gone a lot of the time. I don't know…I just don't like him."

"What about the wedding?" Jack changed the subject to something much more pleasant. "How did that go?"

"Oh, Jack! It was the best part of the whole summer! Genevieve was so beautiful and radiant! And Arnaud looked at her like she was the best thing that ever happened to him. It was so romantic." Rémy's cousin had finally managed to get the much older Arnaud to admit his feelings for her. They had only dated for a few months before he proposed. I was so glad I was able to attend the wedding.

"It sounds nice. I'm glad there was something good about the trip. What about Ireland?"

"It was okay. More of the same: train, talk, train some more. I'm not really sure how much good the training is doing. I don't see any real improvement in my abilities."

"What do you call what you did to me this morning?" he asked incredulously.

"That's different. We've never told the council members, French or Irish, about the extent of our mental abilities. We think it's better to keep that to ourselves for now," I admitted.

"Probably a good idea. From what I've heard, I don't totally trust that either group has your best interests at heart. Do they still think you're going to be the next Oracle?"

I nodded. "Yeah, but we're no closer to knowing for certain. It's so frustrating! I don't want any of this! I just want to live my life!" Elijah whimpered in his sleep and I realized that I had been nearly yelling.

"Shh, babe. It's okay. We'll figure this out. I'm just glad you're back. I can't even begin to tell you how much I missed you. I don't want you to go next summer."

"I don't want to, either." We were silent for a while, enjoying the quiet evening and the respite from watching the children, although we were careful to keep Megan in our sight the entire time.

"Excuse me," an older woman said as she and a man approached. I sat up to see what they wanted. "We just wanted to tell you what an adorable little family you are. It reminded us of when our children were small. Enjoy them while they're young; they grow up too soon," she sighed wistfully. "You two don't look old enough to have two kids already."

Really? Some people might find this sweet, but I found it intrusive and shot a warning look at Jack. I was thoroughly sick of people telling me what I should do. "Well, I got knocked up back in junior high. He's not around anymore. This is my new baby daddy." I leaned against Jack as I said this. I could feel him trying to hold in his laughter. "We're not married or nothin'."

"Oh. Well," the woman said. "Um, have a nice evening." She and her husband rushed away, whispering to each other, no doubt about the shocking lack of morals in today's youth.

Jack chuckled and pulled me down on the blanket with him. "You're awful! That poor woman."

"Poor woman, my foot! Nosy old biddy is more like it. It's none of her business how old we are or how many kids we have. Or don't have. Whatever!"

"Remind me to stay on your good side, querida," he softened his comment with a kiss, so I didn't mind. Since we were in public and supposed to be watching Megan, it was brief. As I sat back up, I got that creepy feeling again that I was being watched. I stiffened, fighting the urge to look around. "What is it? What's wrong?" Jack was always so in tune with my emotions; it was impossible to hide anything from him.

I couldn't stop myself from looking around. I gasped when I caught a glimpse of a dark, hooded figure amidst the trees at the far corner of the park. It reminded me of the dream from this morning. "There!" I pointed to where the figure had been seconds before. "I swear that guy is watching me!"

"Stay here!" Jack ordered. "Watch the kids." He jumped up from the blanket and took off at a run toward the trees. I saw him look around the stand of trees and then disappear out of the park and up the residential street. I made sure I could see Megan on the playground and I scooted closer to the sleeping Elijah, trying to calm my racing heart. Jack was back moments later. He flopped down on the blanket, out of breath from his sprint.

"Did you see where he went?"

Jack shook his head, not willing to meet my eyes. With a sinking heart, I realized that he hadn't seen the figure at all. He had run toward the trees on my word alone. I loved him for it, but dreaded what it meant.

I dropped my head into my hands and groaned. "Am I going crazy, Jack? Why do I keep getting this feeling? That's what my nightmare was about this morning. The one I didn't want to tell you about. What's wrong with me?"

He pulled me against his side. "There's nothing wrong with you, Ally. I don't know why you keep getting this feeling, but it could be all the stress this whole Seer-thing has put you under. I just wish I could make it go away, babe. I really do."

***

Jack, Tara, and I started our sophomore year in college the following Monday. Freshman year had gone well: I got A's in all my English and humanities classes, a B in my science class, and eked out a C in my Math for Dummies class with much help from Jack. I had helped him pass English 101, so I didn't feel completely stupid. I was, thankfully, done with math—hopefully forever. I was required to take a foreign language and decided to begin studying French since I spent so much time over there. Rémy was a huge help/pain in the ass, forcing me to practice simple conversations with him all the time. Last year, Jack, Tara, and I had taken psychology together, which was fun, but we weren't able to get any of our classes together this semester. The University of New Mexico was a sprawling urban university serving upwards of

25,000 students so we had to plan to meet or we would never see each other. Tara was majoring in biochemistry and spent the majority of her time on the north campus where all the science labs were, so I rarely saw her at school any more. The engineering building, where Jack had the majority of his classes, was near the humanities building, where I had several of my classes, so we could meet for lunch, at least. I had more classes this year in the education building, which was on the other side of campus and not at all convenient; I would be getting plenty of exercise this year with all the walking between classes.

I settled into my mid-morning literature class, a survey of Shakespeare's tragedies, which I had hesitated to take after my community college experience with King Lear, but it fit well in my schedule. I was tired and cranky, having been woken at 4:00 a.m. by the recurring nightmare where I searched for something in a parking garage while someone watched me. This time I had followed the shadowy figure, but had awakened right before I reached it. I hadn't been able to get back to sleep, so I had sat on my back porch, watching the sunrise and drinking too much coffee. This is what I blame my bad manners on.

A soft tenor voice asked if the seat next to me was taken. I merely shrugged and proceeded to ignore the tall, lanky guy who took it. I glanced at him when he nudged me with the sign-in clipboard. He smiled shyly, but frowned and looked away when I just raised my eyebrows.

Crap. You just kicked a puppy, Ally, I told

myself. The guy was skinny and awkward, with a large Adam's apple and messy, brown hair falling in his eyes. He seemed to shrink back into himself at my look. *Don't take your sleepless night out on the poor guy. You're better than that.* So, I smiled and said, "Thanks," noting his name, Michael Conner, above mine on the sign-in sheet. He obviously took my change in temperament as license to become my best buddy, judging by the way he chatted continually to me during class whenever there was a break from the professor. I guess he was starved for conversation or something, because he followed me out of class, all the way to the Student Union Building, or SUB, where I was supposed to meet Jack for lunch. I couldn't shake him.

He followed me to a table by the pizza counter. "Why don't you save our table while I get our lunch? What kind of pizza do you like?"

When did this turn into a lunch date? "Just cheese, but I can get my own lunch."

"Oh, no. Let me, please," he begged.

"Okay, fine, but here's some…" I fished in my bag for a five-dollar bill as he raced away to the counter. I sighed in defeat and put my money away.

He returned a few minutes later, holding a tray laden with food. "I didn't know what you wanted to go with your pizza, so I got a side salad, a pasta salad, and a fruit cup." He placed everything in front of me with a hopeful expression. "Do you want the Sprite or the Coke? I got both so you could choose. Or I could go get something else. Whatever you want."

His over-eagerness to please melted my heart and I again thought of a puppy. I was reluctant to stomp on his feelings for the second time, so I said, "Sprite is great. Thanks, Michael. This was really nice of you." I chose the side salad and the cheese pizza he had bought for me and his face lit up with a huge smile. He could probably be decent-looking if he stood up straight, got a haircut, and grew a spine. I cringed at the uncharitable direction of my thoughts, but what had I done to encourage this level of slavish devotion in such a short time? Whatever it was, I needed to reverse it—fast. It was uncomfortable and kind of creepy, to be honest. I was so flustered I had forgotten Jack was meeting me.

"Hey, hon." He came up behind me and leaned over to kiss me as I raised my confused face to his. He quickly took in the situation and took over in his capable way. He sat down, scooted his chair close to mine, put his arm around me possessively, saying, "Sorry I'm late. Who's this?" He jerked his chin in Michael's direction.

"This is Michael. Michael, this is my boyfriend, Jack." I leaned into him, relieved to have an out. "Michael is in my Shakespeare class. We just met." Michael's shoulders slumped as he acknowledged that I was already taken.

"Mike. Nice to meet you." Jack held out his hand. Michael obliged, putting his slender hand into Jack's much larger one.

"It's Michael."

Jack actually smirked.

"So, you're Ally's boyfriend?" At Jack's firm

nod, Michael shrank even more.

An uncomfortable lunch ensued. Jack and Michael barely spoke to each other, leaving the majority of the conversational burden to me. When Jack made a move to get up and buy himself some lunch, I sunk my nails into his thigh. *Don't you dare leave me alone with him!* I used every ounce of mental energy to send him the message. He either heard me or read my body language, because he sank back in his chair and began to eat the pizza slice I shoved in front of him.

We were all silent for several minutes as Jack and Michael ate; I picked at the salad still in front of me. When I could stand the awkwardness no longer, I began to gather my books, saying, "I've gotta run. I forgot I need to stop by and talk to my advisor about my schedule." I leaned over and kissed Jack briefly. "So, I'll see you at home tonight," I purposely overstated our living arrangements, hoping Michael would assume we were living together.

"Sure," Jack agreed casually. "I may be a little late, but don't bother holding dinner. Love you." He kissed me as we parted ways. "See you later, Mike." He stood, watching, as I walked toward my next class and Michael had no choice but to go his own way.

I waited at our usual spot, an alcove by the engineering building, where we frequently met up between classes. I paced back and forth, hoping he would realize that the story about needing to see my advisor was just that: a story.

"Aaah!" I squeaked in alarm as someone touched

my shoulder from behind. I spun around and straight into Jack's arms. "Oh, thank God."

"Hey, shhh. It's okay, sweetheart. I've got you." He smoothed my hair and kissed the top of my head. "What the hell was that back there at lunch? Who was that guy?"

Now that I was away from Michael and the bizarre situation at lunch, standing in the security of Jack's arms, I realized that I had overreacted. Seriously overreacted. I laughed slightly and pulled away to look up into his wonderful face. "I am so sorry about all that. I just…freaked out, I guess. It's nothing."

"Ally, I was there. It wasn't nothing. That guy was weird! Where did you meet him?"

"He's in my Shakespeare class. I was mean to him and I felt bad so I smiled at him and was nice and he wouldn't stop talking and then he followed me to the SUB and bought me all that food—" Jack put his thumb over my lips to stop my nervous chattering.

"I have a hard time believing that you were mean to anyone, querida," he interrupted.

"I was!" I said as I took his hand away. "I was cranky because I had that nightmare again last night and I couldn't get back to sleep afterward."

"Well, it looks like you've picked up a stray. If he bothers you again I will happily kick his ass. I don't want to have lunch with him again. He bought you all that food? That is just weird!"

I nodded. "Ugh! It was embarrassing. I hope he got the hint and leaves me alone from now on. Why would he do that? I don't get it."

Jack smiled. "I do. He would do that because you are beautiful." He kissed me. "And sweet." Kiss. "And sexy as hell." Long kiss. "And mine." Longer kiss. "And now I have to get to class. I love you and I'll see you at your house later tonight."

CHAPTER SEVEN

*"My master through his art foresees the danger
That you, his friend, are in; and sends me forth"*
—Shakespeare, *The Tempest* 2.1

Michael did get the hint, at least somewhat. In class the next day, he apologized for over-doing it on the lunch the day before.

"I am so sorry about that, Ally. I just got carried away. They don't let me out much." He laughed in a self-deprecating way. "I'm really sorry. You must think I'm crazy." He delivered this apology in such a sincere manner, reminding me again of a small puppy, that I readily forgave him.

"It's okay, Michael. No problem. I just…well, I have a boyfriend, so…"

"Yeah, I got that. Loud and clear."

I winced. I hadn't meant to come off as a jerk, but Michael's behavior had freaked me out. Now I wondered if I had overdone it. Had I let my stress and worry about being followed color my reaction to this sad, rather pathetic guy? And who was I to say that he was pathetic? Who was I to judge? I let my shame over my behavior tamp down the warning bells going off in my head as I said, "Hey, there's no reason we can't be friends. If you want."

His smile transformed his face, and I realized that with some help, fashion advice, etcetera, he could be kind of cute. "Sure. Yeah. That would be great."

I tried to relax into a casual friendship with him, which worked, for the most part. I gently let him know that I wanted to eat lunch with my boyfriend. Alone. I softened the blow by asking him to meet me for coffee before class the next day. When he tried to pay for mine, I put my hand on his arm, shook my head, and said, "Friends, remember?" He nodded once and stepped aside to let me pay for my drink.

Michael was a sophomore, like me, and planning to major in English. When I teased him about having no future job prospects with that major, he shrugged and said he would worry about it later. College was for learning to think. This was a great sentiment, but I would never be comfortable with not having a firm career path after college; hence my double major in English and education.

My roommates were mixed in their opinions of my new friend: Tara thought I was too nice and in grave danger of being run aground by my sympathy for the downtrodden. "This is what you do, Ally. This is why Travis hung around, even after he dumped you. You always seem to pick up strays." She had adopted the term from Jack's description of Michael, when he had shared our lunch story over dinner the night before.

Mina took a gentler approach. "I think it's nice."

"Thank you, Mina." The rest of the group rolled their eyes and let loose a collective groan. We were in the midst of a Jason Bourne film fest—it had been Rémy's turn to choose.

"He sounds very much like he needs a friend," she said as she reached for another slice of pizza. My boss, Rudy, also the owner of the restaurant, had handed me a giant box containing one of the 26-inch pizzas he was famous for as Tara and I left at the end of our shift.

"Table that ordered this sent it back. Said they didn't order green chile. You take it home to those boys," he had said gruffly. For some unexplained reason, he had sort of adopted Tara and me, giving us shifts that worked with our schedules, time off whenever we needed it, and he always sent food home, frequently manufacturing a reason why it was extra when I knew good and well that he had made it just for us. Although we were both too young to have a server's license, he allowed Tara and I both to be waitresses, having other waiters deliver our alcohol orders. "I put some slices of cheese pizza in there, too," he finished, knowing that I was a vegetarian.

"Thanks, Rudy," I had given him a hug. He was a good guy.

"Jack, what do you think?" Tara appealed to him. "Are you okay with her befriending this Michael character?"

Jack paused in the act of chewing, wide-eyed. He swallowed and reached for his soda, taking his time before answering, as if sensing a trap. "I am not Ally's boss. She can be friends with whoever she wants."

There was a beat of silence before he was hit in the face with a sofa pillow, thrown by Mat. "What a suck up! Ally, he told me he was gonna kick the guy's ass if he ever saw him sniffing around you again! Oof!" he said as Jack threw the pillow back with greater force.

I intercepted the pillow as it was returned. "Stop wrecking my living room, you two! Jack gets points for a good answer, at least." I settled on his lap and kissed him. "I already knew how he felt about Michael. I don't know how I really feel about him, either, but I can't…" I let my sentence fade.

"We know, chérie, we know," sighed Rémy. "You just don't have it in you to be unkind to someone."

"Hey, don't knock it." Tara now came to my rescue. "That's why you're still around, after all."

I ignored the others and slid off Jack's lap and snuggled into his side. He put his arm around me and pulled me close, kissing the top of my head. "Jack, you know he's not a threat, right?" I whispered. Why in the world would I be tempted by anyone else when I had this amazing guy right next to me? There was absolutely no comparison between him and Michael, either physically or emotionally.

"I know, querida. I just can't help being jealous when I see any other guy around you. It's natural. Sorry," he whispered back.

"It's positively primeval." I giggled and reached

up to kiss him.

"Umm, hello. We're all still here, you know," Tara complained as our kiss went on longer than was probably appropriate in mixed company.

I smiled against Jack's lips. "Later," I whispered.

"Count me in," he said.

***

The nightmare changed that night. Up until now, I had searched frantically for something and then tried to follow the shadowy figure; tonight I was followed. I wove in and out amongst the rows of cars in a parking garage, trying to find whatever it was I had lost. At this point in the dream I usually caught a glimpse of the figure in the black hoodie and started following. Tonight, I heard a noise behind me and turned around, startled, just in time to see the figure dart behind a concrete column. My stomach flipped as I realized the nearest exit was three rows away. I moved quickly around a Toyota Camry—what was it with the car brand recognition?—and toward the elevator that I knew would lead me to the street level. My stomach dropped further as I heard footsteps behind me. My pace increased; so did the footsteps behind me. I began to run, reaching the elevator just as the mysterious figure caught up with me, his hand—I was fairly sure it was male—grasped my shoulder. I screamed in terror.

"Ally! Wake up! You're having a nightmare. God, girl, you need to wake up!" Tara sat beside me, shaking my shoulders.

I sat up, knocking her hands away. "What? Where?" I panted, looking frantically around my bedroom. "Oh, my God," I slumped back against my headboard. "Oh, Tara. I'm sorry. I didn't mean to wake you up."

"You didn't. Don't worry. I was in the living room working on a paper and I heard you whimpering. I was coming to wake you up when you started screaming bloody murder. You scared the shit out of me! Look! I'm still shaking." She held her trembling hands in front of my face.

I took her hand in one of mine, the other wiping the sweaty hair out of my face. "I'm sorry. I had a nightmare."

"The same nightmare you've been having?" I had told her about the recurring dreams several weeks before.

I nodded. "Yeah, but it was worse this time. This time I was being chased. It felt so real, Tara. Why is this happening? I'm so tired of it!"

"I know, sweetie. Hey." She pulled me into her arms. "I'm here. It's okay."

I managed to keep from completely falling apart, but I clung to my best friend, not able to let her go.

"Do you want me to stay with you for a little while?" she offered.

"Oh, no. You don't need to do that. I don't want to bother you." But I didn't let go of her hand.

"Scoot over." She curled up against me on the bed. "I'll stay until you fall asleep." She was still there in the morning. Just another reason why she was my best friend.

***

"Ally, the guy at table four requested you specifically. Can you take it?" Amber, one of the other waitresses asked as she came in the kitchen.

"Um, sure, if you can take over here." I was prepping dinner salads. She smiled and swapped places with me. I wiped my hands and hurried toward the dining room, sure that it was Jack who had stopped in to surprise me. The surprise was entirely on me as I approached table four; it wasn't Jack. It was Luc.

"What are you doing here?" I stopped a few feet short of the table.

"Having lunch. That is what one does at an establishment of this sort, isn't it?" He smiled suavely.

"I mean, what are you doing here in Albuquerque? It's a long way to come for lunch."

"I wanted to speak to you, Ally, without the rest of the Conseil there. You seem like a sensible young woman; I'm sure you will be able to understand what I have to say."

"I have no interest in what you have to say." I turned to go.

"Well, if you are afraid…"

Did he really just dare me? What was this, middle school? And yet, I sat down across from him. Dang it, why did dares always work with me? "Talk. I have a ten minute break, then I'm done."

He inclined his head in acknowledgment. "Very well. I will take what I can get. Ally, I have come to make another plea for you to listen to reason. The

Conseil is living in the past. We are standing at the precipice of a new world of opportunity. You are the next Oracle—"

"Shh! We're in public, you idiot! Do you think I want the people I work with asking about that kind of stuff?"

He looked irritated for a moment before covering it smoothly. "Of course. My apologies." He lowered his voice. "You are the next in line. Everyone knows this. I want you to know that there are options beyond what Kate and the rest of them have in mind for you."

"Options? Like what? What are you trying to tell me, Luc?" I was running out of patience.

He leaned across the table. "The Conseil has no vision! They would have you spend your life hidden away in that mansion, doing nothing but running the family business, making money. With your abilities, you should be running countries! I can help you make that happen."

"Sorry, Luc. You are barking up the wrong Oracle. I have no plans to take over anything. The gods or fates or whatever chose poorly when they picked me." I stood up. "Now, if you'll excuse me, I have to get back to work. I have salads to make." I retreated to the kitchen to spend the rest of my 15-minute break—yes, I had lied to Luc—thinking about what he said. Oh, not so much *what* he said— I truly had no interest in the kind of power he seemed obsessed with—but more *why* he said it to, to me, at least. He had been extremely circumspect this last summer during my visit to Rouen, not starting any of the controversy he had begun during my first visit. In fact, he had been absent more often than not. So why was he here now? And why come to me?

Rémy? I sent my thoughts to him, hoping my long-distance communication skills were up and running. It took quite a bit of concentration for me to talk with him over any kind of distance. Nothing. *Rémy?* I tried again

—I'm in class. Is this important? he finally responded.

—Luc just showed up here at the restaurant, I replied somewhat impatiently. As if I would bother him for trivialities!

—What? Merde! he cursed. *What did he want? Are you okay?*

—I'm fine. He spouted more of that crazy 'let's take over the world' crap.' He's gone now. I just thought I should give you a head's up in case he hunts you down.

—Thanks, chérie. I will keep my eyes open. Can I come by your house later so we can talk about this?

—Sure. See you later.

***

He was waiting for me in the driveway when I got home after my late afternoon class.

"You have a key, Rémy. Why didn't you go on in?" I asked, juggling my book bag and the bag of groceries I had stopped to purchase.

"I was fine listening to music in my car." He took the groceries from me and shut the door of my SUV. "I haven't been here long."

"Thanks," I said, opening the front door. "Come on in. We can talk while I get dinner ready. It's Mina's night to work late, so I'm cooking. Why don't you stay? I'm not as good a chef as Mina, but it's pretty hard to mess up spaghetti. Unless, of course, you have a hot date?"

He laughed lightly. "No date, hot or cold. Thank you. I will be happy to stay for dinner. I assume Jack will be here, as well?"

"No. He has plans with Megan tonight. She's been feeling a bit neglected, so they're going to try and spend more quality time together. It will just be myself, Tara, Mina, and now you."

He helped me prepare dinner, taking over the sauce creation, claiming that he had a secret recipe that would cause us to swoon. He probably just didn't trust me to produce anything edible.

"But you're French. How is it that you have an amazing recipe for Italian spaghetti sauce?"

He scoffed and gave me a disparaging look. "Maybe because I can read a recipe book. The French prepare everything better than you Americans."

"Don't be such a snob, Rémy. Drenching everything in butter doesn't qualify as better cooking. But I am looking forward to your sauce. Mine comes straight out of a jar." I began washing and chopping vegetables for a salad.

"Luc was waiting for me when I walked out of class today," he said as he measured oregano into the pot of sauce.

"And?" I prompted.

"I was civil, at least somewhat. We went for

coffee and I listened to what he had to say."

"Which was?"

"More of the same." He shrugged. "Seers should rise up and take control, we should be running the world, blah, blah, blah."

"Did you just say 'blah, blah, blah?'" I laughed.

"Ah, oui. I've clearly been in America too long. All the wrong things are rubbing off on me. Are you going to keep interrupting?"

"Sorry, Mr. Grumpy Pants. Continue. You left off at 'blah, blah, blah.'"

He rolled his eyes. "So, after I listened to him rant for a while, I told him he was still crazy and could go to hell. Do you have any wine?"

"For you or for the sauce?" I asked.

"For both. One should never cook without a glass of wine," he said, stirring the sauce.

"Is that an old French proverb?" I asked slyly, going to the pantry for the bottle of wine he had given me as a housewarming gift last year.

"It should be." He chuckled. "I can't believe you still have this. It's a really nice merlot. Why didn't you drink it?" He fished around in my junk drawer for the corkscrew he had also given me.

"You do know the drinking age is 21 in America, don't you?"

"It's not my fault you live in a nation of puritanical hypocrites. I am trying to educate you, that's all." He opened the wine, poured a glass for himself, added a few glugs to the sauce, and then handed me a glass. "Here. Tell me what you taste."

I took a small sip and kept it on my tongue as he had taught me. "Umm, blackberry," I said after I swallowed. "And cocoa. It's good. Thanks."

He flashed his signature smirk and took a sip before going back to stirring and tasting the sauce.

"What do you think it means, Rémy? That Luc showed up here? What do you think he wants?"

"I'm not sure. I thought maybe he had gotten over his crazy ideas about Seers being in control, but it doesn't appear that way now. This worries me, chérie."

"Me too. I don't like Luc. He scares me," I admitted quietly.

"Oh, Ally," Rémy set down his wine and came across the kitchen to hug me. "He can't hurt us, chérie. I won't let him. I promise."

Mina came in just then. "Oh, I'm sorry. Excuse me." She started to back out.

Rémy's reaction shocked me. "Where in the hell have you been?" he yelled, dropping his arms from around me and advancing toward her, grasping her upper arms and shaking her slightly. "I have been trying to get in touch with you all afternoon! You didn't answer your phone and you closed your mind off from me completely!"

Mina squared her jaw and faced him. "I was at work," she said calmly, brushing his hands off. "I didn't have my mobile on me." I noticed that she did not address why she had closed her mind to him; he didn't follow up on it.

"Did Luc come to see you?" he asked.

"Luc? From Rouen?"

He nodded. "He came to see both Ally and me today."

"Why? What did he want?"

I broke in. "It was more of his crazy 'Seers should be in control of the whole world' rant from last summer. It creeped me out."

"I haven't seen him," she said. "This is very odd. Why, after all this time, would he come here?"

"I very much fear that he did not give up on his idea. In fact, I believe he has simply been biding his time until he was ready," Rémy said.

"Ready for what?" I asked, not sure if I wanted the answer.

"I do not know." He shook his head. "But I fear he has something planned. Something we will not like."

Tara came in a few minutes later, full of news about her day and oblivious to the undercurrents in the kitchen. She took the glass of wine from me and sipped. "Mmmm. Hell, yeah. This is great. What's for dinner? It smells amazing." None of us mentioned Luc's mysterious appearance to her.

I finished making the salad, Mina slathered the loaf of French bread I had bought with butter and garlic salt, and Tara set the table. Rémy was right about his sauce: it was swoon-worthy. I pretended that it was merely acceptable, though; his ego was big enough. In spite of the upset of the day, we managed to have a relaxing evening, finishing the bottle of wine and talking about anything except what Luc had said. I noticed the increased tension between Mina and Rémy did not totally abate throughout the evening, however. They spoke to the others around them, but never directly to each other. Once, when they reached for the salad at the same time, their hands touched and they both jerked away as if they had been burned. Hmmm. Very, very interesting.

***

I showed up to my midmorning Victorian lit class to find a cancellation note on the door. Yes! It was nice to have an unexpected break. We were currently reading Christina Rossetti's *The Goblin Market*, which was an amazing poem and not really about goblins at all. May I just say the Victorians were obsessed with sex? Nevertheless, I was happy to forego class for the day. The past few weeks had been stressful, with a heavy work schedule, unremitting homework, and the worry over Luc's unexpected visit hanging over my head. I headed back to the Student Union Building, planning to enjoy a latte and maybe a bagel since I had skipped breakfast. I approached the bigger-than-life bronze sculptures in front of the SUB but stopped short when I saw Jack talking to a guy I didn't know. He laughed at something the guy said and I paused to enjoy the sight. Jack was a pretty serious guy most of the time and I loved to see him laugh, the corners of his eyes crinkling in an attractive manner. He wore jeans and a dark blue, long-sleeved Henley that stretched across his broad shoulders. He had pushed the sleeves up to his elbows, which showcased his chiseled, brown forearms, the left one with the compass tattoo. He wore a red baseball cap perched backwards on his head and he hadn't shaved that morning, his jaw scruffy with his black whiskers. I bit my lip in appreciation. And he was mine. He was, thankfully, oblivious to the admiring looks from some of the nearby girls. I smiled, because simply looking at him made me happy. I sauntered over to him, standing at his elbow, not wanting to interrupt.

He saw the guy notice me and looked down. "Hey, beautiful! What are you doing here? I thought you had class right now?" He leaned down to give me a quick kiss.

"Cancelled. I'm free for a whole hour. What about you?"

"This day just got better. I'm free for a couple of hours. Oh, this is Rick. He's in a couple of my engineering classes. Rick, this is my girlfriend, Ally." I still got a thrill when he called me his girlfriend. "You want to grab some coffee or something?"

"Sure, but I don't want to interrupt."

"No problem. See you, Rick." He waved and steered me away.

"I didn't mean to drag you away from your friend, Jack," I began.

"Don't worry about it. I would much rather spend time with you. Besides, I didn't like how he looked at you."

"Oh, really? And how did he look at me?" I asked, amused at his jealousy.

"He was definitely leering. All guys do when they look at you." He sounded so nonchalant when he said this I had to laugh.

We entered the SUB food court area and stepped up to the counter at the gourmet coffee stand. Once we had our coffee and bagels, we found an empty table in the quieter area tucked behind the coffee stand.

"You look great today, querida. I love it when you wear those boots," he said as he took a sip of his drink.

"Really? I didn't know that. I will be sure to feature them more regularly in my wardrobe choices," I teased.

"Mmmm. They already feature prominently in several of my fantasies about you. I don't know if I can take any more," he teased back.

"Fantasies? Ooh, that sounds promising. Are you going to tell me about these fantasies? I would love to know."

"Definitely not." I could swear he blushed although it was hard to tell with his dark complexion. "Is it hot in here?"

I laughed and put my hand over his. "I'm just glad to know you have fantasies about me. Do you want to hear some of mine about you?"

He choked on his coffee and coughed. "Are you trying to kill me, Ally?" He leaned across the table, pulling me slightly to meet him. "I have incredible fantasies about you. Someday, I'm going to act on them. But not today." He kissed me sweetly.

"Hey, lovebirds!" Tara interrupted, plopping down uninvited and unwanted at the moment. "So, there I was, sitting in my bio-chem class, minding my own business, doing today's Sudoku puzzle, when I saw this." She slapped a copy of the *Daily Lobo*, our university newspaper, down between us, open to the personal ads, one circled in red.

To the flame-haired girl in Zimmerman Library Tuesday night: your beauty lit up the study carrels on the 4th floor. Très très beau. Your taste in literature is exquisite. "Like a vessel at the launch/ When its last restraint is gone."

I had to read it three times before it sunk in. "Oh, my God. I think it's me. I mean, I think it's referring to me. I was at the library that night. That's where I like to sit—"

"Yes, of course it means you!" Tara interjected.

"What the fu—" Jack grabbed the paper and read it again. "How could it be Ally?"

"Thanks a lot!" I objected.

'No, I didn't mean…there are nearly 25,000 students here. How could it be…shit! This is you."

"Ally's got a secret admirer!" Tara taunted. "That is so romantic!"

"It's not romantic! It's creepy, that's what it is. I don't want someone creeping around, watching my girlfriend, and putting personal ads in the goddamn paper!" Jack nearly shouted, causing people at the tables next to us to stare.

"Hey, shh," I soothed, placing my hand on his arm. "I'm sure it's nothing. It's kind of weird, yeah, but…" I let the sentence fade away.

"Is this French?" Jack demanded, pointing at the ad. "Did Rémy do this? I'll kill him!"

"No way." Tara shook her head. "This is totally not his style. What do you think that last line means? 'Like a vessel at the launch/When its last restraint is gone'?"

"It's from *The Goblin Market.* It's the poem I was studying that night in the library. I had gone there to work on my literary analysis paper."

"So? Why would they include that line? What does it mean?" Tara asked.

"I don't know. I mean…" I frowned, confused by why the quote had been included.

"What, Ally? What is it?" Jack asked, his jaw flexing as he tried to control his anger.

I hated to make it worse, but knew he wouldn't let it go. "It's just that *The Goblin Market* seems like a children's poem and Christina Rossetti swore that it was. But it has a lot of thinly veiled eroticism in it. If you read that line with that in mind—"

"Son of a bitch!" Jack hissed.

"Eww, that is kind of creepy," Tara agreed. "And if you consider that whoever it was had to be close enough to see what you were reading. Shit, girl. I think you have a stalker."

Jack cursed again under his breath.

"Do you think this could be the same person that's following me?" I asked in a small voice. My stomach sank when I saw Jack and Tara exchange a quick look: nobody but me had ever seen so much as a glimpse of anyone following me. I knew my friends thought I was imagining everything because of the stress I was under trying to figure out if I was the next Oracle. "Well, I didn't imagine this!" I said hotly, gesturing to the newspaper on the table between us.

Tara wouldn't meet my eyes, but Jack shifted closer to me, bringing my hand up to his mouth, kissing my clenched fist. "Hey," he said softly. He lowered my hand and engulfed it between his large, warm ones. "I'm sorry. That was not cool. I believe you." At my disbelieving look he rephrased. "Okay, I'm trying to believe you. I really am. I love you, Ally, and I hate the thought that someone is sneaking around watching you. I really hate the thought that there might be two people doing it."

"I'm sorry, too, Ally," Tara added. "I just don't want to believe that you're being stalked. I really, really hope you're wrong."

I nodded, agreeing with both of them. "What am I going to do, Jack?" I whispered.

"*We*, sweetheart. You're not in this alone. I'm going to help you figure this out."

"Me, too," said Tara.

"I'm so sorry, Jack." I couldn't meet his eyes.

"For what, querida?"

"It's always something with me, isn't it? Aren't you sick of it yet? Don't you want to be with someone who doesn't have all this extra crap?"

He gave me a crooked smile. "Are you forgetting all the crap I came with? You've put up with an awful lot, you know. That's what people who love each other do: they deal with each other's crap."

I tried to smile. "That's really romantic."

"That's me: Mr. Romance," he said before swooping in for a kiss. "I gotta go. Tara, will you stay with her? Make sure she gets to her next class?"

"Sure, Jack."

He grabbed the newspaper before he left, walking with purpose toward the front of the building.

CHAPTER EIGHT

*"I flamed amazement; sometime I'ld divide,
And burn in many places;"*
—Shakespeare, *The Tempest* 1.2

To my Titian-haired beauty: J'adore, ma belle. "He had robbed the body of its taint, the world's taunts of their sting; he had shown her the holiness of direct desire."

I lowered the newspaper with a groan and dropped my head onto my arms. Why me, God? The cheesy personal ads kept coming, at least one per week. Each time there was a French love phrase of some sort and a suggestive quote from one of the books I was currently studying. It was embarrassing and disturbing. Tara no longer teased me about them because she knew how much they upset both Jack and me. Jack didn't talk about it much, but I could tell he was aware of them and still angry. Although I still felt like someone was watching me,

I hesitated to mention it to Jack or Tara, knowing they were inclined to think it was a product of my overly-stressed imagination. I was turning into a nervous wreck: the nightmares about searching for something while being followed disturbed my sleep at least three to four times a week, I still felt like I was being watched in reality, and I apparently had a secret admirer. Crap. I was having a hard time concentrating and was afraid my grades were going to suffer.

"Hi. Excuse me." The voice came from above my head.

I sat up, brushing my long, red hair out of my face.

"Are you her?" A girl about my age stood at the edge of the table.

"Excuse me?"

"Are you her?" She pointed at the *Daily Lobo*, opened to the personal pages, on my table. "Are you the redhead in all those personal ads?"

"What? No, of course not. Why would you think that?" I was appalled someone had connected me to the crazy ads.

"Because you have really red hair, you're pretty, and you have the book the latest ad refers to." She reached down and picked up the copy of *A Room with a View*, which was where the latest quote came from. "I'm just wondering. My friends and I," she gestured to a table behind her, "have been figuring out the quotes for weeks and trying to find who the girl is. A bunch of people are trying to figure it out."

"What do you mean by a bunch of people?" I

interrupted her.

"It's kind of a thing on Twitter right now. See?" She showed me her smartphone. Oh, my God. I had my own hash tag! #RedHairMysteryGirl. "It's you, isn't it?" she said, grinning.

"Nope. Sorry. It's definitely not me. I, uh, I just dyed my hair this color last week. Yeah, it's really blonde. I gotta go." I hurriedly gathered my books and rushed out of the SUB. Oh, great. This was getting out of hand. My humiliation was now trending on social media. Shit. Shit. Shit. I paced and cursed under my breath, wondering what in the world I could do to stop the personal ads.

"Ally! Hey, where were you?" Michael jogged up to where I paced.

"Oh, crap, Michael! I'm sorry." I had been waiting for him in the SUB for our usual coffee date before our Shakespeare class.

"No problem. Are you okay? You look upset."

"No, I'm fine. I'm just irritated by something. It's fine." I managed to dredge up a slight smile. It wasn't his fault, after all.

"Okay, well, let's get some coffee and go over these character analyses. I need your advice on what to write about Caliban. I'm not sure what to think about him."

"Sure. Just, uh, give me a second." I pulled an elastic band off my wrist and looped my hair into a ponytail, which I then stuffed into a slouch hat that I fished out of my backpack. I added a pair of glasses for good measure, which I usually only wore in class to see the board. This would have to do for now; maybe I'd consider dyeing my hair for real. Or shaving my head. This might call for drastic measures.

Once we had our coffee and were settled in an area of the SUB far away from my, ahem, fan club, Michael asked, "So, what's with the disguise?"

"It's that obvious, huh?" I grimaced at his nod. "It's these stupid personal ads." At his blank look, I pulled the latest out of the book I had folded it into and showed him the ad.

"Hmm," he mused. "And you think this is meant for you?"

I flushed. "Yeah, I do. It's not that I think I'm a beauty and all that," I hastened to assure him. "It's just that the first one was very specific about a location. And all the quotes are from the books or poems that I'm reading for my Victorian lit class."

"So, you've got an admirer. Lucky you. Do you think it's your boyfriend?"

"No." I laughed. "This is not Jack's style."

"What? He's not romantic like that?" he scoffed.

"He's plenty romantic!" I rushed to defend him. "He's just not creepy. He compliments me to my face."

"Well, maybe not everyone has that luxury. So, you don't like these ads? You're not flattered or anything?"

"No, I mean, yes—I'm flattered. But I wish they would stop. They border on stalkerish, the way this guy knows what I'm reading—"

"Maybe it's a girl," he suggested.

I had no comeback for that. "I suppose it could be a girl. My point is, they're embarrassing, especially now that I have my own hash tag and people are starting to ask if I'm the mystery redhead." I sighed and took a sip of my mocha latte. "Never mind. Let's look at these character sketches, okay?" We were reading *The Tempest* and had been instructed to analyze two of the characters. I had chosen Prospero and Miranda and felt fairly confident that I had done a good job, but wanted to get Michael's opinion. I finished reading his analysis of Caliban and waited for him to catch up.

"So, what do you think?" he asked anxiously.

"It's good. I'm not sure I'm in total agreement of your sympathetic take on the monster, but you've backed it up adequately. How did I do?"

"Good. I like how you compare Prospero to a chess master, aligning all the people like pawns. You've also pointed out some strengths in Miranda's character that are rather nice."

"Thanks, Michael. Well, let's head to class." As I threw away my empty cup, a chill crept down my spine and I looked up just in time to see someone duck quickly into a nearby alcove, as if they did not want to be caught watching. I didn't hesitate; I darted after the figure, leaving Michael standing by the trashcans. The alcove turned out to be a service corridor. I heard a door slam just as I turned the corner, but every door up and down the entire hallway was locked.

"Ally? What the heck? Who was that guy you were chasing?" Michael caught up to me, slightly out of breath.

I whirled around, backing him up against the wall. "You saw someone?" I demanded. He nodded. "What did he look like?"

"Jeez, Ally! Calm down!" He looked at me as if I were a crazed lunatic.

"Sorry." I backed away, giving him some room. "I was just surprised you saw someone too. Could you see what he looked like? Was it definitely a man?"

"I couldn't really tell anything except, yeah, it was a guy. I just caught a quick glimpse. What's going on?"

"I think this guy has been following me for a while. I catch glimpses, but that's it." I put my hands on my hips, dropped my head back, and laughed mirthlessly. "You must think I'm insane! First, I have a secret admirer placing personal ads in the *Daily Lobo*, and now I'm chasing a stalker. I'm not usually this self-absorbed."

"I don't think you're insane or self-absorbed. Well, maybe a little insane. Come on, crazy girl. We're going to be late for class."

***

"Ally, I have a favor to ask." My dad paused while the waiter placed our desserts in front of us. He still made a point of taking me out to dinner at least once a month when he flew in for business.

"Sure, Dad. Whatever you need." We had built a comfortable relationship, enjoying each other's company, although we would probably never be as close as I was with my mother.

"Well, I need your presence at a fundraiser next week. You know I'm on the board of directors for a homeless shelter here in Albuquerque, right?" I nodded. It was one of the many interests that brought him here regularly. "Well, we have our annual fundraiser next Saturday evening, and I bought a table. I'm having trouble filling it, and empty seats look bad. I need you and Jack to dress up and come be beautiful and charming. There will be good food, entertainment, and even some dancing. What do you say?"

"Of course, Dad. No problem." I was glad he and Jack got along so well; Dad approved of Jack's old-fashioned treatment of me—i.e. we weren't shacking up—and Jack was happy I was able to get along well with my father. He and his dad had a tense relationship at best. "I'll talk to Jack to make sure he's available next Saturday."

***

"I'm going to be out of town next Saturday. I'm sorry, querida. Mat and I are going camping," Jack said as we sat on my couch, doing homework the next evening. "It's okay. I'll cancel. Mat and I can go another time," he offered.

"Absolutely not!" I sat up and took his adorable face in my hands. "You are not to cancel! You haven't had any fun lately! All you do is work and study and do army stuff. You deserve to go camping."

"Ally, it's no problem. I love spending time with you."

That deserved a kiss. "I know you do. You're the best boyfriend in the whole, wide world." That earned me a longer kiss. "What were we talking about?" I asked as I pulled back, flustered as always from his kisses.

He chuckled and kissed me briefly. "I was telling you I don't mind canceling my camping trip so I can take you to your dad's fundraiser. Who else would you go with?"

Aha! I knew he really wanted to go camping. I just needed to convince him I would be fine without his company. "Don't worry about it, Jack. I'll ask Tara. Since you're stealing her boyfriend away, she should be free."

She wasn't free; she was scheduled to work, so I asked Rémy. Jack was less than thrilled at this development; the latent jealousy he harbored against Rémy for our past semi-romantic entanglement occasionally reared its ugly head.

"Jack, you know you have no reason to worry, right?" I was helping him load Mat's truck for their camping trip. The weather had turned colder and this would be their last chance to camp before they had to deal with copious amounts of mountain snow. "He's like a brother to me."

"I know, I know. It's just that the thought of sending my girlfriend off on a glamorous date with a 23 year old French guy rubs me the wrong way. I'm not sure he totally understands the whole 'like a brother' thing, either."

"Hey." I backed him against the side of the truck. "Look at me. You're the one I want to be with, Jack. I love you. And Rémy is in love with Mina. He just doesn't know it yet." I leaned in, pulling him down for a kiss. "Now, go have fun camping with your cousin. Don't freeze off anything important."

***

Rémy picked me up Saturday evening in his gorgeous BMW. "You look beautiful, chérie, as always."

"Thanks, Rémy." I had chosen a sea-foam green cocktail dress—okay, Tara had chosen it for me—and Mina had helped me pile my hair on top of my head in a way I hoped looked sophisticated and not pathetic. "Wow, you look great. You didn't have to rent a tux for this."

"I didn't rent it." Of course he would own a tux. What was I thinking? "Nice roses. Did Jack send them?"

"Yes," I smiled at the arrangement I had made in a crystal vase and placed on the dining room table. The lush bouquet had been waiting on my doorstep when I got home from school, along with a note:

Have a wonderful time tonight. I'll be dreaming of you.

He must have arranged for them to be delivered today before he left yesterday.

Rémy was the perfect date for an occasion like this fundraiser; he was an amazing conversationalist, excelling at the kind of small talk I sucked at. He had our entire table laughing and chatting like old friends in a matter of minutes. He was incredibly gorgeous and his accent drew women like a moth to flame, but he never ignored me, making it clear to all the women who flocked around that he was with me.

"You don't have to stick to me all night, you know." I looked up into his face as we danced to the music of the live band. "I think that woman over there, the anchor from channel 4, would love to dance with you. I can make myself scarce."

"No thank you, chérie. I promised Jack I would take good care of you. I shudder to think what he would do to me if I abandoned you. And I thought we were through with you trying to arrange my love life?"

"Well, I wouldn't have to arrange it if you would just admit that you like Mi—"

"Shh." He put his fingers against my lips. "Don't say it."

"Why? I don't understand. She likes you too. I can tell. What is it with you two?" He wouldn't answer; he shook his head and danced.

He insisted on walking me to my door when he dropped me off. "I thought I left the porch light on," I mused. One of the girls must have accidentally turned it off before they left for work. I fumbled for my keys on the dark porch, suddenly nervous in the unexpected dark. I heard a soft meow coming from the bushes. "Wicky?" My cat ran toward me and wound himself around my ankles. I dropped my purse and picked him up. "What are you doing out?" Wicky was strictly an indoor cat; I never let him out because he had no claws. "Rémy! Something's wrong!"

"Stay here," he ordered as he bent to pick up my

keys. He handed me my purse and used the keys to enter the dark house. He returned a few minutes later. "Call your stepfather. There's been a break-in."

I dialed the phone with cold, trembling fingers. Brian arrived before the units he had sent. "Come on in, Ally." He finally allowed Rémy and me to enter the house. "I need you to look around and see if anything is missing. Your bedroom window was broken, but I can't tell if anything was taken. I need you to do a quick inventory. Okay?"

I nodded and went to my bedroom to check. I had heard of how people who had experienced a break-in felt violated, but I had never understood it before. I knew exactly what it felt like now. Inside my bedroom I saw the broken glass beneath the window and wrapped my arms around my waist to ward off the chill from the cold air streaming in. Nothing seemed disturbed: my bed was still neatly made from that morning, all the bottles and jewelry on my dresser were the same as always. Then I noticed that the top dresser drawer was not pushed in completely. I pulled it out and stared into my lingerie collection. I knew immediately that it had been rifled through. God, I cannot describe the chill that invaded my bones as I thought of some unknown person running his hands through my underwear. I reached in and began sorting. Within about 30 seconds, I realized that a pair of red lacy panties was missing. I backed up until I felt my bed and sat.

"Panties. He took a pair of my panties," I whispered. I was too horrified to be embarrassed.

***

Two hours later, the police officers were gone and my bedroom window was boarded up. I swept up the last fragments of glass, trying to come to terms with the fact that my house, my bedroom, had been invaded by some unknown entity. I was too numb to know what I felt.

"All right, sweetheart. We're done here. Get a few things packed. Your mom insists you come home with me," Brian said.

"No." I shook my head. "I'm not leaving my home. What about Tara and Mina? They don't even know. They'll be home soon. I'm not leaving."

"I'll stay," said Rémy. He and Brian shared a long look before Brain nodded. "Okay. I'll have a unit drive by every fifteen minutes tonight.

I was changing into my sweats when Tara and Mina arrived home. "Hey, sweetie," Tara sailed in and flopped on my bed. "How was the fundraiser? Why is Rémy still here? What the hell happened here?" She finally noticed my boarded-up window.

Several hours and multiple cups of tea–laced liberally with brandy—later, Tara and Mina finally turned in, retreating to their own bedrooms while I got the couch ready for Rémy. I insisted I was fine sleeping in my own room; I didn't want to appear weak. But once in my bedroom with the door closed, I paced, unable to bring myself to sleep in the room where some unknown creeper had been rooting through my underwear. I was furious…and scared. I finally gave up and grabbed my fluffy blanket, planning to sneak in and sleep with Tara. I stopped short of the living room at the sight of Mina and Rémy having a hushed argument.

"You don't know anything!" Rémy hissed at her. The tortured look on his face was heartbreaking.

"Then tell me what I should know! I don't know what I'm doing here, Rémy. I feel useless, unnecessary. I should go home." Mina delivered this speech in her usual quiet way. I was shocked; I had no idea she was unhappy.

"You can't leave," Rémy stated.

"Why not? What's keeping me here? I don't belong—" Rémy interrupted her, stepping forward, pulling her into his arms, and laying an epic kiss on her. She tensed in his arms and tried to push him away before giving in and melting into his kiss. I felt like an intruder and faded back into my bedroom, determined not to disturb their tender moment.

I couldn't bring myself to lay on my bed, so I curled up in the armchair and wrapped my fluffy blanket around me, sure that I wouldn't be able to sleep. I watched my bedside clock change minute-by-minute until 3 a.m. I must have drifted off finally, only to be woken by a soft, deep voice.

"Ally, sweetheart. Wake up."

"Jack?" I couldn't believe my eyes and was sure I had conjured him up in my dreams. The clock on my nightstand read 3:45 a.m.

"Yeah, querida. I'm here." He was really here. I was so glad to see him; he was what I had needed all night long.

"How? I thought you were camping? There was no cell service." To my shame, I had tried earlier in the evening.

"Rémy called me. Not on the phone." He smiled crookedly as he said this. Rémy must have mentally reached out to Jack. I knew I'd be in awe of his powers in the morning; right now I focused on being in Jack's arms. "Mat and I packed up and got here as fast as we could. He's with Tara."

"Oh, God, Jack." I threw myself into his embrace, letting loose the tears that I had kept in all evening. "I was so scared. I still am."

"I know, babe. I'm sorry I wasn't here for you."

"You're here now."

He picked me up and carried me to the bed. "You need to get some rest. Do you think you can sleep for a few hours?"

"If you stay with me. Please? I won't try anything," I promised sleepily.

"Hey, that's my line," he teased. "Don't worry. I'm not going anywhere." I watched as he unlaced and toed off his hiking boots, then discarded his jacket and several layers of shirts, leaving his dog tags lying against his bare chest. His jeans were the last item to go, leaving him in boxers. "Sorry I smell like a campfire," he said as he pulled the covers over us both.

"You smell amazing." I wrapped my arms around him, tucking my chin under his. Oh, I could get used to this. I had seen him shirtless before—swimming and that sort of thing—but I had never had much opportunity to touch. I knew I had to behave; he wouldn't be able to withstand much hand wandering, so I simply flattened my palm over his muscular left pectoral, right above his heart.

He pulled me even closer, tangling his legs with mine. He was so incredibly warm and I felt the fear melt away as I concentrated on the beat of his heart within his chest. "Go to sleep, querida. I'm here now."

***

I woke, engulfed in warmth, with the weight of Jack's arm draped across my body. The dim light in the room told me it was early morning. I watched him as he slept and smiled at how handsome he was. He hadn't shaved in several days and his black beard came in thick. His lashes against his cheek were unfairly long and his lips were full, parted slightly as he slept, a soft snore more adorable than anything else. He must have felt me staring because he rolled toward me and pulled my body close.

"Hey," he mumbled sleepily.

"Hey, yourself."

"What time is it?"

I turned my head to peer at the clock. "7:00."

He groaned. "Three hours is not enough. Shh. Go back to sleep."

The next time I awoke, it was 11:00 and the spot next to me was empty. I had a moment of panic before I realized the bedroom door was open and I heard his voice from the kitchen, along with Mat and Rémy's. The pillow still held the indentation from his head. I hugged it, breathing in the lingering scent of Jack's fragrance—a mix of his aftershave, his own unique essence, with an overtone of smoke—and wondered at the feasibility of never washing my sheets again. I forced myself to get up and took a few minutes to wash my face and brush my teeth before making my appearance.

"Hey, gorgeous," Jack greeted when I slipped my arms around him as he poured himself another cup of coffee. "How are you feeling?" He kissed me and then reached in the cabinet to get another cup for me.

"Thanks." I gratefully took a sip of the strong, dark brew. "Mmm. Better. I'm so glad you came. I'm sorry you had to cut your camping trip short but—"

"You are more important than any camping trip."

I smiled at him as I took another sip of coffee. "Rémy, thanks for getting hold of him. I am in awe of your abilities, by the way."

He smiled, just a bit of a smirk; he looked like he hadn't slept well. "My pleasure, chérie. I know you needed him," he said simply.

Seeing the vase of roses on the table across the room jogged my memory. "Jack, thank you for the flowers. They're beautiful. That was really sweet of you."

"Huh? What flowers?"

With a sinking feeling in my stomach, I got up and walked across to the roses. I detached the small card from the pick and handed it to Jack. "These flowers. You sent them, right?"

He read the card and looked up at me, his jaw flexing. "I didn't send these, Ally."

***

"Why on earth didn't you call me last night?" I didn't bother to answer my dad since he had been ranting and asking the same question for the past twenty minutes. He had shown up about five minutes after I woke up and had been scolding me ever since. Am I ever glad that he didn't show up while Jack and I were in bed together—that would have been a bit awkward. I knew he wasn't angry; he was scared. Close on his heels was the crew to install a state-of-the-art alarm system and bars on every window. My adorable little house was about to become Fort Freaking Knox and I couldn't work up any emotion beyond a numb acceptance.

"Josh, give it a rest, man. She's had about all she can take." Jack and my dad locked eyes in a silent battle.

"Easy for you to say," groused my dad. "She called you." Actually Rémy had called him, but I wasn't about to correct him.

"Jack." I roused myself from my stupor long enough to attempt to douse the rising testosterone level in the room. "Why don't you go home for a while, okay? Get a shower and change." I pleaded with my eyes for him to understand.

He looked hard at me for a few seconds before finally nodding in understanding. I walked him to the front door. "Let me take you out tonight, Ally. You need to think of something else for a while."

"You think you can distract me?" I asked, a bit of my normal spirit fighting its way to the surface.

He flashed me a wolfish grin before swooping me into a fierce kiss, right in front of my father. My dad made a disgusted noise and retreated to the kitchen.

"Mmmm," I said, licking my lips, savoring his flavor. "That was some kiss, Mr. Ruiz." I recovered enough to give him a stern look. "You are not in competition with my father. Be nice."

"Sorry." He had the grace to look a bit ashamed. A tiny bit. "So, I'll pick you up later, okay?"

"Okay. I guess it would be good to get out of here for a while. Where are we going? What should I wear?"

"You always look great." It was what he always said.

"Well, I could wear those boots you like, if you want." I tried to look innocent. "Or sneakers." I shrugged.

He laughed and pulled me in for a hug. "I love you, you know?"

"I know."

***

I wandered into the kitchen to find my dad, Brian, and Rémy huddled over cups of coffee, discussing the case while Mina prepared lunch. Mat had taken Tara out earlier, leaving his truck for Jack. I moved to help Mina make sandwiches, interested to observe the dynamics between her and Rémy since their lip-lock the night before.

The horrid red roses were still in the middle of the table, mocking me with their presence. Brian had stopped me from stuffing them in the trashcan earlier, stating that they and the note were evidence. I wanted them off my table and out of my house, pronto.

"I'll take them with me when I leave, Ally. I promise," Brian said, accepting the sandwich I had made for him. "Thanks, sweetie."

"You're welcome, Dad." I kissed his cheek before placing another sandwich in front of Josh. "And one for you, Dad." I kissed his cheek, as well. They both chuckled appreciatively at my teasing. "I just want those damn flowers gone. They give me the wiggins!" I shuddered and sat down at the opposite end of the table, waving away the sandwich Mina tried to place in front of me. I had not regained my appetite yet. She placed it in front of me anyway, and then gave Rémy one. I expected a special, secret smile or a lingering touch or something! They didn't even acknowledge each other. Seriously? Yikes. What was up with them?

It's a good thing I had no appetite; rehashing the break-in, the personal ads, and the whole being followed thing made my stomach cramp. Brian studied the note, which he had placed in an evidence bag. "The roses were on the front step when you arrived home yesterday? What time was that?"

"Around five."

"Did you see anyone loitering, hanging around? Anyone who didn't quite belong?"

I shook my head. "No, but I didn't really look. I was in a hurry. I was running late."

"I checked with the neighbors. Nobody saw anything." He sounded frustrated.

"You'll find out who's been placing those personal ads, right?" I asked anxiously.

"I'll try, sweetheart, but I'll need a warrant. Newspapers are funny about protecting first amendment rights." Brian didn't look hopeful.

***

I wore the boots. Jack whistled when he saw me, twirling me around to get the full view. "Good Lord, Miz Moran. You look incredible!"

It was exactly what I needed after the events of the previous evening: a night out with my boyfriend, just being young and in love. We didn't do anything fancy or expensive—just dinner and a movie. But we held hands in the car, sat as close together as possible at dinner, snuggled during the movie, and made out in his car before he walked me to my door. It felt like some of our first dates and allowed me to forget, for a little while, the stress and tension I lived under lately.

"Thank you, Jack."

"For what, querida?" He held me close on my front porch.

"For making me remember it's not all bad right now."

"Hey." He lifted my chin. "I know it's tough right now. But I'm here, Ally. I'm not going anywhere." He sighed and pushed my hair behind my ear. "You barely ate anything at dinner."

I shrugged, not able to meet his gaze. "It's no big deal. I'm just not hungry."

"I'm betting you haven't eaten anything all day, either. Is Mina or Tara home yet?"

"I don't think so. Tara's out with Mat and Mina

has the late shift again. Why? Do you have something nefarious planned?" I waggled my eyebrows at him.

"Nope." He took my keys from me and opened the door. "But I'm not going to leave you alone in this house tonight."

"Hmmph. Well, a girl can dream," I said as I brushed by him into the house, hurrying to punch the alarm code into the keypad.

"So can a guy, babe. And I do. Frequently." He sent me to my room to change into my sweats while he made tea and found some crackers and cheese, which he made me eat. He stayed until Tara got home, double-checking all the windows and doors before he left. "Tara, make sure she finishes before she goes to bed, okay?"

"Yes, sir. She will not go to bed until she has licked the last crumb from that plate." She saluted him, clicking her heels together.

"Smartass," he muttered as he mussed her hair. "Good night, sweetheart. Call me if you need anything." He kissed me and left.

"All right, you big baby," Tara took over the chair Jack had vacated. "You're on a hunger strike?"

I sighed and pushed the plate of remaining crackers and cheese away. "No. I just don't have an appetite right now. I'll get it back tomorrow I'm sure. Don't fuss, please. Jack's sweet to worry, but it stresses me out."

"Hey." She rubbed my arm. "I'm sorry. I was just teasing. I know this has been hard. Are you doing okay tonight? Anything I can do to help?"

"You know what? Yes. You can talk to me about anything except all this crap going on. Tell me about you and Mat," I ordered. "How are things with you two?"

"Sounds good. Let's go curl up on the couch and gossip about our boyfriends." She grabbed my hand and dragged me over to the couch, where we each settled into a corner and shared the blanket. "It's going great with Mat. He is by far the best boyfriend I've ever had."

"Why? What is it about him?" I felt like we hadn't had a chance to really talk for ages because we were so busy with work and school. It was ironic that we lived together and yet had less time than ever to talk. Tara was my best friend and I missed the closeness we used to share. I was seriously sick of all this Seer/Oracle/stalker crap taking over every aspect of my life so much so that I didn't even pay attention to my best friend. "I've missed you, Tara."

"Oh, sweetie, you really are stressed out, huh? Okay. Wait here." She leaped off the couch and headed to the kitchen. She returned moments later with two pints of ice cream and two spoons. "This is serious; I had to bring out the big guns. Cherry Garcia or Karamel Sutra?"

"Karamel Sutra." My appetite returned as we dug in and began to catch up on all the girl talk we had been missing for so long. Mina came in, exhausted from her late shift, but revived somewhat when I retrieved a pint of Chunky Monkey for her. There's not much that Ben and Jerry can't solve. "So, Tara was telling me just what it is about Mat that does it for her."

"It could be the way he fills out his blue jeans," Mina said softly.

I froze with my spoon halfway to my mouth. Tara choked on her ice cream. "Why, Mina, you sassy minx!" she said. "Have you been scoping out my boyfriend?"

"No, but I'm not blind. He's gorgeous. So is Jack."

I smiled in acknowledgment. "But Tara's dated a lot of gorgeous guys. I want to know what it is about Mat that makes him so special." I motioned toward her with my spoon. "You've been with him longer than any of them. What is it?"

"Hmmm." She appeared to be thinking deeply. "I guess it's the way he treats me, like I'm the most important thing in his whole world. And we can talk about anything. We never run out of stuff to talk about." She looked dreamy.

"Yeah, I'm sure you spend all your time *talking*," I teased, waggling my eyebrows.

"Hey!" She kicked my foot. "Just like you and Jack, huh? You guys sure do a lot of *talking,* too."

As I laughed, I felt the stress melt away. It felt so good that I was determined to stay this way. I made up my mind then and there that I would not be controlled by my circumstances. I was the next Oracle, for God's sake! It was time to take control of my life.

"What about you, Mina?" Tara asked. "Why don't you let us find you a nice guy?"

She smiled sadly. "Does Jack have another cousin?"

"Probably," I said wryly. "But I think you're already interested in someone else, aren't you?"

She stared at me for a long moment before dropping her spoon into her half-empty carton and setting it carefully on the coffee table. "I'm very tired. I'll see you in the morning."

"Mina, I'm sorry," I called after her retreating figure. She stopped and turned back to look at me.

"What am I missing?" said Tara, her head rotating between Mina and me. She caught on quickly. "Ohhhh. You and Rémy, huh? I should have figured that out much earlier." She looked irritated with herself. She got up off the couch and walked over to Mina. "Come back and sit down." She pulled the reluctant girl back and pushed her into the armchair. "I don't know how you all do it in Ireland, but here in America we talk to our girlfriends about the guys we're crushing on. That's what friends are for. Now spill!" She said it in such a funny, mock-threatening way we all laughed.

"Okay," said Mina. "It's just that I haven't had friends in so long I've forgotten I don't have to keep everything in." I noticed her eyes shining with unshed tears.

"So, you do have a thing for Rémy, don't you? I kind of inadvertently saw him kiss you last night," I admitted. "It didn't look like you were objecting."

She dropped her head into her hands and shook her head miserably. "No, I wasn't objecting."

"Cool. Do you realize all three of us have kissed Rémy?" Tara pointed out.

Mina raised her head quickly. "You too?" she asked Tara. "I knew about Ally, but…"

"Oh, yeah. Rémy and I went out for a few weeks when he first got here. But it was just so he could get close to Ally," she said nonchalantly.

"I'm sure it was more than that," said Mina diplomatically.

Tara softened noticeably. "Aww, thanks, Mina. It was fun—I mean, Rémy is a great kisser, and he's absolutely gorgeous—but it didn't mean anything. It was just for laughs."

"So, let me get this straight," I began. "You like Rémy. Rémy kissed you. It was a great kiss, from what I could tell. So, why are you two giving each other the silent treatment? Why aren't you together?"

The tears she had been holding in now streaked down her cheeks. "I don't know! He always pulls away. He won't talk to me about it. I think it's the prophecy. He's afraid of starting something because of that whole 'heart of the Oracle' thing." She sniffed and wiped her eyes. "He just doesn't feel the same way I do. It doesn't matter as much to him. He could have anybody he wants."

"Oh, Mina. You're so wrong. Don't you see? He does feel the same way. In fact, I bet he feels even more than you. He could have anybody, but he wants you. He just doesn't feel like he can have you. Yet. Be patient, Mina. This can't last forever. We'll figure this out. I promise." I felt like I'd been saying that a lot lately.

"And in the meantime," Tara piped in, "we can make him aware of what he's missing by finding you a nice, gorgeous guy to play with."

Mina looked doubtful, but I felt sure Tara would have someone lined up for Mina in the near future.

CHAPTER NINE

*'My charms crack not, my spirits obey, and time
Goes upright with his carriage.'*
—Shakespeare, *The Tempest* 4.1

I woke the next morning to the tantalizing aroma of coffee wafting into my bedroom. "Tara, you are a lifesaver!" I stumbled into the kitchen, rubbing my eyes. Mina didn't drink coffee in the morning, so I knew it was Tara.

"Sorry to disappoint, chérie." Rémy looked up from his iPad. "Nice jammies."

"God, Rémy!" I ran back to my room to get a robe to cover my tank top and boy shorts. "Remind me again why we gave you a key? Thanks," I accepted the mug of coffee he handed me.

"So I could make sure you get a proper cup of coffee once in a while?" he said with a smirk.

I sneered, but he did make the best coffee I'd ever had. Damn it. I'd had the nightmare again and was tired and cranky. "So, to what do I owe the pleasure of your early morning company?"

He ignored me for a moment while he poured another cup, which he handed to Mina as she appeared in the kitchen.

"Oh." She appeared startled and reached up to smooth her hair. "Thank you, Rémy," she whispered and sipped the coffee, although she usually drank tea.

"You're welcome." He smiled, but she had already turned away. His misery showed for a split second before he schooled his features into their normal superior look. "I talked to my grandparents last night. They're coming for a visit during the Christmas holidays."

"Aww, crap." I guess I shouldn't have been surprised; I had made known my decision to not take my usual Christmas jaunt to Ireland or France. It was way too much to hope for that the overseas Seers would let it be. "Well, I'm not going to spend my entire winter break training with Kate. I have not spent a Christmas here in two years! I'm going to enjoy this one. I'm going to spend it making cookies, shopping, and taking my little brother to see Santa Claus. I refuse to waste my entire vacation on Seer stuff!"

"Calm down, chérie. I know. I told them not to expect you to spend all your time with them."

"Ugh! How long will they be here?"

"Probably through New Year's."

I grimaced. "And when do they arrive?"

"Next Saturday."

"Great. Perfect. Not even a day after finals week to relax!"

"Consider how I feel," he said. "They're staying

with me at my apartment."

"Aww, poor Rémy! This is going to seriously cramp your free-wheeling bachelor lifestyle, huh?" I remarked.

Mina choked on her coffee as she tried not to laugh.

"Hilarious," he said.

"Speaking of freewheeling bachelor lifestyles…" Tara sailed into the kitchen, fully dressed and looking gorgeous, as usual. Jeez, living with someone as beautiful as her could really give a person a complex. I looked down at my ratty robe and reached a hand up to my snarled hair, thinking maybe I should try a little harder. "Clear your social calendar for tonight, ladies. We are going out! I've already talked to Mat, who will make sure Jack's there, and will bring a friend for Mina."

It was Rémy's turn to choke on his coffee.

"Oh, I'm sorry, Rémy. I didn't know you were here," Tara lied. "You're invited too, of course. I'm sure you can find a date."

"I'm sure I can." He looked straight at Mina, as if daring her to say something.

She stared back and the tension in the room was palpable. Finally, she squared her shoulders and addressed Tara. "That sounds wonderful. I'm really looking forward to this evening. It will be good to get out and have fun for a change."

Rémy narrowed his eyes at her and addressed Tara. "I have other plans for tonight. Thanks anyway." He gathered his iPad and left without another word.

"That was fun," said Tara.

Mina visibly deflated. "No, it wasn't. I don't like being at odds with him."

"You'll get used to it. We all do," I offered.

"And you are not backing out," Tara declared. "It will be good for him to know you aren't going to sit around and wait for him forever. Mat's bringing his friend Alex tonight. He's a paramedic too."

"You're right." She sat back up, straightening her shoulders and tossing her hair back. "Why shouldn't I go out and have a good time?"

"That's the spirit! You deserve to go out with a hot guy, Mina. You're gorgeous, and if Rémy can't see what's right in front of his face, then too bad! Come on, let's go decide what you're going to wear tonight. I'm sure I have something you can borrow."

I watched them head off to Tara's room, where I'm sure she would find something scandalously slinky for Mina to wear. They were of a similar height and build—tall and slim, not that I'm bitter—so they were able to swap frequently.

***

Although I had my doubts about it, the triple date turned out to be fun. We all went for dinner at a trendy Asian cafe and then to an 18-and-over nightclub for dancing. Mat and Alex, Mina's blind date, were both over 21, but Jack wouldn't turn 21 for a couple of months and Tara and I were both still 18. Alex turned out to be a nice guy and was immediately smitten with Mina. Who wouldn't be, with her black hair and fair complexion and overall beauty? He was good-looking, as well, and they seemed to hit it off. It looked like Rémy might have some competition.

Jack and I had a good time, although it was slightly out of our comfort zone. We weren't the club types and usually preferred to spend our time together watching movies, taking long walks with his dog, or simply talking for hours on end. We never ran out of things to talk about and could be perfectly happy spending the evening with an endless pot of coffee and conversation. Anyway, it was good to put the stress and tension of the past months behind me for an evening.

***

Mina and I accompanied Rémy to the airport to pick up his grandparents the following Saturday. We had discussed how we would try to keep them busy during their stay to minimize the time Kate would certainly want to spend working us to death. I had finished my fall semester finals the afternoon before, and I had no intention of wasting the majority of my Christmas break training. I had never spent a Christmas with Jack and no Oracle on earth would stop me this year.

"Ally, my dear! It is wonderful to see you," exclaimed Phillipe as Kate fawned and fussed over her grandson. He kissed both my cheeks and then pulled back to look into my eyes. "How are you doing?"

I had always liked Phillipe; he tended to let Kate worry about the Oracle/Seer stuff and spent time talking to me about normal things. I had never known a grandfather, so I was happy to adopt Rémy's. "I'm good, Phillipe, thanks. I'm glad you're here."

Kate swapped places with him, hugged me, and started the inquisition. I sighed inwardly and resigned myself to being immersed in the Seer world, at least for the rest of the afternoon. I smiled at Phillipe and Rémy's reunion; he was certainly the apple of his grandfather's eye. I had realized very quickly that Rémy could do no wrong as far as his grandparents were concerned.

We took them out for lunch so we could have a chance to catch up. Rémy chose a steak house that had semi-private booths so our somewhat odd conversation would not be overheard. Phillipe seemed disappointed that he would not be able to try any New Mexican food—Rémy rolled his eyes and muttered he wasn't missing anything—so I promised him I would take him and Kate to a great Mexican place soon, but we would leave Rémy at home.

"Now, Ally, tell us all about what is happening to you," Kate commanded as soon as we had placed our orders and the waiter departed. "Rémy has told us about the dreams and the break-in, but I would like to hear it from you."

So I spent the time until our salads arrived expounding upon the nightmares I had been plagued with all semester and the creepy feeling I was being followed, and how I would occasionally catch a glimpse of a dark figure that no one else seemed to see.

"Oh," I gasped softly. I remembered something that I had never told anyone else about. "I'm okay," I reassured the rest of table, "it's just that I remembered that Michael saw him too. I forgot to tell anyone. I guess the break-in pushed it out of my mind."

"So, this Michael-person saw who was following you? I can't believe you never told me!" Rémy hissed, irritated.

"Sorry!" I hissed back. "I've had a lot going on. My life hasn't been a picnic lately, you know!"

"I can't help you if you keep important things from me," he replied.

"I didn't 'keep' it from you." I used air quotes and my snarkiest tone. "I forgot."

"Mina, how do you put up with these two and their constant harping at each other?" Kate said, exasperated. "Stop it, children!" We ceased. "Now, Ally, in a civilized manner, please tell us about this Michael and what he saw—without any interruptions from you!" She pointed her finger at Rémy, who started to break in.

"Michael is a friend of mine from school. We had a class together this last semester and he sort of, well, attached himself to me."

"She didn't tell him to get lost when she had the chance," Rémy inserted rudely. "What?" he asked when I glared at him. "Can you deny he annoys you more than anything else?"

I shrugged guiltily. "No, I guess not. But he's a nice guy! I feel bad for him. He's well, he's uh—"

"A complete dork?"

"Rémy!" exclaimed Kate.

"No, he's right." I put my head in my hands. "Michael is definitely awkward and, yes, he kind of bugs me. But I think he needs friends."

"That's kind of you, Ally. Continue, please," Kate said.

"We meet for coffee before class a couple times a week. A few weeks ago, we were in the SUB—the Student Union Building—going over our *Tempest* essays when I felt that chill I get. I knew someone was watching me again—that's how I know. Anyway, I turned around and saw him—the guy. I ran after him, down a hallway. Michael followed me and asked who the guy was. Don't you see? He actually saw someone! I'm not imagining it!"

"Of course you're not imagining it, Ally," Mina said in her quiet, assured way.

"Jack and Tara think I am."

"No, Ally. They're just worried about you. Something is happening to you, and they want to help, but they don't know how," she said.

"Mina, love, you are wise beyond your years." Phillipe spoke for the first time since we sat down. "Ally, my dear, something is indeed happening to you. Why do you suppose someone is following you?"

"I have no idea! To drive me crazy?"

He smiled. "That's probably simply an unfortunate side effect. But why you, of all people? What could someone gain by stalking you?"

I shook my head. "I don't know."

"Stalking is about fear and power. Do you have any jealous ex-boyfriends?" Phillipe asked.

"No. My only ex-boyfriend now has his own

boyfriend. They're very happy. He is definitely not stalking me." I thought of Trevor and his current boyfriend, Ricky, and had to laugh.

"Then the only other thing I can think of is that this stalker is somehow connected with the Seer world. It is well-known in certain circles that you are the heir-apparent to the Oracle. There are those who would wish to control you."

"Well, crap. This just keeps getting better and better. And you wonder why I'm not chomping at the bit to take over for Kate?"

"I know, Ally, and I'm sorry." Kate reached over and touched my hand. "We don't get to choose. It chooses us."

The arrival of our entrees saved me from giving my true opinion of this sorry situation.

As we ate and I tried to avert my eyes from the bloody mess of Rémy's prime rib—he always ordered it rare—Kate questioned me about the details of the break-in. "So, tell me exactly what was taken, Ally? What was disturbed?"

I sighed and pushed my veggie plate away; talking about the break-in always twisted my stomach in knots. I was going to end up with an ulcer if my life didn't calm down pretty soon. "The only area disturbed was my bedroom. The intruder broke the window to get in. I noticed my top dresser drawer wasn't closed all the way and I could tell my underwear had been rifled through. A pair was missing."

"And what—"

"Grand-mère," Rémy interrupted. He leaned toward her and began speaking in rapid French, too rapid for my beginning skills to make sense of. She seemed to argue with him for a moment before giving in to whatever it was he wanted and sat back in her seat.

"Ally, I am sorry. My grandson has reminded me of my table manners and that we should speak of less weighty issues so as not to interfere with our digestion." She looked meaningfully at the plate I had pushed away.

I looked at Rémy and raised my eyebrows. What an aggravating man! One second he was harassing me, the next he was looking out for me. He winked at me and shoved another disgusting chunk of meat in his mouth.

***

Rémy was true to his word and kept his grandparents as busy as possible during their two-week stay. He took them to all the touristy sights: Old Town, the Tram, and the Breaking Bad locations—it turns out Phillipe was a huge fan of Walter White. He even took them to Santa Fe for a weekend, which gave me a nice break. I made good on my promise and took them out for Mexican food, since I knew Rémy would steer them away from it. I dragged Jack along and we took them to El Patron, one of our favorite restaurants. In addition to good food, it had mariachis, which no self-respecting tourist should miss. They were highly amused by the Mexican kitsch, and Phillipe loved the food. Kate was more reticent about trying the chile and seemed to share her grandson's prejudice against

American food, although she was much nicer about it. They were eager to meet Jack, since I had talked about him for the past two summers.

"So, Jack…" Kate began the interrogation as soon as the chips and salsa had been delivered. "Ally tells us that you are in the army?"

"Yes, ma'am. I'm in the reserves right now, in officer training, and I'll be regular army after I graduate."

"What are you studying?" Phillipe asked.

"I'm a mechanical engineering major."

"Ah, you must be very intelligent, then. Engineering is considered a difficult field." Phillipe tried to butter me up by complimenting my boyfriend.

"Yes, Phillipe, he is," I said. "In fact, he's brilliant."

Jack rolled his eyes. "No, I'm just good at math and physics. I can't write to save my life. That's Ally's field."

"So, when will you be graduating?"

"Well, I started college with a lot of credits from community college, so I could probably graduate at the end of next year if I really worked at it. But that would leave me very little time to spend with Ally, so I'll probably just take the full four years."

Kate smiled at both of us. "Well, I can certainly understand that. You are very lucky to have her, young man."

"I know that," he said as he took my hand under the table. "I'll do whatever it takes to keep her."

"I'm the lucky one," I said. "Jack has put up with so much over the past few years with all this Seer business."

"You're worth it," he replied simply and leaned in to kiss me briefly, regardless of our audience. "Besides, are you forgetting what a bad bet I was when we first met?" At Kate's inquisitive look, he continued, "I was on probation when Ally and I first met. I got arrested and spent nearly a year in juvenile detention for selling drugs. Ally never told you that, huh?"

"That's because it's not important. It's not who you are," I said staunchly. I hated when he referred to his past as if he had been some kind of criminal. He had such a tender heart and had suffered so much when his mother was killed that he had gone crazy for a few years. He still bore the emotional scars from that time and probably would for the rest of his life.

"Well, she could certainly do better, but I kind of hope she doesn't figure that out," he said gallantly.

I was about to answer back when a vision struck, taking me by surprise. I couldn't catch my breath and gasped for air like a fish. It wasn't clear like most of the visions I'd had in the past; it was nothing but a series of disjointed, terrifying images.

Darkness…cold…screaming…blood. Lots of blood, on my hands, on my clothes, on my face. I could smell the coppery tang hanging in the air, surrounding me, encompassing me, smothering me.

"Ally!" Jack shook me. "Breathe, babe, breathe!"

I finally took a huge breath and slumped against him. I felt cold wetness against my cheek as he dipped his napkin in his water and wiped my face. "I'm okay," I whispered, trying to believe it.

"What happened, querida? A vision?"

I nodded and looked up to see Kate and Phillipe staring at me, concerned.

"What did you see, Ally?" demanded Kate.

I shook my head, refusing to speak of it.

"Give me your hand." Kate held hers out to me expectantly. I reluctantly put my cold fingers in her warm palm. She squeezed it, bringing her other hand up to cover and chafe warmth into mine, as she concentrated on seeing into my mind. "Oh, my dear. I'm so sorry that you have to see these things. I wish I could take this from you."

"What? What did she see?" Jack demanded, pushing my hair aside to wipe the back of my neck with the cold napkin. "She's white as a ghost."

"She saw images for the most part. Blood, darkness. Nothing was very clear. Did you know that she can hear and even smell in her visions? I've never heard of anyone having such clarity. Oh, my gracious!"

"Yeah, well, do you see what this does to her? Do you see why she doesn't want this? Goddammit! I hate to see her like this!" His ferocity probably shocked Kate and Phillipe.

"Jack, I'm all right, I promise. It was just so sudden." I sat up and returned the wet napkin to the table. I made up my mind not to let the awful vision ruin what had been, up until a few moments ago, a perfectly lovely evening. These stupid visions had already ruined enough for me—I was not about to let them win. Besides, I had learned that there wasn't a whole hell of lot I could do about them anyway. "You know what we need? Fried ice cream."

Jack took my face in his hands and stared hard, looking to see if I was just putting on a brave front. I was, but it would have to be enough for now. He obviously decided the same thing because he nodded and said, "Okay. Fried ice cream it is." He caught the attention of a passing waiter and put our order in.

"What in the world is 'fried ice cream'? How is that even possible?" Phillipe puzzled.

I laughed, glad to move past the terrifying vision and into the culinary delight that was the staple dessert of Mexican restaurants across America. "It's amazing! They take a scoop of ice cream, cover it in this crispy, honey cornflake-type coating, and then deep-fry it. Then they pour on chocolate sauce and whipped cream and top it with a cherry. You're going to love it!"

"It sounds, um…delightful, dear," Kate said with a disbelieving look at Phillipe. When the desserts arrived, it amused me to watch her poke at it with her spoon, trying to break through the outer coating to get to the ice cream within. She ate enough to be polite before surrendering the rest to Phillipe, who seemed to like it well enough.

Just as we were finishing, the mariachi band came to our area of the restaurant and Jack requested they play *Paloma Querida* for me. They stayed at our table, conversing in Spanish with Jack for a while. He also asked them to play *Las Mañanitas* for me since my birthday was the following week.

"A Christmas birthday?" Kate asked, surprised. "How do you like that?"

"It's okay," I began.

"As long as she gets separate presents," Jack cut in, teasing.

"That's right. No Christmas/birthday presents allowed."

"That's one of the first conversations we ever had. Do you remember, Ally?" Jack asked, putting his arm around me as the mariachis played.

"I remember you freaking out and backing off," I accused.

He chuckled. "Yeah, well, that's because I found out you were only 16 years old. I was 18 and had it bad for you. All I could think was 'jailbait.' Of course I was freaked out."

"I went home and looked up the law online to make sure it was legal."

"You did? I never knew that."

"I had it bad for you too, Mr. Ruiz." I realized that we were ignoring our guests, so I squeezed his hand and turned back to Kate and Phillipe.

***

"Jack, I really think Megan would love the unicorn dress we saw at Macy's." Jack had picked me up from work an hour earlier and begged me to go to the mall with him for a last minute gift for Megan. I was exhausted from a busy afternoon at the restaurant and wanted nothing more than to go home and put my feet up. Tara and I had driven together as we were scheduled for the same shift, but she had gone home early, saying she didn't feel well, so I had called Jack to pick me up. "Jack, slow down, please!" I struggled to keep up with his much longer legs as he strode through the mall.

"Sorry, babe." He slowed down for me. "I just want to look a little more, okay? I'm not sure about the color on that unicorn dress."

What? Since when did Jack *ever* care about the color of any type of clothing? For that matter, I had never known him to even think about choosing clothes for Megan, preferring to have Trina, Shelly, or even me do that. "I thought you already bought all of Megan's Christmas presents," I accused, suddenly suspicious.

"Uh, yeah, but I want to get her a, um, a dress. Yeah."

I guess I should be glad that Jack is a terrible liar; he'll never be able to get away with cheating on me. "A dress? Okay." I decided to play along and see where he went with this.

Another hour and the original unicorn dress later, we were finally done and headed toward the parking lot. I saw Jack check his phone right before he detoured us to Barnes and Noble, saying he wanted a cup of coffee.

"Coffee? Now? Really, Jack?" Liar, liar, pants on fire.

"Yeah. I'm parched. Shopping makes me really thirsty," he declared as he dragged me to the coffee counter in the bookstore.

I waited until we were seated, waiting for our coffee order. I had ordered my usual mocha latte and pondered why Jack had ordered a white chocolate caramel mocha, extra hot, extra shot of espresso, in lieu of his usual cup of whatever was freshly brewed. Was he trying to stall for more time?

"What?" he sounded guilty.

"Who are you and what have you done with my boyfriend? Clothes shopping? Fancy coffee? Really? What is going on?"

"Shit," he muttered. "I told her I couldn't pull this off."

"Told who? What is going on?" I demanded.

"Okay, look, sweetheart. I'm really bad at this. I promised Tara I would keep you away from the house for a while. Please don't ask me why. Just go along with it. I'm begging you. She's going to bust my…uh, *chops* if I screw this up."

"Why would she need me away from the house? I thought she was sick?" I pondered what Tara could possibly be up to and suddenly remembered the calendar. Duh. My birthday. "A surprise party? Are you guys throwing me a surprise party?"

"I can neither confirm nor deny that. Are you mad?"

"Mad? Why would I be mad? Nobody has ever thrown me a surprise party, Jack. This is so sweet! No, I'm not mad. I know I don't usually love parties—"

"Understatement of the century," he muttered.

"But when it's for me, I can make an exception."

"Can you please act surprised? Tara is going to kill me."

"Don't worry. I'm so excited it'll look like I'm

surprised. Who all is coming?"

"Oh, no you don't! I'm not telling. At least you'll have something to be surprised about." He refused to tell me anything else. "Ugh." He grimaced as he took a sip of his white chocolate caramel mocha. "This is disgusting. Way too sweet. You want it?" So, I alternated between sips of each flavor, thinking I would never get to sleep tonight with so much late afternoon caffeine.

***

I thought I did a fairly decent job of acting surprised, but I tried not to overdo it. I was surprised by how many people were there: my family, quite a few members of Jack's family; my friends—including Travis and his new flame, Rick; Rémy and his grandparents; Mat, and even Alex. He and Mina had been dating for a few weeks now; the attempt to make Rémy jealous had turned into a romance for real. I didn't know how I felt about it, since I knew she had deep feelings for Rémy, but figured it was none of my business and hoped she could grab some happiness where it was available.

I was in the kitchen, refilling the chip bowl, when Tara finally cornered me. "So, he couldn't pull it off, huh? How long did it take you to figure it out? Give me that. This is your party. You don't have to replenish the refreshments." She took the chip bag from me and finished refilling the bowl.

"How could you tell? I thought I did pretty well when everyone popped out and yelled 'surprise!'"

"You did okay, but Jack looked super guilty. I

didn't know for sure until now." I threw a chip at her. "Hey! You should be glad that he's a wretched liar."

"Oh, I am. I just hoped I was better. So, you thought it was a good idea to get Rémy and Alex in the same room, huh? Just gotta stir stuff up, don't you?"

"He's in love with Mina, you know. And I think she's in love with him too. I'm just trying to get them to see it."

"What about Alex? He and Mina are dating. She's with him now." I needed Tara to see there was another person involved in this; her predilection for match-making could hurt someone this time.

"Ally, it's not always a forever thing like it is with you and Jack. It's not always true love."

"I know that! I'm not naïve. But people have feelings, Tara." We stared at each other across the kitchen. "Hey, I'm sorry. This is a great party. I love it. Thanks." I crossed the room and hugged my best friend. "Just be careful, okay?"

"Okay. Point taken." She hugged me back. "Now get out there and enjoy your party! You haven't been here for your birthday in years! I wanted to do something special. You deserve it, Ally." She hugged me again and shoved me out of the kitchen.

***

Later, after most of the guests had left, I headed to the family room to collect empty cups. I stumbled upon Mina and Rémy arguing. I am ashamed to admit I ducked back behind the entryway to listen.

"I don't owe you any sort of explanation, Rémy!"

"Really, Mina? And you are dating this man, this Alex? What do you know about him?"

"I know everything I need to know! He is handsome and kind to me. I like spending time with him."

"Do you love him?"

"Love him? What are you talking about? We have only been going out for a few weeks!" I had never heard Mina sound so angry; she was usually so soft-spoken.

"Are you sleeping with him?"

"This conversation is over! You can go to hell, Rémy!"

"So, it's not serious then?"

"I didn't say that. It's truly none of your business, you know. You have no say in the matter. You don't own me."

He cursed in French and I heard him start to walk away. I realized too late that I had no good escape route, so I just stood there, looking guilty. He stopped when he saw me. "Maybe you can talk some sense into her. Or do you applaud what she is doing?"

"I, uh, I…"

He threw his hands in the air and walked away, still muttering in French.

***

The rest of the guests finally cleared out around

midnight and the three of us girls finished cleaning up the kitchen. Mina slammed cabinets and put the dishes away with much more force than necessary.

"*What is going on with her*?" Tara mouthed silently to me.

"*Rémy,*" I mouthed back. I set my dishtowel down with a sigh and walked over to Mina, took the stack of plates out of her hand, and led her to sit at the table. "Hey, talk to us. I overheard your fight with Rémy earlier."

She stared at the table briefly before dropping her head to her arms and screaming. "He makes me so angry! He doesn't want me, but no one else can have me, either! What a hypocrite! He goes out all the time!"

"He's a pig, what can I say?" Tara offered. I gave her the look that said she wasn't helping. "Besides, he does want you. He just doesn't think he should."

"Why? Because of the stupid prophecy? Nobody knows what it really means! Ugh! I'm so sick of living my life in accordance with that fucking prophecy!"

"Tell us how you really feel, Mina," I said sarcastically.

"I'm sorry," she said, somewhat calmer. "That was uncalled for."

"No." I shook my head. "It was definitely called for."

"But I don't understand why he's letting it get in the way," Tara said. "I mean, you haven't let it come between you and Jack."

"No, but I've been with Jack since before the

prophecy. I think Rémy feels much more bound by it for some reason. He really tried to make a romance happen between us that first summer, tried to go along with what his grandmother wanted. But even he couldn't deny how awkward our kiss felt. I take it there's no awkwardness when he kisses you, Mina?"

"No. Awkward is certainly not how I would describe it."

"What about Alex?" I asked. "Where does he figure in all of this? He's a nice guy and I'd hate to see him get hurt."

She dropped her head back to her hands. "I don't know. He *is* a nice guy and I like him. But…"

"He's not 'the one'?" Tara asked.

"No. I don't think so. Can we finish cleaning this up in the morning?"

"Sure," Tara and I said in unison.

Mina nodded. "Goodnight." She left the kitchen and went to bed quietly, just as she did everything else in her life. I wondered if I would ever really know her.

***

The day before Kate and Phillipe left, my presence was requested/required at a private luncheon with Kate. I dreaded going because I knew a private tête-à-tête with her meant I would hear some stuff I didn't want to hear. I was right, but she lured me in and disarmed me with high tea, complete with scones and Devonshire clotted cream at the St. James Tea Room. It was a sneaky, sadistic grandmother-type trick and I totally fell for it.

"Would you like another cup of oolong, Ally?"

"Thanks, Kate. This is great. I've heard about this place, but I've never been," I said as I looked around the tearoom, admiring the frilly, fussy decor. It was a total chick place; I could just imagine Jack cringing if I ever brought him here. It felt a little bit like I was on the set of *Downton Abbey*. Grams would adore it and I began to make plans to bring her here for her birthday.

"I'm so glad you like it. Ally, I wanted to have a chance to talk to you privately before I left."

Oh, great. I knew it. The vast amounts of tea and scones in my stomach started churning. I had always put my stress in my stomach; lately this meant my stomach was constantly upset. "Sure, Kate. What did you want to talk about?"

"Ally, we need to talk about your future."

Crap, crap, crap, crap, crap. "Okay," I said it more as a question.

"My dear, I feel you are, well, floundering a bit. I think it's time for action."

"Action? What do you want me to do? I don't have a lot of spare time, you know, between college and work."

"I'm concerned with your lack of training opportunities here. I'm glad you and Rémy and Mina are together, but I feel that, as the next Oracle, you should be spending a lot more time with me." She poured herself more tea as she spoke, then skewered me with her laser-like stare over the rim of her tea cup.

"So, you and Phillipe are going to stay here in

Albuquerque for a while?" I asked hopefully.

"No, dear. That's not possible, I'm afraid."

I shook my head as I tried to keep the food I was stupid enough to eat down in my stomach where it belonged. "No, Kate. I can't go back to traveling to Europe every few months. I can't do it!"

"I don't want that, either." She patted my hand and then sat back in her pink armchair. "That's why I think you should move to France. I've made arrangements for you to spend next year studying at the university in Rouen. It will be a wonderful opportunity for you."

What? No friggin' way! "Kate." I tried my best to stay calm. "I appreciate the thought, but I have no intention of moving to France for a year. My life is here. My family is here."

"What about Rémy? His family and his life are in France. Is he to be forever uprooted because you are not willing to compromise?"

Holy shit! How long had she been keeping that in? "Kate, I'm so sorry. I feel terrible about that, but I don't want—"

"It's not just that, Ally. You, Mina, and Rémy are bonded in some way, but I need to spend time with you all in order to understand why. I have been having more visions, much like yours, that make me think this situation is moving toward a crisis of some sort. We need to stay together."

I excused myself to go the bathroom, where I threw up the beautiful cream tea I had consumed. It was certainly not anywhere near beautiful the second time around, but I immediately felt about a thousand percent better.

"God, Kate. This is a lot to lay on me," I said when I returned to the table. "What does Rémy have to say about this?"

"He will do whatever you want. He is utterly devoted to protecting you. He will, however, be finished with graduate school in the spring and be ready to take on the reins of our business." Rémy had explained his family business was a fairly vast import/export empire, hence his international business degree.

"Okay, Kate. I get it. I really do, but I need some time to think about all this. Please?"

"Of course. Why don't we finish our tea and speak of other, more pleasant things?"

I sipped a little tea to get the awful taste out of my mouth, but refused to eat anything else. I wondered if the ache in my stomach was a permanent addition.

CHAPTER TEN

*"My master through his art foresees the danger
That you, his friend, are in, and sends me
forth,—"*
—Shakespeare, *The Tempest* 2.1

I guess I shouldn't have been surprised when I got the call from Fionnuala. It was, after all, too much to hope that she hadn't heard of her sister's visit to the U.S. She informed me she and Caoimhe would be arriving in Albuquerque the following week and that they would be staying with me. I argued that Rémy had a spare bedroom, but she said they weren't comfortable staying with a bachelor. So, Mina emptied a few drawers for them and moved into my room for the week. I might as well have gone to Europe over the break for all the time I was spending with the various Seers in my life. Argh! Jack, usually so laid back and easygoing, actually expressed his irritation over all the out-of-town visitors.

"Jesus, Ally! We haven't been able to spend any

time together! Can't you tell them no?" He kissed my neck as he said it, so I had to re-focus my thoughts before answering him.

"Jack, you know that renders me speechless and witless." I reluctantly pulled myself out of his arms and sat on the opposite side of the sofa. He pulled my feet into his lap, pulled off my socks, and started rubbing them. Just one of the many reasons I loved this man with my whole heart. "I tried, I really did, but you can't argue with Fionnuala. She is a force of nature. I swear I won't let her take all my time, though. She's Rémy's aunt, so he can take sight-seeing duty." I hadn't told Jack that Kate was lobbying for me to move to France for a year; I had no intention of actually doing it so I didn't think it was worth upsetting him. I could hardly wait to see what Fionnuala and Caoimhe had in mind for me. "I'm sorry I've been neglecting you." I pulled my feet away and crawled over to him. "Let me make it up to you," I whispered against his lips. He gladly took me up on my offer, pulling me into his arms and kissing me senseless. He pushed me down into the couch cushions and moved his hand up under my shirt to caress my back—he never let himself go too far, more's the pity. I was thinking how nice it was to have my own house where we could do this, uninterrupted by parental units, when we were interrupted by my roommate and her boyfriend walking in and plopping down on the love seat across from us.

"Get a room, you two," Tara said. Mat just grinned at his cousin and winked at me.

"We have a room," I groused, not letting Jack

pull away from me. "It's called *my* living room. Go away."

Jack kissed me quickly and sat up, smoothing my shirt down in the back. "Great timing, as usual, Mat. Why aren't you at the apartment, kissing your girlfriend on our couch?"

"Because I'm having a hard time stopping at just kissing, to be honest. I thought it was a good idea to come over here and watch a movie. Looks like we're just in time, huh, *primo*?"

"Yeah, yeah, I know," Jack muttered. I didn't fully understand the pact that the two cousins had made to not push Tara and me into a more physical relationship, but they both felt we were still too young, at least compared to them. I was already 19 and Tara would be in a few months, but Jack was nearly 21 and Mat had just turned 22. It was very sweet, but Tara and I were both starting to get frustrated, in more ways than one!

"So, is Trina throwing you a big birthday bash for your twenty-first, Jack?" Tara had obviously been reminded of the age difference, as well.

He shrugged and sighed. "Probably. She never listens when I tell her I would prefer a quiet family dinner."

"But you get so many more presents when you have a big party!" My extroverted best friend could never understand how someone would prefer a small group gathering.

"I don't need any presents. I've got everything I need right here." He kissed the top of my hair. Tara and Mat made gagging sounds, but I pulled him down for a well-deserved kiss.

"So, I guess that means I can return the gas cap I got you for the 'Stang," said Mat with a smirk. Jack's had been stolen a few weeks before in the UNM parking lot.

Jack threw a pillow at him. "Well, I guess I can put up with a party. I really want that gas cap."

***

Fionnuala and Caoimhe arrived a week later, sweeping in majestically and declaring their intention to spend every spare moment with Mina and me. Over my cold, dead body! I knew they were just trying to make sure they got equal time with us; there was truly no useful purpose to the visit, except the invitation they issued for Mina and me to spend a semester in Ireland. I noticed the invitation did not seem to include Rémy. We spent several afternoons with them before I foisted them off on my grandmother, who was only too glad to entertain them, taking them to see whatever it was old ladies liked. Imagine my surprise when I came in late from work one evening to find them gathered around the kitchen table, downing shots of tequila and laughing uproariously.

"No, no! The blond's was much bigger! I swear it was!" Fionnuala exclaimed.

"No way! The one with the tribal tattoo had a much bigger—"

"Grams!" I interrupted, seemingly in the nick of time. "What are you all doing?"

"We are just enjoying a wee nip before I head home." She spoke very precisely, intent on correctly pronouncing her words; I had no intention of letting her drive anywhere tonight.

"So, where did you all go this evening?" God only knew when Grams was in control of the agenda.

"Oh, your grandmother took us to one of those Indian casinos and we saw the loveliest show: Thunder from somewhere or other…" She fumbled and drank another shot.

"From Down Under?" They all nodded and giggled. Good God! My grandmother had taken Rémy's aunt and her friend to see a male strip review. "Well, I'm sure that was educational," I quipped. "And it's 'Native American,' Fionnuala. Please don't say 'Indian' in public, especially around here." I confiscated their half-full bottle of Patrón Silver.

"It *was* educational! You have no idea, Ally!" Caoimhe piped up. "All the dancers were slick and hairless like a bunch of greased-up infants! I wonder how they do that?"

"Lots and lots of waxing, most likely," I said, taking their shot glasses. Where did those come from? We didn't have any.

"They looked more like naked mole-rats," Fionnuala added. They all laughed drunkenly.

"Okay, ladies. It's time for bed. Let's go." I pulled Fionnuala and Caoimhe up and started hauling them to Mina's bedroom. "Oh, no, you don't." I propped them against the wall and zipped over to pry my grandmother's car keys out of her hand. "I'm certainly not letting you get behind the wheel in your condition. You taught me better than that." I pocketed her keys and finished helping my Irish guests to their room, where I laid each on the bed, removed their shoes, and covered them with a quilt.

I tucked Grams in on my couch while she protested that she certainly wasn't drunk, but was maybe the slightest bit tipsy and would just take a short nap. Yeah, like an eight-hour nap.

I was pouring coffee the next morning when Jack let himself in, slipped his arms around me from behind, and nuzzled my ear. "Is that your Grams asleep on the couch?" he asked and then spied the tequila on the counter next to the shot glasses. He looked at me with raised eyebrows. "Did I miss a drinking party last night?"

"Yes, and so did I, apparently." I handed him a cup of coffee and told him how my grandmother had taken my two senior citizen guests to see the male strippers. He choked on his coffee.

"Wow. She is nothing like my grandmother."

"You should be grateful for that," I said.

"Oh, I am. Believe me. God, I guess her asking me if I carried a condom on our first date was mild compared to this, huh?"

I laughed in agreement and sipped my own coffee, then leaned against the counter, thinking. "Did you?" The words popped out of my mouth before I could stop them.

"Did I what?" He looked at me, confused.

"Did you carry a condom on our first date? Do you now?"

He just stared at me like I had grown another head.

"I'm sorry. It's none of my business. Sorry." I concentrated on drinking my coffee.

He sighed and put his cup down on the table, then walked over to me, took the cup out of my hand, and set it on the counter next to me. "Look at me, Ally." He lifted my chin with his finger. "It is absolutely your business. Since the very first day in English class, when I dragged you to the bathroom after you had that vision, it's been your business and only your business." He kissed me tenderly. "And yes. I have carried a condom in my wallet since I was fourteen."

"Fourteen?" I squeaked.

"Shh." He kissed me again. "I was an idiot. I did a lot of stupid things back then, Ally. The smartest thing I ever did was ask you out."

"Did you ask me out? I don't remember it like that."

"Oh, and how exactly do you remember it, Ms. Moran?"

"I remember you backing me up against your car and kissing the crap out of me."

"Is that right? Kind of like this?" We didn't speak for several minutes as he ravaged my mouth.

"So, you still do?" I asked when he pulled back.

He rested his forehead against mine. "You're not gonna let this go, are you, babe? Why? What's going on? This isn't about my past, is it? You've really never had a problem with it. What's up?"

"I just…we've been going out for more than two years, Jack. Why don't you want to, um, well, you know—take our relationship farther?"

"Maybe because you can't bring yourself to say

it yet." He took the sting out of his words by pushing my hair behind my ear, which he knows I love. "Ally, sweetheart, I want to make love with you more than I can possibly say, and yes, I carry a condom just in case there comes a time when I absolutely cannot resist you one second longer. But," he forestalled me as I opened my mouth to speak, "I hope I can resist for a little longer. Ally, it's not just about the physical pleasure with us, although I'm positive that will be phenomenal. It's about the commitment. When we take that step, I need it to be always and forever. I know that's incredibly old-fashioned—"

"Archaic, actually," I inserted.

"But I need to be able to hold you all night long and wake up next to you the next morning. Every morning. We aren't ready for that quite yet. Almost, but not yet." He looked into my eyes. "Can you understand that? Can you be patient for just a little longer?"

I melted at the pleading look in his eyes. "Of course, Jack. I guess I just needed to know that it's as hard for you as it is for me."

"That's an appropriate choice of word, querida. More than you know."

"What? What word—oh. Sorry," I whispered.

He laughed and hugged me. "Oh, Ally. I absolutely adore you." He kissed me again, thoroughly. "Please trust me on this. I never want us to feel guilty about anything we do together. I want it to be pure joy."

What could I possibly say to that? I don't know what I had ever done to deserve this incredible man, but I knew a good thing when I saw it. "I absolutely trust you, Jack. About everything." This time I kissed him.

This was, of course, when Grams decided to stumble into the kitchen, groaning and clutching her head.

***

I guess I shouldn't have been surprised on the first day of the spring semester to find Michael in my Feminist Literature class. We were both English majors, and were bound to run into each other in upper level classes like this. I had finished all my core classes finally, and was able to concentrate on education courses this semester, with room left for one lit class. Of course, the education building was all the way across campus from the humanities building, so I would get plenty of exercise.

"Hey, Ally, how was your break? What else are you taking this semester? Can we still get together before class for coffee?" He finally stopped for a breath.

"Um, hi, Michael. I'm not sure which question to answer first. Break was good, I guess. Busy. I worked a lot. I'm taking mostly education courses and yes, we can still meet in the SUB for coffee. How did I do?"

He ducked his head, embarrassed. "Sorry. I got a little carried away, I guess. I'm just glad to see you. I missed you."

Awww, how...awkward. He looked so hopeful. Great. This was all I needed: he still carried a torch for me. I needed to nip this in the bud quickly. "Thanks, Michael. So, what did you do over the break? I spent a lot of time with my boyfriend." I watched his face fall. Jeez, way to go, Ally! Hit him over the head with it, why don't you?

"Oh. Same one? Or a new guy?"

"Same one. Jack." I bit my lip, feeling sorry for him. He was a really nice guy, just kind of awkward. "So what did you do? Any new ladies in your life?" I teased.

"Yeah, right." He grimaced. "Like that's gonna happen. No, I mostly just played video games. Hung out. Played D & D some."

Wow. He was like the poster child for nerds. But even nerds deserve some love, so I went through my mental contact list, looking for someone who might be a good match for Michael. Bingo! One of the waitresses at work always talked about anime, video games, and other nerdy stuff and she was pretty cute. Maybe I could work out a meeting between the two of them. "That sounds fun," I said, hoping he wouldn't see through my fake enthusiasm.

"Yeah! Hey, do you play? I bet I could get my dungeon master to let you in our group."

Nope, he didn't see through it. "Um, that does sound great, but I don't really have time for anything else right now. Sorry. So, this seems like a cool class, huh? I can't wait to see the reading list." I desperately tried to change the subject.

The reading list turned out to be interesting, with books I hadn't read. I loved studying literature and looked forward to someday teaching it. Too bad it doesn't pay much.

Later that afternoon, after a full day of classes, I walked toward my SUV after the shuttle dropped me off. The bad thing about an urban university was the parking nightmare—my parking permit was for a lot so far away they had to provide a courtesy shuttle. As I neared the car, I noticed a red, long-stem rose had been tucked under the windshield wiper. I smiled as I removed it and sniffed its delicate perfume. How sweet of Jack to do this on the first day of the semester.

Me: Thanks for the rose! It made me smile at the end of a very long first day back! Love you!

Jack: What rose?

My smile faded as I read his text and my hand trembled as I replied.

Me: You didn't leave a rose on my windshield?

I already knew the answer as the bouquet of roses left on my doorstep weeks ago finally flashed through my mind.

Jack: No.

Then my phone rang.

"Jack? There was a rose on my windshield. It was him, wasn't it? The guy who broke into my house and left the bouquet and stole my underwear? Wasn't it?" I was babbling and crying, probably not making much sense.

"Where are you now, Ally?" He sounded grim and I could hear him cursing under his breath.

"I'm still in the parking lot. I just got in the car."

"Lock your doors. Now."

"Okay." I did, then rolled down the window just enough to throw the rose to the ground outside; I couldn't stand having it in the car with me one second longer.

"I want you to drive straight to the shop, okay? Don't stop anywhere, promise me? Ally?"

"Yes. I promise." I hung up and, with shaking hands, put the car in reverse and backed out of my spot. I concentrated on not hyperventilating while I drove. I couldn't stop the tears from flowing freely down my face and my stomach immediately started to hurt. Jack was waiting for me in front his uncle's auto body shop, pacing, when I pulled up. He waited impatiently while I unlocked the door, then wrenched it open, barely waiting for me to undo my seatbelt before pulling me into his arms.

"Are you okay?" he said against my hair.

I nodded. "Yes. I'm just scared. Why is this happening?"

"I don't know, babe, but I'm going to kill the son of bi—" His words were drowned out by the squeal of Rémy's tires as he sped into the parking lot and parked next to my car. Of course. When my thoughts went crazy like they had when I discovered the rose, I couldn't keep anything from him. I'm sure my fear transmitted to him like a homing beacon.

"Is she all right?" he demanded.

"Yeah, just scared. Rémy, can't you do anything

about this? Can't you, I don't know, get vibes or something from the rose about who it is?" Jack asked.

"Probably not, but I can try," he shrugged. "Let me see it."

"I threw it out. I didn't want it in my car." I pulled away from Jack and wiped my eyes. "Sorry."

"It's okay, chérie. Don't worry about it. If it happens again, though, save it."

"You two must be getting sick of rescuing me." I sniffed, searching through my coat pockets for a tissue.

"No, chérie. It's my job," Rémy replied as he handed me a handkerchief. I know, a handkerchief? And, yes, it was monogrammed.

"Actually, it's my job," Jack spit out through gritted teeth, his jaw flexing in irritation.

"I was speaking of the prophecy," Rémy said. "You don't own her, you know."

"Okay, you two. Let's dial it down." I stepped between them, hoping to deflect a little of the free flowing testosterone. "I don't want it to be anyone's job. I want to stand on my own two feet. I hate this!" I nearly stamped my foot in frustration.

Rémy put his arm around me and pulled me in for an awkward side hug, probably to keep Jack from slugging him. "Ally, you are one of the strongest people I know. This is too big for one person to handle. If, as my grandparents think, it concerns Seers, then it also involves Mina and myself. Don't be afraid to lean on us. We want— no—we need to help."

I hugged him briefly and then stepped back into

the shelter of Jack's arms. "Querida, don't make me tell you why it's my job," he warned.

"I know. I just don't like feeling helpless."

"You are the least helpless person I know. Nobody who has been knocked flat on their ass by your blue light power-thingy would ever think you're helpless," Jack assured me.

"That's for sure," Rémy muttered.

"Rémy, will you follow her home? I'll come by after work, Ally, okay?"

"Yeah," I said, trying to smile. "Stay for dinner. I'm not cooking, don't worry. It's Mina's turn so it will be delicious."

"You're not that bad a cook. Anyway, I just want to be with you."

"I'm a terrible cook and I know it. Rémy, you should stay too."

"We'll see. Are you ready to go?"

***

To my flame-haired minx: Tu es ma joie de vivre. "What is one man's and one woman's love and desire, against the history of two worlds?"

"Son of a bitch!" Jack exclaimed, throwing the *Daily Lobo* on the table in aggravation. "This has got to stop!" The creepy personal ads had picked back up the second week of the semester at least once and sometimes twice a week. "Is the quote from a book you're reading?"

I didn't say anything; I just gestured to the book

that sat on the tabletop, *Four Ways to Forgiveness* by Ursula LeGuin. It was one of the creepiest aspects of the ads, the fact that the writer always knew what I was reading at the moment. I stopped reading the paper, sick to death of the personal ads and the unwelcome notoriety that went with them. People still stopped to ask if I was the red-haired girl referred to in the ads, and although I always told them no, it still annoyed me to have random strangers accost me in the SUB.

"I am going to find out who is placing those ads," Jack promised. "I'm fed up with this."

"Jack, forget it. There's no way to find out. Brian has tried, but without probable cause he can't get a warrant. It's fine. There's really no harm being done."

"No physical harm, maybe, but it's doing a number on you mentally, Ally. You don't say much about it, but I can tell it adds to your stress."

He was right, but I kept quiet. My stress was at an all-time high and it was all I could do to keep functioning on a daily basis. The roses continued, as well, often appearing on my windshield, other times waiting for me on my front porch, once even delivered to me at work. Although Rémy and I had both tried to sense where they came from by holding them, all we got was a blank. Rémy was convinced this was proof that Seers were somehow involved because any normal item would have some residual energy; the roses were a completely blank slate.

"Okay," Jack sighed, standing up. "This is me not talking about it anymore. What do you want for lunch?”

“Um, just a bottle of water, please. I’m not hungry right now.”

He sat back down and took my hand, waiting until I looked up. “Wrong answer, babe. You need to eat. I know this makes your stomach hurt, but you gotta eat something. You’re losing weight.”

I smiled crookedly. He was concerned about my stomach issues and lack of appetite, as was my family. “Sure, okay. Get me a sandwich. Thanks.” He brought me back a veggie wrap, which I used to love, but didn’t look appetizing in the least at the moment. I knew he expected me to eat it, so I made an attempt, nibbling at one half before I realized I would throw up if I continued. “I swear I’ll eat it later, Jack. I just can’t right now. That stupid ad,” I finished on a whisper, ashamed to feel tears building. I sniffed and tossed my head, determined not to let the stress, the ads, or the stalker win.

“Okay,” he said grimly. “It’s okay, babe. Hey,” he changed the subject, “you remember that I have training this weekend?”

I nodded. “Yeah, and I’m going to miss you.”

“I wasn’t fishing for that,” he said. “Why don’t you do something fun while I’m gone? Go have a spa day or something with Tara and Mina. Maybe spend the weekend with your mom and Brian. You haven’t seen Elijah in a while.”

“Yeah. That sounds good. I’ll do something.”

“Ally, promise me, please? I need to know that you’ll do something for yourself, something that will relax you. You’re wound so tight, babe. I’m really worried.”

"Hey, it's me," I tried to joke. "I'm strong, remember? I thought we already established that."

"Promise," he pressed.

"I promise."

***

I kept my promise, but not in the way he expected. Sunday night I stood in the kitchen of his apartment and put the finishing touches on what I hoped would be a delicious enchilada dinner to welcome him home after a long, hard weekend of army training. When he returned from these monthly training gigs, he always headed over to my house to spend time with me, regardless of how exhausted he was. Tonight, he would be able to relax in his own apartment and not have to drive anywhere. I had made Tara promise to keep Mat away until much later in the evening. I heard the key in the lock and the door open, accompanied by the sound of the thud of his duffle bag as he dropped it on the floor.

"Mat? You here? What's cooking? It smells great—" He stopped short in the doorway of the kitchen, surprised to see me setting the table. "Ally? What are you doing here? God, you're a sight for sore eyes!" He pulled me into his arms for a long, deep kiss. "Sorry. I know I reek, but I absolutely could not resist. What are you doing here?"

"You smell fine." He didn't, but it wasn't important. "I made you dinner."

He smiled. "You didn't have to do that. I eat at your place twice as much as I eat here, you know."

"I know, but this is a special dinner. It's almost certainly edible. Why don't you take a shower while I finish up here?" He kissed me quickly and headed off to the bathroom. I heard the shower start as I peeked into the oven to check the enchiladas. I stirred the rice and beans, double checked the table, and went to check on Jack. The shower had cut off a few minutes before, so I figured he should be dressed by now. "Hey." I knocked on his half-open bedroom door. "You about ready?" I peeked around the door as he was zipping up his jeans.

"Yeah, I just gotta grab a shirt." He rummaged through his dresser drawer, looking for a clean t-shirt.

I sauntered in and sat on his bed, enjoying the sight of his strong back as he leaned over the dresser. I looked around his bedroom, noticing that most of the furniture had come from his room at Manny and Trina's; he still had the same twin bed and mismatched nightstand. There were a couple of movie posters on the wall, a small bookshelf crammed full of novels, mostly spy thrillers, and that was it. He certainly didn't go in for the over-decorated look. I inhaled, enjoying how his scent clung to the bedclothes.

"You're playing with fire, querida." He leaned against his dresser, t-shirt forgotten, arms crossed, watching me through narrowed eyes.

"What?" I really tried to sound innocent. "I'm just sitting here on your bed, minding my own business."

"Oh, yeah? Minding your own business, huh?" he said as he uncrossed his arms and stalked over to the bed. He sat down beside me and framed my face in his big hands. "You are going to get us both in trouble." He leaned in to kiss me, pushing me down onto the bed. We lay side-by-side, kissing for several long, glorious minutes before he pulled back and stared down into my face, running his fingers through my hair, spreading it out on his pillow. "Well, this will certainly fuel my fantasies for the next several months."

I smiled up at him. "You say the sweetest things, Jack." I played with the dog tags hanging from his neck, running my fingers through the dark hair sprinkled on his chest.

He ran his fingers down my neck and onto my collarbone, pushing my shirt aside to kiss my shoulder. His hand left that spot to run up under my shirt in the back, over my ribs. For once he dared to run them up the front, and just as I thought things were about to get truly interesting, I realized what he was actually doing.

I pushed his hand away and looked into his face. "What are you doing? Are you...God, are feeling my ribs?" I sat up, wounded that our tender, almost passionate moment had turned into something else.

"Ally." He sat up and pulled me back to him. "Don't be mad, sweetheart. I'm just concerned, that's all. You're so thin. You've lost a lot of weight in the past few months, and you don't have much of a reserve."

I knew I had been losing weight: just that morning I had pulled on a pair of jeans that fell right back off. "Well, I'm sorry if I'm too skinny for you! I didn't know it was such a turnoff! I'll just take my skinny ass and—" I vaulted off the bed and stomped to the bedroom door. He was on his feet instantly and slipped around me to block my exit. "I would like you to move," I said coldly, not able to look at him.

"Ally, please." He waited. "Please look at me, babe." I finally relented and peered into his face, only to see worry and concern clouding his eyes. "I'm so sorry. I'm just so worried about you; we all are. I know you're barely eating anything because your stomach hurts all the time and you're throwing up a lot, aren't you?" I looked back down at my feet and nodded. "Sweetheart, please, please go to the doctor. This is not normal and it's not going away. There has got to be something they can do to help you. I need you, Ally. I can't stand the thought of something happening to you." His voice caught as he choked up.

My anger melted as I realized the depth of his concern. "Okay." I nodded and wrapped my arms around his waist. "I'm sorry."

"You'll make an appointment?"

"Yeah. I'll go in to the clinic tomorrow after class."

"Okay. Good." He leaned down and kissed me. "I love you so much. I know you're going through hell right now. I wish I could do more to help you."

"For now you can come eat this magnificent meal I've made and you can rave over it, even if it sucks. And maybe you should put on a shirt."

He laughed and pulled on a t-shirt, then led me to the kitchen. "It smells great, so I know it won't suck. It smells like something Trina would make."

"Well, it should; it's her recipe. I spent the day with Trina and Megan, two of my favorite people in the whole, wide world. We went shopping, had lunch, and got our nails done." I flashed my sparkly pink nail polish at him.

"Very nice," he commented wryly. "What color did Meg go with?"

"She couldn't decide, so she got a different color on each nail."

"Wow. I'm sure that looks…"

"Awful!" We both laughed. "But she's happy and she's only eight, so who cares?" I dished out food on both our plates and brought them to the table. "I asked Trina for some of your favorite recipes and she wrote them out for me and told me exactly what to do. I've never made enchiladas before. I've eaten them plenty of times, but never made them. I hope they turned out okay."

"You're not having any? Should I be worried? Maybe you're trying to poison me or something," he joked, noticing that I had only served myself a small helping of rice and beans.

I bit my lip. "No, I'm not trying to poison you. It's the chile, Jack. I know it will kill my stomach and I want to be able to enjoy this evening with you. I guess it *is* time I get to a doctor about this."

He took my hand and brought it up to his lips. "It is. Okay, I'm done harassing you for the night. Let's just enjoy."

I smiled and dug into my dinner. Jack did the same and swore it was even better than Trina's. I called him a liar and he just laughed. It must have been all right, though, because he ate an enormous amount. He told me all about his weekend, part of an advanced leadership training program he had been chosen for. We also made plans to attend Megan's first communion in two weeks, which would, of course, involve a huge gathering of family and friends at Trina and Manny's.

As I drove home much later that evening, I thought about how lucky I was to have a guy who cared enough about me to push me to go to the doctor and who was willing to risk my awful temper to get me to see the necessity. Glaring headlights in my rearview mirror distracted me from these thoughts; jeez, that guy was close! I tapped my brakes to get him to stop tailgating. What a jerk! I got a little nervous when he didn't back off. Instead, he sped up. Oh, my God, was he trying to force me off the road? What if this was my stalker? My blood froze and my fingers were ice-cold and trembling as they clutched the steering wheel. What should I do? I sped up. So did the car behind me. I slowed, hoping the car would tire of the game and pass me. No such luck. We kept up the speed up/slow down routine for several miles as I became increasingly annoyed and scared. I struggled to reach into my back pocket for my phone so I could call 911. Just as I wrangled the phone out and began to dial, trying very hard not to wreck, the car behind me sped past, nearly scraping the side of my car. I screamed and dropped the phone. Oh, no he did not! I accelerated, determined to catch up—God only knows why! I have no idea what on earth I planned to do if I caught up, but I was determined to get a license plate number at the very least. I lost sight of the vehicle when I stopped for a red light that the car in front blew through. I drove slowly, looking vainly for any sign of the car. Damn it! I turned onto a busier street, figuring I would head home. I realized I was in an area of town I rarely ventured into and decided I better get out of it post haste. I had just managed to get my breathing back under control when the car came out of nowhere, nearly sideswiping me as it passed, forcing me off the road into the gravel. I barely managed to keep my SUV from flipping as I braked to a halt. I fumbled to open the door and ran around to the side away from the road, where I promptly threw up what little dinner I had been able to eat. I stood leaning against the side of my vehicle, panting and crying. *Okay, Ally, think! What just happened? You got scared, that's what. You're okay, your car isn't damaged. You were just scared. Calm down and think. What did the car look like?* I frowned as I tried to remember if I had seen the car. All I could remember was a vague impression of a large, dark SUV of some kind. As I began to calm somewhat, I realized that some of the clamor in my head was Rémy and Mina, who had felt my terror and were now trying to communicate.

—*I'm okay, guys. I just had a scare.*

—*Where are you?* Rémy asked. *I can be there in a few minutes.*

—*No. Stay home. I'm fine. Really. I'll be home before you could get here. I'm not far. Please, Rémy.*

—*All right. I'll meet you at your house. Are you at home, Mina, or are you out on yet another date?*

He directed the last bit to my roommate, who had broken up with Alex, only to find herself being asked out regularly by other guys.

—I'll have some hot tea waiting for you, Ally. Be safe. I noticed that she didn't even bother to respond to Rémy.

He was waiting for me in the driveway as I pulled in. I threw myself into his arms, needing to be comforted after my scare. "God, Rémy! When is this going to be over?"

"Soon, chérie, soon. Let's get you inside. Mina has tea for you."

I refused to let anyone call Jack; he had been falling asleep on the couch when I left and I knew he would rush over even though there was absolutely no reason. Mat was still at my house and I made him swear not to tell Jack when he got home later. I would call him in the morning and probably have to suffer through him yelling at me for not calling him immediately. Rémy made me go back over the whole event in minute detail as he paced back and forth across the kitchen floor.

"That's all I remember! I was seriously freaked out at the time and didn't manage to get a license plate number! Sorry!"

"Rémy." Mina put her hand on his arm, stilling him. "Come sit down, please." He stared at her hand resting on his arm and I swear I could hear him gulp. He came and sat beside me.

"Sorry," he said. "Things are developing, Ally. I have a feeling this will be over soon."

"What does that mean? The visions I keep getting are terrifying, full of blood and darkness!

I'm afraid of how this is going to turn out, Rémy! I'm so scared!"

***

I called Brian as soon as I calmed down. He volunteered to come over, but said there was little the police could do since I hadn't seen the license plate. I told him to stay home; there was no need for everyone to rush over when there was nothing to be done. It seemed like the stalker knew exactly what he—I assumed it was a he—could do to stay off police radar and yet still drive me slowly crazy.

As predicted, Jack went crazy when he found out and yelled at me over the phone for a full two minutes. I let him vent, knowing he was simply scared for me.

"I can't believe you didn't call me! I should have been the first one you called, but NO! You called Rémy! Do you have any idea how that makes me feel?"

"Jack, I'm sorry! I didn't call Rémy. He just knew." I cringed as I admitted this, knowing Jack still had some major jealousy issues because of the mental connection Rémy and I shared. "Mina knew too. I didn't call anyone. I wasn't going to…"

"You weren't going to call anyone? Why the hell not? You were run off the road, Ally! You should have called the police immediately!"

"I did call Brian when I got home, but there was nothing he could do." I pulled the phone away from my ear as he began yelling in Spanish, mostly curse words.

"Ally?" He finally calmed down after a few minutes. "Are you still there? I'm sorry, *querida*. I shouldn't have yelled at you. It's not your fault. I just…"

"I know, Jack. It's okay. I don't mind you yelling. You were so tired last night and there was nothing you could do."

"I could hold you! I need to be there for you when stuff like this happens!"

"Well, sometimes I need to take care of you, Jack. With all this craziness, sometimes I need to be the one taking care of someone else."

He sighed. "Okay, okay. Just please call me next time. Please, Ally?"

"Yeah, I will. Do you still want to meet for lunch?"

"Jesus, Ally, of course I still want to meet. I'm not mad at you. I'm mad at this whole situation." He muttered another curse under his breath. "You're still going to the clinic today, right?"

"Yeah, right after my last class. And yes, I will call you as soon as I get done. I promise."

***

I don't know what I expected from my visit to the clinic, but it certainly wasn't the barrage of tests that were ordered: an abdominal X-ray, an MRI, and a complete blood panel. The first test they did, right in the clinic, was a pregnancy test, although I told them it would be an immaculate conception if I was. Sheesh, you'd think they would have a better sense of humor working on a college campus. They then sent me directly over to the university hospital for the other tests; I guess that's one of the advantages of attending a tier-1 research university with a medical school and teaching hospital. Several hours later, I found myself back with the doctor, who gave me instructions and prescriptions for irritable bowel syndrome—gross—and gastro-esophageal reflux disease, thought to be exacerbated by stress. The doctor gave me a list of foods to avoid and told me to eat small, frequent meals. He was most concerned about my weight loss and prescribed some Ensure shakes. When he asked what I was doing to manage my stress, I almost laughed uncontrollably, but held it in for fear he would send me straight to therapy. I would love to visit with a therapist about everything that was going on, but somehow I didn't think talk of prophecies and Seers would go over too well. He recommended I try yoga.

Jack waited for me at home, keeping Mina company while she cooked. She had put him to work chopping vegetables. I apprised them of everything the doctor told me. "So, you're going to be okay?" he asked as he put down the knife and wiped his hands. "If you do all that stuff, you'll be okay?"

"Yeah, it's just something I have to learn how to manage. Small meals, cancer patient shakes, and the little purple pill are part of my foreseeable future. Oh, and stress management. I told the doctor I'd get right on that."

He pulled me into his arms, squeezing me tightly. "Oh, thank God. We can handle all that.

Well, the stress may be a challenge, but we can do the rest." He insisted on going to the grocery store to pick up the Ensure, Prilosec, and the prescription that had been called in. "It will help me feel useful," he said. "Oh, call your mom and grandma," he said as he ducked out the door.

What a rat! Leaving me to deal with my family while he escaped to the grocery store. Oh, well, better get it over with. I dialed the phone and spent the next half hour reassuring Mom and Grams that I was okay.

CHAPTER ELEVEN

"I have bedimmed
The noontide sun, called forth the mutinous
winds,
And 'twixt the green sea and the azured vault
Set roaring war."
—Shakespeare, *The Tempest* 5.1

My health improved slowly over the next few weeks as I learned what foods and in what amounts I could handle. I tried to ditch the disgusting Ensure drinks—they triggered my gag reflex—as soon as possible, but Jack was a harsh taskmaster, handing me one out of the refrigerator every time he came over. Then he watched me drink it, often withholding kisses until I was finished. I cooperated because I knew he was worried, but the second the scale showed I had regained five pounds, I declared my independence from the shakes and refused to drink any more. I still mourned the loss of chile in my life and was determined to get to the point where I could eat it again. What kind of New

Mexican doesn't eat chile? I signed up for a yoga class three nights a week, and surprisingly, to me, at least, it really helped with the stress management. Nothing in my life had changed: the personal ads were still coming, the roses kept appearing, I still had the nightmares, an occasional vision, and often felt someone following me, but I handled it better now. Jack loved the yoga outfits I wore and I was a huge fan of the fact that he seemed unable to keep his hands from running over interesting parts of my body when I was wearing the tight pants.

A few weeks before the end of the semester, I was enjoying a cup of herbal tea—coffee was another tragic casualty of my stupid stomach issues—with Michael while we hashed out ideas for our feminist lit class final papers. There was no final exam, thankfully, just a fifteen-page paper. I always prefer a paper to an exam because I feel like I can be sure of getting a good grade if I put the time in, whereas a test is much more in the hands of the professor. Yes, I'm aware of my control issues, thanks.

"So, I'm thinking I'll do mine on sex and gender roles in advertising," Michael said. "Or do you think that has been done to death? Ally?"

"Hmm? Oh, sorry, Michael. I thought I heard…" I had heard a laugh that I knew, but one that didn't fit in this context of the Student Union Building. I stood up and peered over the planter we were sitting behind and looked around until I found what I was looking for: Mat. I would know his laugh anywhere, but what was he doing here, in the middle of the day? He had probably come by to meet Tara, so I started to walk over and say hi. I stopped dead in my tracks when I realized it was indeed Mat, wearing his paramedic uniform and sitting at a table laughing and holding hands with, well, definitely *not* Tara. Oh, my God! Was Mat cheating on Tara? It certainly appeared so. Why else would he be holding hands and laughing and flirting with another girl? I never in a million years would have thought he would do something like that. Why would he cheat on her? She was absolutely gorgeous and I thought they were doing fine, just last night they were cuddling on the couch while we watched a movie. What should I do? My first impulse was to march over to his table and demand some answers, but making a scene didn't appeal, especially when I was trying to maintain a low profile in the wake of the personal ads people kept asking me about. So, I turned and walked back to my own table, sinking down into my chair and blindly reaching for my tea.

"Ally? What's wrong? Who was that? You look…weird," Michael asked, concern written all over his face.

"I, uh, I don't really know. No, I'm okay," I hastened to assure him, "I just, um, I thought I saw someone I know. We probably better get to class." I stewed about it all day, wondering what on earth I should do. By evening, I was no closer to an answer, yet dreaded going home to face Tara.

She was painting her nails at the kitchen table when I walked in. "What do you think?" she asked, holding her hand up for inspection. "Glitter top coat or just plain?"

"Um, glitter. Yeah."

"Seriously? You always say plain and I always go with glitter." She cocked an eyebrow at me.

Crap! That's right! Was she suspicious? "Just trying to mix it up," I said and chuckled lamely.

Her eyebrow rose farther. "Are you okay? Shit, did you find another rose? I swear to God, I'm going to—"

"No, no rose. I'm fine. It's just—"

"Does your stomach hurt? I can get the Mylanta for you." She started to get up.

"No, Tara. I'm fine. Really." I tried to slip past her to go change out of my yoga capris.

"Stop." She put her leg in front of me, blocking the door. "Sit." I sat, of course. You don't mess with her. At least I never had. "Spill."

Crap, crap, crap! "Okay, but you have to promise me you won't freak out."

"Oh, I make no promises. You better spit it out, Ally." Her voice dropped about an octave as she realized she would not like what I had to say.

"I-saw-Mat-in-the-SUB-today-holding-hands-with-another-girl," I said in a rush, just wanting to get it over with. "I'm so sorry, sweetie."

"Mat? My Mat?"

I nodded miserably.

Her face hardened into granite; she was not the kind of girl to dissolve into tears. "Oh, he's the one who's going to be sorry! I assure you of that!" She dialed her phone as she spoke, but I noticed her hands were trembling. "Shit!" she yelled when she misdialed twice. I took the phone from her without a word, dialed Mat's number, and handed it back to her.

I heard him answer with a cheerful, "Hey, babe, what's up?"

"Mateo Jimenez," her voice was icy, "would you care to explain to me why you were at the SUB today, holding hands with a girl who is not me?" She hung up while I could still hear him talking on his end. "He's on his way."

Not a full five minutes later, Jack's Mustang roared into our driveway. Mat jumped out before the car even came to a complete stop. I held Tara back from confronting him in the front yard, thinking the neighbors didn't need a show tonight.

"Tara, babe, please let me explain," he begged, taking her hands in his. It was not a good sign that she flung them away from her in distaste.

"Who is she, Mat? Why would you cheat on me?" I could hear the tears behind her words. "Are you tired of me?" She whispered this last question, choking.

"She's no one! I'm not cheating on you, Tara! God, I'm gonna kill you, Jack! I knew this would backfire and get me in trouble!" He turned toward Jack, who backed away with his hands in front of him.

"What is going on here? Jack, what do you have to do with this?" I asked, perplexed. Was this more than a simple case of a cheating boyfriend?

"It's his whole fucking fault!" Mat yelled, running his hands through his hair. "Babe." He turned back to Tara. "I would never cheat on you. I love you."

"Somebody better start explaining right now,"

Tara growled.

"Okay, okay! Everyone just calm the hell down!" Jack yelled. "All right. Sit down and I'll try to explain." We all remained standing, arms crossed, staring at him expectantly. "Okay, fine. He's right. It's my fault. That girl is the receptionist at the *Daily Lobo*. I asked—"

"Forced!" yelled Mat.

"I may have been somewhat insistent that Mat pretend to flirt with her so he could pump her for information about who was placing the personal ads," Jack explained.

"Oh, my God!" exclaimed Tara.

Ow!" Jack rubbed his arm where Mat punched him. "Sorry. Poor choice of words. He *flirted* with her to obtain information. That's what I meant."

"Did you sleep with her?" demanded my psycho best friend.

"Of course not! God, babe, do you think I'd do that? We had coffee! That's it!" Mat protested.

"Ally said you were holding her hand!"

Mat turned and glared at me.

"Well, I'm sorry!" I said. "How was I supposed to know you were on some undercover mission for Jack? Wait a minute, why didn't you do it yourself, Jack?" I rounded on my boyfriend. "Why did you make Mat do the dirty work?"

"Because she had already seen me when I was in there demanding to talk to the editor. And they might have threatened to get a restraining order if I ever entered the building again. And because I couldn't pull it off. I don't have any idea how to flirt and be charming. Mat's always been good at that kind of stuff. I'm sorry, Tara. I didn't think you'd ever find out. It was a shitty thing to do, but I was desperate to figure out who was placing those ads so I could put a stop to it." Jack leaned his forearms on his knees and rubbed his hands over his head. I reached over and rubbed his back, knowing he felt bad and realizing he had done it for me. He and Mat both had.

"Did you kiss her?" Tara wasn't quite ready to let it go.

Mat sighed and got up out of his chair to kneel before her, taking her hands in his and kissing them. "No, I did not kiss her. I don't even like her. Since the night we went on our first date nearly two years ago, Tara Scott, these lips have kissed only yours. And my grandmother. She always kisses me right on the mouth. I can't stop her." She smiled slightly, as if she was trying to hold it back. "I am completely and totally in love with you. I only met that girl for coffee and pretended to flirt with her because Jack made me. He's going crazy trying to figure those ads out. We were hoping she would tell me who was placing the ads. I'm sorry, Tara."

She uncrossed her arms and leaned forward to run her hands through his black hair. "I love you, too, Mat Jimenez. I just about died when I thought you were cheating on me." She leaned forward and kissed him. "But since you were doing it to help Ally, I guess I can get over it." He stood up, pulling her into his arms for a full-on make-up kiss.

"So, did she tell him?" I asked Jack while Mat and Tara made up.

Jack shook his head. "No. It was a stupid idea."

Tara pulled away and smiled up at Mat. "You mean you couldn't talk her into telling you who was placing the ads? Are you losing your touch?" she teased. "You talked me into going out with you and I had no intention of ever doing that."

"Well, maybe my heart wasn't really in this." He pulled her back in for another kiss.

"Could you, though?" she asked when he let her up for air.

"What?"

"Could you get her to tell you?" Tara asked. "You really are good at wearing people down. If you went out with her again, do you think you could get her to tell you who's placing the ads?"

Mat looked at Jack and me as if we might have some idea why Tara would suggest something so crazy. We both shrugged. He was on his own with this one.

"Babe, what are you talking about? I'm not going out with her again. Not that I went out with her before! We just had coffee! I swear!"

"I know, Mat, calm down! What I'm asking is, could you get her to tell you if you really tried?" She held his face in her hands. "This could be the break we need in the case!" She still watched way too much CSI. "What?" She looked around at the rest of us. "Just because I know about it, he should stop? That's crazy! This is our best chance, you guys!"

"Let me get this straight," said Mat. "You want me to, what, ask her out so I can keep trying to get her to tell me who is placing the personal ads about Ally?"

"Yes, but I have a few rules: no kissing; hand-holding only. And I want to be there."

"No way! I can't go on a date with another girl while my girlfriend is watching," he objected.

"Okay, fine. Then I want Ally to be there. I'll feel better if she's there."

"You want it to be a double date with Ally and Jack? That won't work because she knows who Jack is," Mat explained.

"No, not a double date. Ally will already be at the restaurant where you will take this girl—what's her name, anyway?"

"Teresa."

"Okay, so you will take this Teresa out to dinner at a restaurant where Ally will be—you can make Rémy go with you—and you will wine and dine her, only holding hands, mind you, and you will get her to tell you who the fuck is placing those goddamn personal ads. Got it?" We all got it. Nobody argued with Tara when she was like this.

"Okay, babe. Got it. Dinner, handholding, and info. I think I can get her to spill; she's pretty gossipy and I think she's dying to tell someone. I'm the perfect candidate because I don't have anything to do with the university." He pulled her close again. "Are you sure about this, Tara? I don't want to go out with that girl again. I just want to be with you."

"I know, sweetie. Just do this for Ally. One last date, okay? You don't have to enjoy it. In fact, I'd rather you didn't. I'll make it up to you later." She kissed him as she finished saying this.

How did this go from Mat being in deep trouble

to Tara promising to make it up to him?

"Why does Tara have to make it up to him? I thought she was mad at him?" Jack whispered in my ear.

That's just one of the many reasons I love him so much: we think the same. I laughed and pulled him out of the chair and into my arms. "I love you, you know?"

"I know."

***

So that's how I ended up at Antiquity, a gorgeous restaurant in Old Town, dressed to the nines and sitting across from Rémy, who was also dressed to the nines. I was enjoying my stuffed mushroom appetizer and trying not to look at Rémy eating his escargot while keeping my eye on the door to see when Mat and Teresa came in. We were ensconced in a cozy, candlelit booth for two, but had a decent view of the entrance; this would be a truly romantic date if I were with my actual boyfriend. This was one of my dad's favorite places to bring me when he was in town, which was how I knew it would be perfect for this occasion. There were absolutely no vegetarian entrees on the menu, but I knew the chef was happy to put together a plate of veggie sides. Rémy had, of course, ordered an expensive bottle of wine, which he insisted on sharing. I guess a swanky place like this didn't quibble over little things like underage drinking. Rémy told me I looked at least 22, so it wouldn't be a problem; he still had a hard time understanding

American drinking laws.

"I still don't understand why I need to be here," I said as I stuffed another mushroom in my mouth.

"Because Tara can't be here. And she obviously does not trust Mat to be alone with another girl. Are you sure you don't want to try one? They are not as good as French escargot, but they will do." He impaled a snail on his tiny fork and held it out to me.

"A world of no. If I won't eat a chicken or a cow, I'm not about to eat a bug," I shuddered. "And she does too trust Mat. God, you're so curmudgeony! She trusts him, now that she knows he's not cheating on her," I explained.

"That makes no sense, even from you." He poured more wine into my glass as he spoke. "Regardless of why we came here, I am glad we have a chance to be alone."

"Great. You're plying me with wine and you want to talk to me alone. This can't be good." Nevertheless, I took a rather large sip of fortifying wine.

"Ally, I want to discuss what happens when the semester is over. I'm graduating soon and I need to return to France, at least for a while. Phillipe needs me for the family business. At the same time, I need to protect you. I am torn, chérie. I cannot be in two places at once. I know your life is here, but I am wondering what we are to do."

"Yeah, I know. I know you need to go home; your life is there in France. My life is here. I don't know what to do, Rémy. I'm sorry."

"Have you given any thought to what my

grandmother suggested? That you spend a semester in France?”

“I have. I don't want to leave. I want this all to be over, Rémy. Why can't it just be over?” I pushed my plate away.

He smiled at me sadly. “I don't know, chérie. Maybe it will be soon. I don't want to pressure you, Ally. I just want you to consider it.”

“You know Fionnuala is pressuring me and Mina into spending a semester in Ireland, don't you?”

“Yes, I know. I also noticed the invitation did not include me. I don't think I have to tell you how little regard I have for that suggestion. Now, we will talk of it no more tonight. Mat and his date have just arrived and I want you to enjoy this fine meal we are about to have.” He pushed my plate back in front of me.

He was a charming dinner companion for the rest of the evening, making me laugh and telling interesting stories until dessert, when he ordered my all-time favorite chocolate mousse for me. I decided to risk the caffeine in the chocolate just this once. Rémy really was an amazing guy and I wished he and Mina could figure out their differences; I wanted him to be happy and I had a feeling that his happiness depended upon Mina. Sigh. Why did life have to be so complicated?

I watched Mat and Teresa as their ‘date’ progressed. Mat was obviously charming the socks off of her, judging by the rapt look on her face. She was a cute girl, not stunning like Tara, but the kind of girl who would be flattered to have a good-looking guy like Mat paying attention to her. The more they talked and laughed, the worse I felt; both of them were being used just so I could find out who was placing the personal ads. It had seemed like such a great idea when we planned it. Now it just seemed pathetic and mean. The worst part was this innocent girl who thought she was on a real date. My stomach started aching as I deeply regretted the chocolate mousse. And the mushrooms. And the veggie plate.

We were finished with dessert, drinking coffee—why the heck not, as I would probably throw it all up anyway—when I noticed Mat acting a bit strangely. He kept turning around to look at me, without trying to look like he was looking at me. I grabbed my phone and sent him a text.

Me: What are you doing? You're going to blow it! Did you find out?

Mat: Yes. We'll be leaving soon. Meet me at the house.

We waited until they left, then Rémy paid our bill and we left. I tried to pay, since I had invited him, but he brushed off my suggestion with a shrug. I had given Mat the money to pay for his and Teresa's dinner earlier in the day. I couldn't let the poor guy pay for an expensive date he didn't even want to go on. His behavior at the end of dinner had been so odd it made me a little afraid of what he was going to tell us. Everyone was waiting in the living room when we got home and Jack was pacing while Tara and Mina looked worried.

"Mat? What did you find out? What is with you all?" A frisson of cold crept down my spine.

"It's that Michael guy. Michael Conner," Mat said.

I looked at Jack in horror. "Michael? My friend, Michael? No," I whispered.

"Oh, God, Ally." Jack came and folded me into his arms. "I am so sorry, babe."

***

I was numb with shock. How could he do that to me? I thought we were friends! He knew how much the ads upset me! The feeling of betrayal was so intense I extracted myself from Jack's hold and ran to the bathroom, barely making it to the toilet before barfing epically. Oh, God, stuffed mushrooms, assorted veggies, chocolate mousse, all topped off with red wine was not a pretty sight the second time around. Of course, Jack was right there, holding my hair back until nothing was left but dry heaves. I finally finished, flushed the toilet, and sank back, exhausted, against the tub.

"Why do you always see me at my absolute worst? Thanks," I said as I took the cool, wet washcloth from him.

He sat down next to me, leaning against the tub. "This isn't your worst, Ally. I mean, it was pretty bad, what with that red wine, but definitely not your worst," he teased.

"Thanks, that makes me feel so much better," I sighed.

He put his arm around me and pulled me snug

against his side. "I'm just kidding. Mina is making you some hot tea. Why don't you go get some sweats on and meet us back in the kitchen so we can figure out what to do about this." He stood up and pulled me to my feet.

I entered the kitchen a few minutes later and froze as I heard Jack's voice.

"I'm going to kill the son of a bitch, that's what!"

"You can't literally kill him, Jack," Mat said. "They put people in jail for that. I'm pretty sure Ally doesn't want to visit you in the big house."

I sat down at the table and sipped the tea Mina had thoughtfully prepared for me. I gratefully took the painkiller Jack handed me, along with a glass of water. "Yeah, I've heard they can be really stingy about the conjugal visits." Everyone laughed, which helped diffuse some of the tension in the room.

"Well, I can kick his ass at the very least. He deserves it for what he's done to Ally. God, I can't believe he's behind all the crap Ally's been going through this year!"

"I don't think he is," said Rémy quietly.

"What?" the rest of us exclaimed.

"I believe he is the one responsible for the personal ads, but not the rest."

"You don't think he left the roses? Or that he broke into my house and stole my underwear?" I asked.

"No. He's a sad, confused boy who has a crush on you, but I believe a Seer is behind the roses and the break-in. Remember there was no residual energy trace on the roses. This Michael could not do that."

"Shit," Jack muttered.

I just sipped my tea, devastated by the thought that this wasn't over.

"Okay," Mat said. "We can at least deal with this little asshole and his personal ads. And no, Ally…" He held up a hand to forestall what I was about to say. "I won't let Jack hurt him. We'll just scare him. I guarantee there won't be any more personal ads."

***

He was as good as his word: the personal ads stopped. Jack told me they confronted Michael as he was leaving class and pulled him aside for a "word." Jack swears they didn't touch him. He also said that Michael swore he only placed the ads and knew nothing about the roses or the break-in. Jack and Mat believed him, which was good enough for Mina, Tara, and Rémy, but I still wondered. The next day in class, I pointedly sat across the room from the seat Michael was saving for me and refused to even look at him. He waited for me after class, but I held up a hand.

"Don't, Michael. Just…don't. I have nothing to say to you. Ever." And I walked away.

CHAPTER TWELVE

"Thunder and lightning. Enter Ariel, like a harpy; claps his wings upon the table, and, with a quaint device, the banquet vanishes."
—Shakespeare, *The Tempest* 3.3

Things settled down somewhat as the semester raced to a close. The roses stopped appearing and I hadn't felt like I was being watched or followed for several weeks, which made me wonder if Rémy was wrong after all, and Michael really had been behind it all. I still avoided him like the plague, but after a few weeks I started to feel guilty as I watched him sit by himself in class. I know, I know! What the little creep had done was pretty awful, but was I any better, the way I had used people to find out who placed the ads? Mat felt terrible about what he had done; he said the scene when he dropped Teresa off at her door was not pleasant. She had clearly been expecting a kiss and the offer of another date. Instead she got the classic "I'll call soon" line from Mat. We all did stupid things without thinking about the effects on other people's lives and I wasn't too sure I had the moral high ground on this one.

I finally sat down with my mom and Grams to talk about what Fionnuala and Kate each wanted me to do with respect to spending a semester abroad. They were understanding and helped me craft a logical pro and con chart so I could weigh my decision. The fact that my stalker seemed to have disappeared helped me decide I would be fine without Rémy as my constant watchdog so he could return to France to begin his career in his family's import/export business. I sat him and Mina down one evening to let them know my decision. He actually took it fairly well and said we could at least give it a try and that he could be on the next overseas flight should I need him. He looked less pleased that Mina said she had decided to stay in the U.S. and look for a job now that she had her associate's degree in computer web design. I wondered if they would ever get their relationship sorted out. I felt independent and empowered to have made such a momentous decision and was ready to move on with the next chapter in my life.

Jack was a huge fan of the new plan and I had high hopes that he would see this as an opportunity to move our relationship in a more serious direction. You know, the kind of direction with diamond rings? Not that I needed diamonds, mind you. Any nice gem would do. I was ready to be with him more than just a few evenings per week. I thought he was ready for more too, but all of the unsettled Seer stuff in my life kept us from moving forward.

At least I assumed that's what was holding him back from proposing. Maybe he really didn't want to marry me. Maybe he was rethinking our relationship. Maybe he was—ahhh! For God's sake, stop! I took a few deep breaths, realizing I did this to myself regularly. It was time for some of that stress management the doctor had prescribed, and that meant either yoga or ice cream. A quick trip the freezer told me that it was going to be yoga. Maybe I could stop by the grocery store on the way home from yoga. Double stress management. Nice.

***

I had completed all my finals for my education courses and just needed to turn in the paper for the feminist lit class and I would be done with my sophomore year. I had been running late this morning, too late to mess with the shuttle from the distant parking lot where my pass allowed me to park, and had decided to splurge on an expensive spot in the tall parking structure right across from the Fine Arts building. I was glad I had gone with that decision as I walked toward my car much later that afternoon. It had been a very long day with two finals, a meeting with my advisor, and a follow up appointment at the clinic to refill my meds. I had just turned in my final paper and was looking forward to a quiet evening at home with Jack. I walked up the stairs of the parking garage to the fourth floor, where I had been lucky to find a spot earlier that morning. It was still fairly full as I walked the long aisle to the back where I had parked. I passed a bright green Mazda 2 and something about it made me frown. My stomach dropped as I recognized the sound of footsteps behind me. Realizing it was most likely just someone walking to his or her car, I nevertheless turned quickly to look. Nothing. Crap! Was it starting again? I whipped back around and screamed as someone appeared directly in front of me.

"Michael! What the hell? You scared me to death!"

"Sorry. Sorry. I didn't mean to scare you." He held his hands up in front of himself in surrender.

"What do you want, Michael? If you hadn't noticed, I'm not speaking to you."

"I know. Please, Ally. I just want to apologize. Please just give me the chance to explain and apologize," he begged.

I crossed my arms. "Fine. Go ahead."

"Oh, okay." I guess he had been expecting more of a fight. "Listen, I'm really sorry about the personal ads. I didn't mean to upset you. I just…"

"You just what? You knew they upset me! You knew people were harassing me about them! You knew, Michael! You betrayed me! I trusted you!"

"Ally, I'm so sorry! I just got carried away."

"What? What do you mean?" I uncrossed my arms and put my hands on my hips.

"I wrote the first one because, well, I really liked you and I hoped you might realize you liked me back. I wanted to show you I could be romantic."

"Romantic?" Creepy, yes. Romantic? Not so much. "But you knew I was with Jack."

"Yeah, I know, I know. I just hoped that you might see that we're…well, soul mates, I guess." His shoulders sloped down in defeat. "And then I saw how popular the ads were. Everyone was talking about them, trying to figure out who they were for and who was sending them. It was nice. I liked the feeling. Pretty stupid, I know."

Well, yeah, but I didn't need to say it. God, soul mates? I thought he had a little crush on me, but, yikes! "Did you break into my house, Michael?" I demanded.

"No! I swear I didn't! Just the ads."

"So, you didn't leave the roses?"

"No! I told Jack and that other guy it was just the ads. I swear to God, Ally! I would never do anything like that!"

I heard a car accelerating around the corner toward us and I stepped back to get out of the way. I reached out to grab Michael and pull him out of the way, as well. We were close to the corner and the car sounded like it was going too fast; I didn't want either one of us to get hit. As the vehicle rounded the corner and drove past us, several things happened at once. In a movie, the next few seconds would be in slow motion; in real life it happened blindingly fast. I looked up at the car because it was cutting the corner too close. It was a large, black SUV of some sort and the back passenger window was rolled down. A man sat in the seat, leaning forward and holding something in his hands. I thought I recognized the man from somewhere, but it was such a quick glance I couldn't be sure. I heard a loud pop and Michael tripped toward me as

I reached for him; he fell against me, knocking me into the car behind me. I hit my head on the bumper, hard, and just before I blacked out I heard the SUV tires squeal as it roared away.

I came to a few minutes later; at least I thought it must have been just a few minutes because Michael was still out, collapsed against my legs. We must have fallen into a puddle, because my legs felt wet. "Michael? Wake up." I shook his shoulder. "Michael? Are you okay?" He had fallen forward and I feared he might have hit his head harder than I did and was really hurt. I pulled my legs out from under him, feeling the warm wetness again, and knowing in the back of my mind that was not right. "Michael?" I rolled him over, expecting to see damage on his face, but there was nothing. Just his open, vacant eyes. *Oh, God, oh God, oh God!* "Michael!" I screamed and shook him. That's when I noticed the front of his shirt was wet, as well. A coppery tang permeated the air and it finally penetrated my fuzzy brain that he was drenched in blood, as was I. I held my hands in front of my face in the dimness of the parking garage and saw what I had assumed was a puddle of water was actually a puddle of blood. Michael's blood. I screamed.

***

"Ally, drink this, sweetheart." Brian handed me a bottle of water. I raised the bottle to my lips, but noticed there was still blood on my fingers. I lowered the bottle and reached for the tissues Brian had given me, scrubbing ineffectively at the stains with trembling hands.

"It's okay, Ally. We'll get you cleaned up later." He reached to still my shaking hands. "Just drink now."

"Where's my mom? I want my mom. Can you get my mom?" I knew I was babbling, but I couldn't seem to stop. I also couldn't stop the deep trembling that began soon after the paramedics had loaded Michael onto a gurney and into the back of an ambulance. They had worked over him while I huddled on the cold concrete and I didn't know if he was alive or dead.

"Soon, sweetheart. She's going to meet us at the hospital, okay?"

"Okay." I nodded, and then shook my head. "Is Michael going to be okay?"

"I don't know, Ally. Can you tell me what happened here? I know you're upset, but I need to get a statement as soon as possible."

I nodded again and, in broken sentences, told him what I could remember. "The car, the SUV, came around the corner. It was black. I saw, I saw a man. There was a sound, like a pop or something. Then Michael tripped. He fell on me. I fell. I fell and hit my head on that car." I pointed at the blue Ford Fiesta and was fascinated to see blood on the bumper. I reached back to feel the back of my head and winced when I felt the lump. My hand was bloody when I brought it back around to my face. "Ow," I said and stared at my hand stupidly.

A second ambulance pulled up then and Brian was pushed aside as they started to attend to me. "Ally?" Mat was one of the paramedics leaning over me.

"Mat?" I threw my arms around his neck. "Oh, Mat! I think they shot him!" I realized what had really happened and what the man in the SUV had held in his arms was a gun. I started crying hysterically.

"Ally." He hugged me briefly and pulled back. "I need to check your head, okay? Brian says you hit your head and passed out, so I need to check you." He looked at the wound on the back of my head, checked my pupils, pulse, and some other stuff, all while I sat crying. I soon found myself on a gurney of my own with a really uncomfortable collar immobilizing my head and an oxygen mask over my mouth, being loaded into an ambulance. Mat hopped into the back with me.

"Mat?" My voice was muffled by the oxygen mask.

"Yeah, sweetie?" He tucked a blanket around me, which felt amazing.

I pulled my arm out of the blanket and reached up to lift the mask off my face. "Can you call Jack, please?" I had managed to control my hysteria for the moment.

"Brian was going to do that. I'm sure Jack will meet us at the hospital."

"Okay." I sniffed. "Is Michael dead?"

"I don't know, cariña. I'll find out when we get to the hospital, okay? You just rest right now." He replaced the mask and patted my arm.

Once we got to the emergency room, things happened in a rush: my bloody clothes were cut off and bagged as evidence. Apparently patient modesty is not a concern in the ER. I looked around frantically to make sure that Mat was no longer in the room, but the collar got in my way. "Mat? Mat?" I yelled, pulling the mask away again. I did not want my boyfriend's cousin to see me naked. In retrospect, I can't believe I was worried about it in that moment.

"Okay, Ally." Someone in scrubs appeared above my face. "Calm down, sweetheart. We need to make sure you're okay and then we'll get Mat for you. Is he your boyfriend?"

"No, he's his cousin—ow," I whimpered as I felt a prick in my arm. "Where's Michael? Is he dead?" I started crying again, the sobs bubbling up from deep in my chest. I needed to get off this table and find out what happened to Michael. I pulled the mask off, getting it tangled in my hair and whimpering when it hit my head wound. I gave up on it and tried to remove the collar while trying to sit up. I don't know where I thought I was going, wearing only my underwear and bra with IV tubes connected, but it didn't matter at that moment. I struck at the hands that were trying to interfere and I started screaming again.

"We need some help in here!" one of the doctors yelled. "Grab her hands! Give her .5 of Lorazepam, stat!" I screamed as the hands pushed me down on the table. Things started to get fuzzy and my screaming deflated to crying, then whimpering, then nothing.

***

I opened my eyes to see fuzzy faces hovering over mine. I frowned, realizing that my head was throbbing.

"She's waking up." Brian's voice. "I'll get Jack. Here, Jen, sit here."

"Ally-bear, can you hear me?" I smiled at the old pet name, but couldn't fight my way to the surface. I closed my eyes again and slept.

***

The next time I opened my eyes, my head still hurt, but I was slightly less fuzzy. I heard the beeping of my heart monitor and gingerly turned my head, glad the awful collar was no longer around my neck. Ow. I hissed. My head really hurt.

"Ally?" Jack walked into view. I smiled at his rumpled appearance and scruffy, unshaven face.

"Hey," I whispered. My throat felt scratchy and I was incredibly thirsty.

"Here." He poured some water into a cup with a straw and held it up to my mouth.

"We've got to stop meeting like this," I said softly.

"I completely agree." He took my hand in his and brought it up to his lips. "How do you feel?"

"My head hurts. And I feel fuzzy. I'm really sleepy," I mumbled. "What's wrong with me?"

"You hit your head. Again. Seven stitches this time. And a nasty concussion. They're going to keep you for at least 24 hours." He seemed so grim and I wondered what he wasn't telling me.

"That's it? I'm going to be okay, aren't I?"

"Yeah, babe. You're going to be fine." He leaned forward and kissed my forehead.

"Is my mom here? I thought I heard her earlier."

"She was. She had to get home to Elijah, but I promised to call her when you woke up."

"Jack." I caught his hand as he started to pull away. "What is it? You seem…sad."

He sighed and sat on the bed next to me. "What do you remember, Ally?"

I tried to remember how I had hit my head, but everything was still vague. "There was a blue car. I think I fell against it. I fell because…Oh my God. Michael." It all came rushing back. "Where's Michael?" Jack squeezed my hands and frowned. "No. Jack, no!"

"I'm so sorry, Ally."

"No. No. He's not!" I was escalating again, unable to accept what I knew in my heart was true.

"Okay, hon. Calm down or I'll have to call the nurse."

"They shot him, Jack! They shot him! He's not dead! He's not!" I sobbed and tried to pull out my IV, hysterical and making no sense. I knew Michael was dead, but I didn't want to believe it and apparently thought screaming and throwing a fit would help. I guess those drugs they had me on were messing with my mind.

"Ally, you've got to calm down! Babe, please!" He reached across me and pushed the call button repeatedly, while trying to keep me from pulling out my IV. Several nurses rushed in, one pushing Jack away to hold me down while another injected something into my IV. The last thing I saw before I fell asleep was Jack's devastated face, tears tracing their way down his cheeks.

***

Weak sunlight streamed into my room when I woke up for good. I opened my eyes and looked around the room for Jack. No one was there. I tried to lift my hand and realized both my hands were strapped to the bed. I remembered my hysterical outburst of the night before with shame. I was sane and in my right mind now, but didn't like having my hands tied.

"Hey! Hey! Can I please get my hands untied? Please? I won't go crazy again! I promise!" I called out.

"Ally! You're awake, finally." My mom peeked in the door. "Let me get a nurse to undo your restraints. I'll be right back."

She brought a nurse back with her and I was freed from my bonds quickly. The nurse did a brief check of my vitals and then left me alone with my mom.

"Mom," I whispered.

"I'm here, baby." She sat on the bed and pulled me into her arms. "Oh, Ally. I'm here. It's going to be all right." She rubbed my back and then pulled back to brush my hair out of my face.

"Michael's dead, isn't he?"

"Yes, he is. I'm so sorry, Ally."

My face crumpled and she pulled me back into her arms. I cried softly, no hysteria in sight. I didn't want to be drugged and tied down again. Sheesh, crazy much? "He was shot, wasn't he?"

She nodded. "That's what Brian said. God, Ally, you could have been killed!" Now she was crying. We sat there, weeping in each other's arms until I had nothing left.

"Where's Jack?" I asked after I drank an entire cup of water and wiped my face with a tissue.

"I made him go home and get some sleep. He'll be back soon, I'm sure. He didn't want to leave. I had to swear to stay with you every second. He can be quite fierce about you, you know?"

I smiled slightly. "How long have I been here?"

"Almost twenty-four hours. The um…the shooting was yesterday afternoon. It's almost five o'clock now. That last dose of tranquilizer was pretty strong. You've been asleep for a long time."

"I'm sorry about the whole crazy thing. I don't know what got into me." I was so ashamed of how I had behaved.

"Oh, sweetie! Don't worry about that. I can't even begin to imagine what you went through."

"How long do I have to stay here, Mom? I want to go home."

'I know, baby. They just need to make sure you're okay. I think you'll get to go home tomorrow if…" She didn't finish.

"If I can convince them I don't need a straitjacket?"

She laughed mirthlessly. "Yeah, something like that. Do you think you could eat something?"

"Um, sure. I'll try." She went to tell the nurse that I would need dinner. I lay back against the pillows and thought about what had happened.

Michael had been gunned down in the parking garage at the university. I had seen the man that had shot him and he looked familiar somehow, but I couldn't place where I had seen him and it made my head ache to think about it.

"Is your head hurting, sweetie? Do you want something for it?" Mom came back in the room. "I told the nurse you wanted to try some dinner. Let me tell her you want some painkillers."

"Just Tylenol! I don't want any sleeping pills or anything."

She smiled and nodded.

I was halfway through my tomato basil soup and crackers when Jack came in, showered, shaved, looking much better than the last time I'd seen him and holding a bouquet of flowers—not roses, thank goodness. He set them on the table next to my tray and sat on the edge of the bed next to me.

"How are you feeling, querida? Better?"

"Yeah." I couldn't quite meet his eyes; I was ashamed of how I had been the last time he had seen me. "No more crazy. Sorry about that."

"Ally, look at me." He lifted my chin and kissed me so softly. "I know you're not crazy, babe. I love you. I'm sorry I wasn't here when you woke up. Your mom made me go home. She can be pretty scary, you know?"

"That's funny. She said nearly the same thing about you."

"Oh, ha ha, you two. Listen, Ally. I need to go check on Elijah. I can come back tonight," Mom said.

"Oh, Mom, I'm fine. Stay home, please. Elijah

needs you. You don't need to watch me sleep."

"I'll be here, Jen," said Jack. "I'm not going anywhere."

"Thank you, Jack." She hugged him before gathering her purse and leaving.

"I'm not letting you stay all night, either," I said as the door closed behind her. "You need your sleep. I'm fine now."

"We'll see. Now finish your dinner like a good girl."

"Do I get another kiss if I do?"

"You can have one now." He leaned in for a kiss. "And another when you finish."

"Mmmm." I nuzzled against his neck. 'You smell so good. I love how you smell."

He chuckled and pulled back slightly. "Those *were* some good drugs they gave you."

I smiled crookedly. "Yeah." I went back to eating my soup, embarrassed at my lack of filter.

He watched me until I finished the last spoonful, then pushed the container of green Jell-O my way.

"Nope." I shook my head. "Gelatin. Horse hooves. Gross." I swished water around in my mouth and the swallowed. "Okay, I'm ready for my kiss."

"Oh, you are, huh?" he teased. He pushed the table aside and leaned over me.

"Unless you want me to brush my teeth first. Yeah," I pushed at him, realizing that I hadn't brushed my teeth since yesterday morning. Yuck! "I should definitely brush my teeth. And I have to go to the bathroom. Ugh, I'm all tied up, Jack." I fought with the IV lines, trying to figure out which way to get out of the bed.

"Okay, babe. Slow down. I got you." He helped me out of the bed, untangling the plastic IV lines and rolling the stand for me.

I felt a distinct breeze on my backside and reached back to clutch the hospital gown closed. "Oh, for God's sake! Where is my underwear? Did you see?" I looked up at Jack's face. He bit his lip, trying not to laugh. "Ugh!"

"What? I couldn't help it! It was just hanging out there. Oof!" he exclaimed as I elbowed him in the stomach. He caught my hand and brought it to his lips to kiss it. "Don't be mad, querida." He laughed. "You have a beautiful butt. It was the highlight of my day."

"Oh, for God's sake," I groused again as I shut him out of the bathroom. I could hear him laughing through the door.

He helped me back into bed, tucking the covers around me before leaning over. "Do I finally get that kiss now?" I nodded and he sealed his lips over mine.

"I see you're feeling better, Ally," my doctor said wryly from the doorway. "This is your boyfriend, I assume?"

Jack smiled at me and wiped his thumb over my lips before getting off the bed and standing aside for the doctor.

"Nope. I've never seen this guy before in my life. He just wandered in and I thought he was pretty cute, so I kissed him." I winked at him.

"I'm Jack Ruiz, ma'am." He shook the doctor's hand. "And I am Ally's boyfriend."

"Nice to meet you, Jack. Can you give us a few minutes?"

"Sure. I need to call Tara and Rémy anyway. They want to come by, if you're up to it, Ally." He raised his eyebrows questioningly.

"Yeah. Hey, tell Tara to bring me some underwear. And pajamas. And my robe. And ice cream. Please?"

Jack looked to the doctor for assent. She nodded, amused, and Jack left the room to make the call.

***

Rémy, Mina, Tara, and Mat arrived within half an hour. Tara went with me into the bathroom and helped me get my pajamas and robe on so I didn't feel quite so exposed. The doctor had removed my IV, thankfully, so I could get my arms through the sleeves.

I came out of the bathroom and hugged Mat. "I'm so glad you were there in the parking garage, Mat. Thanks. I didn't say it before."

He hugged me back tightly. "I'm glad I was there too, sweetie. You gave us all quite a scare. I'm glad you're okay."

I released Mat and turned to hug Rémy. "What happened? I saw the man who sh—" I choked. "Who shot Michael and I know I recognize him, but I can't remember where I saw him."

"Shh, chérie. We'll figure it out, don't worry. For now, just concentrate on getting better."

"Were they trying to kill me, Rémy? Did Michael die because they were trying to kill me?"

Tears spilled down my cheeks.

"Okay, sweetie." Tara pulled me out of his arms. "Time for all that later." I could see them exchanging worried glances.

"I'm okay, guys. I'm not going to freak out again, I promise." I realized I was exhausted and dizzy from my jaunt to the bathroom. I reached for the wall, stumbling a bit. Jack was at my side instantly and scooped me up in his arms.

"Tara, pull the covers down," he ordered before placing me gently in the bed. "You need to take it easy."

I nodded, appalled at my weakness. "Did you bring the ice cream, Tara?"

She smiled and rifled through her tote bag, producing a small paper bag and a pink plastic spoon. "Here you go, hon. I even brought your favorite pink spoon." She handed me a pint of B & J's Mint Chocolate Cookie.

"You are a life saver, Tara. Jack tried to make me eat Jell-O."

"Gross. Even I won't eat that," she said.

"Sorry, I didn't know. Rookie mistake." Jack rolled his eyes.

"Mmmm. This is awesome," I closed my eyes and savored the creamy, minty sweetness. I could only eat a few bites before I was full. The nurse was nice enough to store the rest in the freezer for me. My eyes were starting to droop and I fell asleep listening to the buzz of my friends talking.

***

I pushed my way throughout the overgrown vegetation, searching for...what? Where was I? It looked familiar, but different...somehow. I looked down and saw I still wore the hospital gown, which was flapping open in the breeze blowing through the wild garden. Oh, great! I looked down again and I was wearing the pajamas and robe that Tara had brought me. Well, that's better. I didn't need to be wandering through my dream flashing my naked, white butt everywhere. It was dusk, with a chill wind in the air. As I moved farther down the path, I realized I was in Kate's garden in Rouen, but it was not the neat, tidy garden I remembered. I paused as I heard voices up ahead, just around a corner. My heart beat faster in fear as I recognized them.

"You realize you killed the boy?" Luc asked.

"Collateral damage. You said to frighten her. This should have done the trick." I recognized the voice. And I knew they were speaking French, but I somehow understood it.

"Fine. Maybe she will realize no one is safe near her. The goal is to get her here where we can control her."

I rounded the corner to see Luc in conversation with the same man I had seen him with in the garden in Rouen at the end of my first visit. It was the same man I had seen in the backseat of the black SUV. Michael's killer. Now I knew where I had seen him before.

"Ah, Ms. Moran. So lovely of you to join us, finally. You're a bit underdressed for the occasion, but no matter. Come, we have much to discuss."

"No! You killed Michael! You shot him!" I tried

to turn and run, but my feet felt like they were mired in molasses. "No!" I screamed.

***

"Ally! Wake up! God, sweetheart, wake up!"

I opened my eyes to Jack, sitting on my bed, looking sleepy and worried. Apparently he hadn't gone home like I asked him to. I launched myself into his arms, tears streaming down my face. I clutched the back of his shirt desperately and tried to calm my breathing. I could hear my heart rate monitor beeping crazily at my bedside. "I'm okay. It was just a dream, wasn't it?" But I knew it had been more than a normal dream. I sat back and cupped my hand around his scruffy jaw. "I need you to call Rémy." My head hurt too much to try to communicate with him mentally. Jack looked at me, hard, but didn't question me. He just got his phone out, dialed, and handed it to me.

"Rémy? I know who did it."

He arrived within fifteen minutes, looking rumpled and sleepy. I realized I had never seen him less than perfectly groomed. He sat on the edge of my hospital bed and I reached to stroke his unshaven cheek.

"Thanks for coming so fast."

"Of course, chérie. Tell me." He held my hand.

"It was Luc—I mean, he wasn't the shooter, but it was the guy I saw with Luc last summer." I explained to both Jack and Rémy how I had stumbled upon Luc talking with a man I had never seen before in the back gardens of the estate in

Rouen. I told them about the dream I had just had that was obviously more than just a dream. "I think Luc sent him to follow me, to scare me. That's who's been stalking me all this time. It wasn't Michael. He just sent the ads. They want to control me. No one around me is safe, Rémy."

"Okay, chérie, calm down. Jack will kick me out if I get you upset." He tried to lighten the mood.

"Rémy, all the dreams, the visions I've been having, they've all been about what happened in the parking garage. They never help. They never goddamn help!" I stopped, aware that I needed to calm down or I would find myself tranquilized yet again. The doctor had told me she wanted to keep me another full day for observation because of my crazy bouts—she referred to them as hysterical reactions—so I knew I needed to relax. "We need to go to France. We need to tell them what Luc did. We need to stop him."

"I'll make the arrangements," Rémy said and got up to leave.

"After the funeral. I want to be here for the funeral."

"Of course."

CHAPTER THIRTEEN

"They all enter the circle which Prospero had made, and there stand charmed;"
—Shakespeare, *The Tempest* 5.1

Brian came the next day to finish getting my statement. He came by himself, knowing my statement would involve stuff about Seers that would never make it to his final report. I told him everything I knew, holding nothing back; he eventually sighed and closed his notebook.

"Well, shit. That's just great. You know who it was, but you don't have a name. And the guy is French and probably back safely in France by now."

"Sorry, Brian," I whispered.

"Hey, it's not your fault, Ally. I just don't know what I'm going to put in my report. Have you told anyone else about this guy?"

No." I shook my head, "Just Jack and Rémy."

"Okay. I know you'll tell the rest of the Scooby gang, but no one else, please. I think I can pass this off as a random drive-by."

"What about Michael's family? They don't get justice? They'll never know what really happened to their son?" I asked, horrified.

"I don't see any way around it right now, Ally. I wish there was some way, but…"

"I know. It just really sucks."

"Yeah, it does. Your mom is coming by in a little while, so if you need anything you should text her. She says you're going to be staying with us for a few days while you recover."

"She doesn't think I should be alone yet. I tried to tell her that I'm anything but alone at my house, but she couldn't be swayed. I'm looking forward to spending some time with Elijah, though. He's growing so fast!" I didn't really mind spending a few days at my mom's house. She would spoil me and I would get to play with my little brother, whom I adored. I must say the feeling was mutual: I was one of his favorite people.

"We love having you, Ally. I hope you know that. You could sell your house and move in and make us all happy, you know," my stepfather said.

"Thanks, Brian. That was really nice."

***

I finally got a few moments alone later that afternoon. No doctors, no nurses, no well-meaning friends or family. Mom and Grams were due in an hour or so and I had sent Jack home to get a shower and a shave and hopefully some sleep. He promised to come by later in the evening.

I closed my eyes and thought about the events of

the last twenty-four hours. I felt the tears leaking out the corners of my eyes as I pictured Michael, lying in a pool of his own blood, eyes vacant and staring. I had since realized that he was already dead when I turned him over and the paramedics had been working in vain. *Collateral damage.* That's what Luc and the unknown man had called him. As if his life was unimportant. As if what was happening in the Seer world, who the next Oracle would be, was more important than a human life. Michael—poor, awkward Michael, who just wanted someone to like him—got in the way. They had used him as a tool to frighten me and ultimately control me. The guilt washed over me, through me, taking root deep in my soul. Michael's family would never know what had really happened to him; they would be told it was a random drive-by shooting, just another statistic of Albuquerque's gang violence problem. I opened my eyes and wiped my tears on the sleeve of my robe. *I would find justice for Michael somehow. Of that I was determined.* Rémy, Mina, and I would go to Rouen and tell the rest of the Conseil what Luc had done. He would not be allowed to get away with it. We would make sure he and the man who had shot Michael faced justice. Then I could come back. Then my family, my friends, Jack would be safe. Until we stopped Luc, no one I loved was safe. If they thought so little of killing Michael, they would think nothing of hurting or killing anyone else I cared about.

***

Michael's funeral was held three days later. I sat in the church, staring straight ahead and dry-eyed, holding tightly to Jack's hand. The minister spoke of a brilliant young man whose life had been cut tragically short. We were among a fairly small group of mourners: his family, a few friends of the family, Jack and me. That's it. Michael had not been a popular guy and he'd had few friends. For some reason, this made me feel even guiltier. The casket was open and I paused in front of it, looking down into the face of the boy who had thought, hoped I was his soul-mate.

"I'm so sorry, Michael," I whispered. Jack said nothing, but put his arm around my shoulders and guided me away.

The ladies of the church hosted a reception after the service. I was sipping the hot tea Jack had just handed me when a middle-aged woman approached me.

"Are you Ally?" she asked. I nodded. "I'm Michael's mother."

I handed my tea to Jack. "Oh. I'm so sorry."

"Thank you for being here. It would have meant a lot to Michael. Are you doing okay? I heard you were in the hospital."

"I'm fine. I got out a few days ago." I could think of absolutely nothing else to say to her. I was alive and her son was dead. What do you say to that?

"Well, I'm glad. Thank you for coming," she said again and moved away.

"Take me home, Jack. Please." He set my unwanted tea on a table and ushered me out of the church.

***

He held me on the couch until late in the evening. I was back in my own house and Rémy, Mina, and I were leaving in a few days for France. I hadn't changed out of my dress, but just kicked off my high heels and curled my feet under me. Jack pulled an afghan over me and let me cry, knowing I needed to release some of the emotion I held inside. We didn't speak much; he knew I needed to go to France to confront Luc, but he was worried. It was difficult for him to trust my safety absolutely to Rémy but I knew he was trying to be supportive. I couldn't possibly have loved him any more than I did at that moment, but the only thing I could do was hold him. Finally, around midnight, he picked me up and carried me to my bedroom. He helped me unzip my dress and pull on my sweats. When he kissed me and made a move to leave, I held tightly to his neck and whispered, "Please stay. Please."

"Okay, babe. Okay." He kicked off his shoes, removed his shirt and tie and pulled me down next to him on top of my comforter. He reached down and pulled up the blanket I kept folded at the foot of my bed, covering us with it as he spooned around my back. "Try to sleep, Ally. I'm here."

***

I sat beside Mina in first class on the flight to

Paris. Rémy sat across the aisle from us, reading a French newspaper the flight attendant had given him. Jack had driven us to the airport in my SUV and leaving him had been more difficult than ever.

"I don't want to go, Jack," I said, hugging him tightly before I went through security.

"I don't want you to go," he replied. "But I know you need to tell them about Luc and make sure he never does this again."

Rémy had decided not to let anyone know we were coming so that Luc could not be forewarned and disappear.

"I'll be back soon," I promised.

"You better be." He kissed me and left, taking a good chunk of my heart with him.

I felt a hand on mine and glanced over to see Mina looking at me, concerned. "I'm okay, Mina. This all just seriously sucks. I'm so over this whole Seer thing."

She smiled crookedly. "Yeah, for sure." I couldn't help but smile at her attempt at American idioms, which sounded ridiculous in her charming Irish lilt.

I read for a few hours. *Sense and Sensibility* was one of my all-time favorite comfort books and I was able to lose myself for a while in early 19th century England and the trials and tribulations of Elinor, Marianne, Edward, and Colonel Brandon. Their lives seemed so simple and pastoral compared to mine. I slept the rest of the way, not waking until I felt the landing gear being activated.

It was early morning in Paris, and Rémy navigated the rental car through the busy streets without a problem until we were on our way to Rouen. He talked strategy nearly all the way: how we would enter the estate quietly and talk privately with Kate and Phillipe before any of the rest of the Conseil, who happened to be in residence, were even aware we had arrived. They would know how to handle Luc, how to make sure he and the unknown man were brought to justice. I didn't add much to the conversation, but just stared out the window, hoping it would all be over soon.

When we arrived at the estate, Rémy pulled around to the back entrance and we entered through the kitchens. He greeted the staff that were cleaning up from breakfast and asked them to keep our arrival quiet until we had seen Kate. André, the butler, checked to see that the hallway was clear before we emerged into the living quarters and made our way to Kate and Phillipe's private sitting room, where André informed us they were to be found.

Kate was flabbergasted to see us when she opened the door to Rémy's soft knock. She stepped aside to let us all enter and then pulled her grandson close in a hug, murmuring to him in French and kissing his cheeks. "Oh, Ally!" She hugged me when she finally released Rémy to his grandfather. "Thank you for bringing him home. I have missed him so much! How long are you staying? Why did you not tell us you were coming? What is with all the secrecy?"

"Grand-mére, we need to talk," Rémy said.

Kate and Phillipe listened in growing horror as he told how the events had unfolded since

Christmas, when they had been in Albuquerque. He told them how the ads had started up again with the new semester, as had the roses, the visions, and the nightmares. He told them how Jack had made Mat flirt with Teresa to get her to tell him who was placing the ads. Then he told them about the parking garage. I got up and wandered over to the windows, looking out on the colorful gardens and trying to tune out his voice as he told them of Michael's death, of how I recognized the man who had shot him, of how I had dreamed of Luc and the man speaking of Michael as collateral damage and of controlling me, controlling the Oracle.

"That's why we did not tell you we were coming. We didn't want to alert Luc. Grand-mére, I know you will know how to deal with this, how to stop Luc from doing anything like this again," Rémy finished.

I turned, expecting to see an angry, determined look on Kate's face as she realized what one of her Conseil members had done in his quest for power. Instead, she was white and shocked. "Oh, my God! I can't believe this! How could he do something so terrible?"

"Kate." I strode toward her and knelt down in front of her. "You have to stop him. You have to make him pay for what he did to Michael."

"Oh, my dear." She looked blankly at me. "I don't know where he is."

"What?" The three of us yelled it at the same time.

"He hasn't been seen for months. He said he was staying at his house in town for a while, but he never returned. I went to visit him a few weeks ago, to ask him why he had not been to the estate in so long, but his house was empty. No one knows where he is. He has disappeared," Phillipe explained.

I lifted myself from the floor and walked woodenly back to the window. Tears streamed down my face as I looked out, seeing nothing of the garden. Instead I saw the faces of my loved ones, parading across my mind: Mom, little Elijah, Brian, Grams, Tara, Mat, Trina, Megan. Jack. We had come here to bring a killer to justice, but you can't have justice if you can't find the killer. I felt Rémy behind me, his hands on my shoulders. Mina came to stand beside me and put her hand in mine. "I can't go home," I whispered.

The End

Acknowledgments

Taking on the adventure of writing a series takes a lot of help! More than anything, I want to thank all those who encourage me to keep writing. It's a scary thing sometimes to open my heart and my stories to the big, wide world, but so many people in my life keep telling me they enjoy reading about Ally and Jack. Thanks especially to Lacey for calling them her bridge to sanity. Thanks also to Sheila for saying what a good book boyfriend Rémy is. I completely agree!

Kelly, I would have been lost without your excellent translation skills, and any errors are certainly my own. Gracias & merci beaucoup!

I couldn't do this without the love and support from my Limitless family, including Jennifer, Lori, Toni, and all my fellow authors who send their congrats and share on social media. You guys ROCK!

Most of all, I want to thank my wonderful family. They are my beta readers, my sounding boards, my personal chefs, and my housekeepers. Lyle, I can't even begin to say how much I love you for all you do.

About the Author

Amy Reece lives in New Mexico with her incredible husband and two ridiculous mutts, Greta and Sodapop. When she's not writing, she's teaching high school English and social studies or maybe wandering through a thrift store in search of the next lucky teapot for her vast collection. She is an unrepentant bookaholic and has overflowing bookshelves in nearly every room of her house. Her favorite authors include J.R.R. Tolkien, J.K. Rowling, and C.S. Lewis–must have something to do with initials! She loves to travel and is hoping to need many research trips for future writing projects.

Facebook:
https://www.facebook.com/areeceauthor

Twitter:
https://twitter.com/AReeceAuthor

Blog:
https://amyreece.wordpress.com/

Goodreads:
https://www.goodreads.com/author/show/13884337
.Amy_Reece

Pinterest:
https://www.pinterest.com/alreece12/